DEAD DROP

EVA MACLEAN

BOOKS

By Eva Maclean

Detective Miranda Murphy

Vinci Books

vinci-books.com

Published by Vinci Books Ltd in 2025

1

A CIP catalogue record for this book is available from the British Library.
Paperback ISBN: 9781036700737

Prologue

HE STOOD and looked at her on the bed, so still, so defenceless. And thought of murder. So easy. No resistance. Nobody would wonder, nobody would even query it. She didn't have long anyway, blessed release they would say, all that sort of thing. So convenient, this end-of-life stage. You could massage it to suit your own ends. The nurses came and went, lots of different faces, overworked and underpaid, looking forward to the end of their shift. Get back to feed the kids and put their feet up. A small mistake with the dosage perhaps, but even that would not be noticed and, if it was, nobody would say anything. Under the carpet. The NHS didn't need any more negligence claims. Death certificate signed by some doctor who would probably never even look at her. Just sign here, doctor. Nobody would ever know. Except him. He would know.

At that moment she stirred and opened her eyes and he smiled and went to hold her hand, caressing the bony knuckles, brushing her hair back from her face. Such a trusting face.

Chapter One

FRANCINE HAD that morning come across Nancy Brophy's essay *How to Murder Your Husband*. If anybody looked into her internet history, there it would be. First mistake. In some ways it was an interesting idea. Life without Justin would certainly be less stressful. She wouldn't have to wonder what mood he was going to wake up in, she wouldn't have to cook dinner and hope it met with his approval. She could just eat something simple with Danny, feed Tommy and then go to sleep with the kids. At the thought of all those extra hours in bed a wave of longing came over her. The insurance would pay off the mortgage and probably give her some sort of payout and when Tommy was a bit bigger, she could start taking in more work again. It was definitely something to consider. Well, so much for that. Life was not quite like that. If something was to happen to Justin, she'd probably find she was devastated. She would think of all the good things, not the bad ones. And, of course, the ultimate crime hadn't turned out too well for Nancy.

They were getting near the school now. Danny liked to stand on the back of the buggy, which made it heavy to push up the hill, but Francine always walked unless it was raining. It was important to get your exercise when you could and she didn't want the kids to grow up expecting to be driven everywhere. She knew she wasn't a successful school gate mum. There were a number of groups and she didn't seem to belong to any of them. It was a skillset she'd never mastered, standing around, lots of news to exchange, gossiping about other people, or whatever it was that went on. The only people likely to talk to her were Brenda, who was actually a grandmother, and Marion, who was a grown-up rock chick and also avoided the cliquey groups. Right now, Francine couldn't see either of them so she just waited for the bell to ring so that she could beat a retreat.

And now they've got this birthday party tonight. Why did Justin insist on having a party? Is forty really such a big deal? Should she be buying him a present? Probably. Maybe she should. Perhaps if she made a bit more effort, he would be a bit different too. Perhaps they could salvage things for the sake of the boys. After all, he hadn't seemed like that when she first met him. There were none of these moody silences. It's probably all her fault. He just doesn't seem to like her any more, maybe she's no longer likeable. What she really needs to do is to get back to work, but she's not ready to leave Tommy yet. It's not good to be financially dependent on a man she's not sure she still wants.

————

JUSTIN SAT IN HIS OFFICE, scrolling through the market reports. Returns were a bit low at the moment. Could he make that point to his clients? They were as capable of looking at Bloomberg as he was, they'd be expecting a hit to the bottom line. It would give him a bit of breathing room. Cargill's secretary walked past and he smiled at her. She didn't smile back. Was that significant? Justin knew he was still good-looking (or he hoped he was). Good, muscular body, brown eyes, blondish hair that flopped winningly across his eyes. Most women appreciated it when he smiled at them. He'd never had any trouble in that department. Had Cargill said something to Julie about him? He had a distinct feeling of being kept at arm's length, no more summons to meetings. Everybody hated meetings anyway, but you didn't like to feel that you were being kept out of the information loop. Maybe Cargill suspected something. No, that wasn't possible. But he would have to manoeuvre his way out of it all at some point, he couldn't just keep grabbing short-term solutions. He was badly over-leveraged. Somehow or other he would have to unwind it, but to do that he needed funds, and ideally, he needed them from a source that wouldn't dig him further in. As long as nobody asked to withdraw, that was the immediate danger. Perhaps he could reduce the rate by half a percent, but then he wouldn't get the new business. These are not stupid people – except in one regard of course – and they all monitor the rates.

His phone pinged. It was a message from Louise. He'd told her not to do this, all he needs is for Francine to see one of these messages. But she wouldn't of course. She's not the sort of woman who would check his messages. Sometimes that worries him – maybe she doesn't care enough to be suspicious. Maybe she's planning to leave him. No, she knows she can't. He's made that clear to her. She knows what the consequences will be and it's not as if he doesn't keep her well provided for. That's probably how he ended up in this mess. He needs to divest himself of Louise – that relationship has really run its course – patch things up with Francine and then figure out how to get out of this much more serious mess. It's all bloody Stanley's fault. Perhaps he'll die soon.

———

STANLEY SET about the wheel arches with a scrubbing brush and watched with satisfaction as the soapy water turned grey. A labour of love, that's what it was. Funny to think of love, after everything that had happened. But nothing could dampen his good mood now. He was beginning a new chapter of life – a bit late, but never mind. He was still fit, that's what matters when you get into your sixties. A lifetime of fresh air, exercise and no junk food. But poor Shirley had been fit too, and the cancer had come for her just the same. Maybe luck had a lot to do with it. In which case he would make the most of the luck he had left.

He could remember being a kid with a motorbike, and this feeling is a bit like that. There are men his age who ride motorbikes, but he's not going to be one of them. It's too late now for that. He was sad for so long after Shirley died, it felt like a long black tunnel, but now he's at the other end and it's all thanks to the van. Just like the kid with the motorbike, he's going to spend endless hours working on the van. Well maybe not endless, because it's all pretty much done now, but he can always find odds and ends to get on with. There's always something you can take to pieces.

The van is a converted Ford Transit. A VW microbus would have looked cooler of course, much more Al Guthrie and the gang, but they go for cool prices these days. The Ford has everything he needs – a bed, a cooker, a TV and a shower. It has a side awning for warm days when he'll be parked up in some beauty spot, sitting in a deck chair reading a book. He's studied every video on YouTube about how to convert your van, how to do running repairs, what equipment you need to carry with you. He's researched all the places you can park up, all over Europe. He's ready for the off, he's got everything he needs. Apart from internet, he'll have to go into cafés for that. And he's got the very best fishing equipment, all the expensive gear he's wanted for years, he has it all now. That's an investment, he can write it all off against tax. He's going to be an ageing Jack Kerouc, on the road, maybe without the drugs. And his first trip will be up to London, not quite the sort of trip he had in mind, but he'll do it anyway. He's not particularly looking forward to this party, but it will be lovely to see Francine and Danny and the baby — Justin not so much.

Chapter Two

ADAM WATCHED the furniture being carried in and realised he'd have to acquire more. The contents of the flat would just rattle around in a house like this. If he'd known how much difference having money made, he might have pursued it a bit earlier, not that he'd ever been involved in anything that made money. It was a revelation. When you have money, everything in life suddenly becomes easy. He decided he wanted a house in this street and bingo – one was suddenly available. And when you are able to pay well over the asking price, no need to worry about the competition, nobody was going to be gazumping him. It's a far cry from the early days with the band – on the road, staying in crappy places, doing crappy gigs, even sleeping in the van sometimes – that was bad. Sometimes he thinks Bert and Lennie talk about him and he's noticed them looking sideways at him once or twice. He knows why. They're afraid that he's been corrupted by it, that he's going to become part of the establishment, not keep the faith. They think he's on some downward slope that will end up with him becoming a Tory donor or something. They thought it was weird that he wanted to buy a house in this ultra-respectable bit of North London, told him he'd be mixing with bankers and assholes like that. What was wrong with Hackney? You could get a big house there, plus a cool vibe. He acknowledged that, but told them he had his reasons. He wasn't going to explain the reasons, or reason singular in fact, as there was only one. Moving here was like his destiny, it was where he was meant to be, here in this street, because what he now realised was that what he wanted was here. He should have realised it years ago, but that was another story. He couldn't say any of that to Bert and Lennie, they'd think he was completely off his head. But really, it didn't matter what they thought, because he was the man with the money. Without his money, the band would have folded months ago and now, thanks to him, they didn't have to sleep in the van anymore.

Of course, Rebecca was not too pleased either. She couldn't understand why they weren't staying in the flat in Notting Hill. She was happy there. All her favourite shops and the place where she gets her nails done and her hairdresser and the cool venues she goes to with her friends. Rebecca made her protest but it didn't work. The look of surprise on her face was almost comical. She stepped on the gas and nothing happened. Rebecca was the sort of girl he had always thought would never look at him – pretty in a natural, unadorned kind of way (although the adornments increased a lot when they moved to Notting Hill), intelligent, worried about the fate of the planet. He'd learned a lot from her, tried hard to get his level of social awareness up to match hers. For a long time, he felt as though she'd made him a better person. But perhaps the money had changed him after all. She thought it had made him more 'establishment'. She was probably right. It was the ultimate in unearned income, and he knew what his younger self had always thought about that.

The rich are different, they have to be. Being in charge of a large amount of money was a responsibility after all. You couldn't go on behaving like a teenager. The money had given him a voice. Rebecca wasn't always the one who knew best now, he had decisions to make that she couldn't help with. She used to be the one with the ethical job and the decent salary, so she had supported him financially and he had fitted in with whatever she wanted. Now he didn't need her salary anymore and he was starting to wonder if he needed her. It was bad to think like that. She was a good person who had stood by him when he didn't have much to offer. She deserved better. If things worked out the way he really wanted them to (and that was a big ask) he would have to let Rebecca go. But she'd be OK, he'd make sure of that.

———

FRANCINE WAS BURPING THE BABY, taking the delivery from the caterers and wondering if they had enough glasses when a large white van pulled up outside. The caterers were driving off and Francine was about to shut the door when a figure climbed out of the van and waved to her. Stanley marched up the path, kissed her and took Tommy out of her arms. Even the baby looked pleased to see him.

Francine stared out at the street. 'What on earth are you driving Stanley?'

'Isn't she beautiful? That's my new home. I've sold the house and everything in it.'

Francine laughed. 'You're on the road? That's amazing. I'd love to be able to do that.'

'Well, when these kids are grown up you can.'

She led the way into the house. 'Maybe. Anyway, I'm so glad you're here. I'm not looking forward to tonight, I'm sure the arrangements I've made will be all wrong. Tom and Louise are bringing some new neighbours, so I guess that will be good, meet some new people. I'm hoping they might have kids. I don't know why I'm worrying so much, it's only a party.'

'There's nothing to worry about. Give people enough to drink, they won't notice anything else. What time are you collecting Danny?'

'In about an hour. You going to come?'

'Yes, why not?'

While Francine fed Tommy, Stanley got the glasses ready. Then he walked around the house. The inside looked beautiful of course, but what about the outside? It was pretty much what he would have expected. Justin hadn't had the gutters cleared and he could see some deterioration on the window frames. He buys an expensive house like this and then doesn't bother to maintain it. Justin would no way be able to do any of these jobs himself, as far as Stanley knew he'd never hammered a nail in his life, or changed a lightbulb, come to that. He probably didn't own a single tool. Stanley knew Justin wouldn't want him hanging around, he made that clear at Christmas, but Stanley wasn't too bothered about what Justin wanted. He would have been happy to cut Justin loose, but, as soon as he met Francine and Danny, he knew he wanted to look out for them. Towards the end Shirley had asked him to do that, to take care of Francine and Danny. Nothing about Justin, as if she knew. They both knew Justin wouldn't need anybody to look out for him. He was much too good at looking out for himself.

Chapter Three

RON AND WENDY were the first to arrive, bearing flowers and wine. Wendy was a no-nonsense woman who wouldn't give any thought to ideas of fashionably late and Ron did as he was told. Francine often suspected herself of latching onto surrogate parents and Ron and Wendy were certainly one set of them.

'Place looks lovely, darling,' said Wendy, looking around. 'Open the wine, Ron.' Ron picked up the bottle and set to work with a corkscrew. Francine noticed that his hands didn't look too painful today, but she was still worried that he might scratch them on the corkscrew.

'Don't mind him. He's fine,' said Wendy, following her line of sight.

'See what I have to put up with?' said Ron. 'A woman of no sympathy. One of these days, I'll walk out on her.'

Wendy rolled her eyes and held out the glasses.

Francine came back from depositing their coats, and saw Tom and Louise walk in with two new people. These must be the new neighbours. The woman had hair done in multicoloured layers and tied up on top of her head and she was wearing a white shirt and black cigarette pants – very chic. Then Francine's gaze passed onto the man and her stomach dropped with a lurch, just like sitting in a plane during turbulence. It couldn't be him. We've all got a double somewhere and this is his double. That's all it is. But her stomach was not quite convinced by this line of reasoning and she walked swiftly back into the kitchen to recover. In a few moments somebody would introduce him to her, and then she'd know. How dare he reappear like this? Or maybe he doesn't know that she lives here, she has a different surname after all. And maybe she should just stop over-thinking this and get on with it.

She fixed a smile in place and walked back into the room. It was Louise that brought them over – Adam and Rebecca. Francine smiled and shook hands and said how nice to meet them and she's sure they'll like it here. She sounded to herself as if she was just babbling rubbish, but they didn't look too alarmed, so it must have made sense. It was him alright and he seemed to be fixing her with some kind of look, which she was definitely ignoring. Checking that they had drinks, Francine swept them along merrily to meet Justin, who cast an appraising eye over Rebecca (or maybe Francine was imagining that, not that she was going to fret about it).

———

STANLEY HAD WATCHED this little exchange from across the room. Francine seemed a bit nervy, but these people looked friendly. That's what she needs, he thought, more friends around. Stanley had found himself quickly drifting towards Ted, two men of a certain age, and while he didn't like being pigeonholed like that, as far as he was concerned, Ted was probably the most interesting person here. They had one particularly sad fact in common, or almost, as Ted's wife was not yet dead, just slowly making her way there.

'It's contrary to all nature in some ways,' said Ted. 'We're the ones who are meant to go first.'

'That's true,' said Stanley. 'But we have to deal with things as they are, not as we think they ought to be. I spent a long time feeling that I shouldn't still be around. Then I bought a van.'

'Motorbikes were my thing,' said Ted. 'BSA Bantam, that was my favourite. A light bike of course, but a great top speed. Had an accident and wrote the bugger off, but I'd had some great rides, down to Cornwall, sleeping on the beaches. What it was to be young.'

Stanley took a swig of his beer. 'Triumph Bonneville,' he said. 'Got rid of it when the kids came along, but what an engine. 0 to 70 in two minutes. Always thought I'd get another but it never happened.'

———

JUSTIN ALWAYS FELT a bit awkward around Tom, but he hoped he didn't let it show. It's hard to relax in the company of a man you're cuckolding, although, when he mentioned this to Louise, she expressed the view that Tom wouldn't particularly care. That probably didn't say too much about their relationship, but who knew, really. You would never know what goes on inside somebody else's marriage. Maybe Tom was also playing away. Maybe they had an arrangement and Tom knew all about it, maybe she discussed his performance with Tom. At this thought, Justin felt a certain shrinking in the nether regions, but he brushed it aside. He couldn't control what Tom did or didn't know, but it was important that Francine didn't suspect. There was no sign that Francine suspected. True, she didn't seem to have much interest in him at the moment, but she had a baby to deal with, so that was maybe understandable. Justin dragged his attention away from all of these considerations, put on his best smile and started to circulate with the bottles. Tom clapped him on the back and wished him a happy birthday (which was a good sign) and told him some things about the new neighbours that were definitely interesting.

———

REBECCA LOOKED around the room and thought they all looked old. Well maybe not all of them. And that's what happens when you move into a neighbourhood like this. You have to mix with old people. There was an old couple that had introduced themselves as Ron and Wendy, they were friendly enough but boring. The couple that had brought her and Adam along were called Tom and Louise. He apparently worked in financial services, which was pretty boring, but they were not quite so old. Louise was definitely attractive and Rebecca had been aware of Tom casting a few glances in her own direction, so he was not past it. The man whose birthday they were here for seemed to have pinned Adam into a corner and looked to be making some kind of pitch. He was a good-looking man, something familiar about him, or maybe she was just familiar with the type. She wouldn't kick him out of bed. And now coming towards her was the man's wife. She was really pretty, but she didn't seem to have made any great effort with her appearance – eyebrows needed doing, and the nails. Rebecca looked up and smiled.

'How are you settling in Rebecca? Do you have lots to do?'

Rebecca waved a hand. 'Not so much. The house was in pretty good nick, but just very old-fashioned. We're getting the decorators in and some new lighting, stuff like that.'

'Yes, Tony and Dorothy were there for years and they had it the way they liked it. But it probably does look old-fashioned now.'

'This house is lovely.' Rebecca thought she'd better make an effort.

'We were lucky,' said Francine. 'The people before us had put in a lot of work, so we didn't have to do much. Just as well, as Justin isn't really into home improvements and we didn't need a load of disruption with a new baby.'

Ah yes, the baby. Rebecca could see that she and Francine were not going to have much in common.

'That must be very tiring,' she said. And looking more closely at Francine she could see that it was actually true. That was how Francine looked. Tired.

'Not really,' said Francine brightly. 'Well maybe, a bit, but they're so much worth it. And this is a great area for schools.'

That said it all, Rebecca thought. Definitely not going to have anything in common. Adam seemed to have extricated himself from the master of the house and headed off in the direction of two old men. And the man himself was heading in her direction.

'I'll leave you with Justin,' said Francine. 'I need to check stuff in the kitchen.' So, she was happy to pass her husband onto a slightly younger and better-maintained woman. Interesting.

Chapter Four

STANLEY REALLY WANTED to be out fiddling with the van, that's what Saturday mornings were for after all, but a well-behaved guest turns up for breakfast, so he sat at the table with Francine and the kids and chatted with Danny about frog spawn. Francine seemed a bit distracted. Danny had to ask her twice for more Rice Krispies and, in the end, Stanley got up and fetched them. Justin appeared a few minutes later, looking like a man who had had a bad night. He was getting on now, Stanley thought, too old for booze and late nights. This thought gave him some obscure satisfaction, but he acknowledged that it was unworthy.

Justin seemed to brighten up after his second cup of coffee and embarked upon an analysis of the previous evening. Francine didn't respond to any of his observations and Stanley was busy looking at his phone (shouldn't be allowed at mealtimes of course, but maybe one of the privileges of age). He was scrolling through some very interesting data when some statement of Justin's snagged his attention.

'...looks like a roadie, but he's loaded. Serious money. I just have to reel him in before Tom does.'

Francine was now looking alarmed and well she might, Stanley thought. Justin really should not be allowed near money, especially not other peoples' money. And he was well-prepared for the question that would be aimed in his direction as soon as Francine was out of the way. At that moment she picked up Tommy and headed upstairs and Stanley waited for it.

'Stanley, things are a bit tight at the moment, so perhaps you can advance me some money? We can treat it as a loan or an advance, whatever suits you.'

An advance against what he thinks will be coming his way when I die, Stanley thought savagely.

'I'm afraid not, old chap' he said, trying to sound avuncular, which didn't come off too well. 'The money from the house is tied up in a long-term loan arrangement and the rest – well – I put it in bitcoin and, as you know, that did not end well.'

Justin stared at him. 'Bitcoin? You cannot be serious. You put it in fucking bitcoin?'

Stanley shook his head and indicated Danny still sitting there and looking from one to the other.

'What on earth possessed you? You didn't discuss it with me.'

'I didn't need to discuss it with you, Justin, it was my money. And I decided to do it after a discussion with your neighbour at Christmas.'

'My neighbour? With Tom? The bastard, I'll kill him. You can't be serious. You've gambled away my mother's money? Tell me it's not true.'

'It was my money to gamble Justin. I don't think access to easy money does anybody any favours. That money is now gone and the rest, when it matures, will go to charity. I live very simply now and that suits me better.'

Justin slowly stood up. 'You self-righteous old prick. Well, that's a good thing you want to live simply, because you're not welcome here. You can go back to your bloody van. Get out of my house.'

'No.' Francine had walked back in. 'Stanley is our guest, he's Danny's grandad. I want him to stay.'

'You're wrong. He is in no way Danny's grandad.'

Justin marched out and slammed the door. A few moments later they heard the engine start and he drove off.

'Sorry about that,' said Stanley. 'He always was a bit given to tantrums. And I think he's right in one sense. I did sound a bit bloody self-righteous.'

Francine shrugged. 'It's not your fault. Justin has a preoccupation with money that worries me. He has a good job and he keeps telling me everything is OK, but I'm afraid it isn't.'

'He went through a gambling period when he was young,' said Stanley. 'Shirley had to bail him out several times. Right now, he has a good job, as far as I know, and he should have plenty of money of his own, but he's still looking for more. I want you to know' he said, looking directly at her, 'that I will always make sure you and the kids are OK. It's just that giving money to Justin doesn't seem like the best way of doing that.'

'That's kind of you Stanley, and I hope it won't come to that. I don't like being dependent on Justin and as soon as Tommy is a bit bigger, I'm planning to get back to work.'

'That's a good idea love. In the meantime, I'll do what Justin suggested and set off home.'

Francine shook her head. 'No, I want you to stay for a

few days, we see very little of you. Justin will just have to get over himself.'

Stanley smiled. 'If you're sure it's what you want, then I will. I suppose the money being gone is good in one way. Justin will have no reason to murder me now.'

Chapter Five

JUSTIN DROVE at top speed towards central London, slowing fractionally for a zebra crossing and wishing it had been Stanley walking across it. Hit and run. Can't be that hard. Except for the bloody cameras. He went past the sign for the Ultra Low Emission Zone and realised he had probably already been clocked. He'd have to pay the charge. And there would be nowhere to park. Fuck everything. Probably time to go back. Maybe the old bastard would have done as he was told and cleared off. Not that his departure would solve the problem. There was still the small matter of Justin's money, the money he was entitled to, his birthright. Stanley had no right to throw it away. Just thinking about it was giving him heartburn. And Tom, another bastard. Did Tom know? Was that why he had done this? Perhaps he should pay Tom a visit. He took the next right turn and headed back uphill.

Tom was just putting out the bins when Justin strode towards him and shoved him inside.

'Justin. What the hell?'

'You know exactly what the hell. You got Stanley to invest in bitcoin. Made good commission on that did you?'

'What are you talking about? I don't trade bitcoin.'

'But you told him it was a good investment. At that party at Christmas. That's bollocks, and you know it. He's lost the lot.'

Tom shrugged. 'We were just chatting. It was a party for fuck's sake. I'd probably had too much to drink. I didn't expect him to go off and just do it.' Tom hesitated for a moment. 'Do you mean he put it all with that outfit that went down?'

Justin narrowed his eyes and saw the beginnings of a laugh, hastily suppressed, creep across Tom's face. That did it.

Justin had never had much exposure to street fighting and his punch went in too low, missing Tom's jaw and smacking into his throat. Tom went down like a bunch of skittles, holding his throat with one hand and clawing the air with the other. At the same moment Justin heard a key in the front door. There was no hope of making any kind of escape, so he didn't try. The door to the kitchen opened and there stood Louise. For once in his life, Justin didn't know what to say. He just stood there looking at his handiwork. Louise bent over her husband, who seemed to be still breathing, and then Justin heard her calling 999 and asking for an ambulance. She was describing it as an assault. Justin thought that was a pretty fair description.

The paramedics arrived ten minutes later, which was very impressive on the whole. They must have been just passing. Ten minutes during which Louise knelt over her husband, who had conveniently manoeuvred himself into the recovery position, and Justin and Louise, who were after all very familiar with each other, did not exchange a word.

Louise was obviously too appalled to speak to him and Justin couldn't work out how this exchange was supposed to go. He wondered if Louise thought that the argument had been about her. She'd probably be disappointed when she discovered that it was something completely different.

The paramedics arrived and reassured Louise that Tom was alive and breathing, but it looked like concussion so they were taking him in. The operator had also called the police and a uniformed constable turned up before the ambulance had left with Tom and Louise. Louise gave him her version of events and he then called up a squad car to take Justin to the station.

'Really officer,' Justin said, as they lowered his head in, 'this is a gross overreaction. It was simply an accident.' They ignored him and set off. At the station he was identified, fingerprinted and then left alone in an empty room. The hours ticked by. They'd taken his phone, so he had nothing to look at but his watch, which wasn't telling him much. Fucking Stanley. It was all his fault. He'd blighted Justin's life ever since he'd arrived on the scene. Grasping old bastard. This will give him a good laugh. But never mind Stanley. What will Francine think? She'll be horrified. And what about Louise? Will she ever speak to him again? And if they charge him, will it get in the papers? What about his job? Will this give Cargill the excuse he needs to force him out? The consequences seemed to multiply the more he thought about them. For God's sake, it was only a punch. People in movies punch each other on the jaw all the time, they don't bloody fall over. Why the hell did Tom have to collapse like that? Why couldn't he take it like a man, maybe punch Justin back? Then it would have been a fight, that would have seemed more honourable. As it was, Justin had started a fight and Tom had wimped out, making it look like an assault. But maybe he won't lead with that story, he'll stick to the accident. First, if anybody ever appears, he needs to demand his phone call, get Martin Sanger down here. He'll have him out of here in five minutes.

MARTIN SANGER TURNED up an hour later, looking like he'd been dragged away from something more important. He agreed with Justin that the accident explanation was their best bet, but didn't seem too optimistic about whether it would work. It was important to bat back any suggestion of premeditation or intent to injure. Justin didn't find this attitude reassuring. God knows, he'd be paying through the nose for this. He had the right to expect his solicitor to be putting in the effort.

Two hours later, two expensive hours, as Justin reminded himself, they were joined by two plainclothes police officers. The woman was middle-aged and jaded-looking. Justin thought she really should be giving some attention to personal maintenance. Her hair had had some bad colour job, her eyebrows were all over the place and her nails were short and unvarnished, although, now he thought about it, really posh women didn't have long nails. Probably interfered with the gardening. But this one wasn't posh, she was just a lower-level cop. At that moment she looked up at him and he experienced the uncomfortable feeling that she had just read all of his observations, as if they were tattooed across his face. The other officer was younger and better-dressed, and looked like one of Justin's juniors at the bank. He was obviously the clever one.

The young officer set up the recording equipment and then the woman gave the names of those present. Justin

Beattie, Martin Sanger, DI Murphy and DC Wilcox. Justin was shocked. She was the DI and the smart young man was the junior. Who could have guessed?

DI Murphy turned to Justin. 'OK Mr Beattie. You've been brought in here following an assault. Quite a serious assault, as the victim has been hospitalised. Would you like to tell us how this happened?'

Justin spread his palms and hoped he looked sincere. 'It was an accident,' he said.

DI Murphy looked puzzled. 'An accident?' she repeated. 'Your fist accidentally connected with Mr Fraser's throat? How did that happen? Did you maybe trip over and fall forward with your right arm extended and your hand bunched into a fist, perhaps in some kind of revolutionary salute, and then Mr Fraser's neck happened to break your fall? Was that how it happened?'

Justin was suddenly very angry. He knew the accident explanation wouldn't wash. Why hadn't his bloody expensive solicitor come up with something better? And now he had to sit here and be politely ridiculed by this woman who looked like his office cleaner. Martin Sanger was signalling to him to say nothing, but he ignored him.

'No, that wasn't how it happened,' he snapped. 'We had a disagreement. I hit him and I expected him to hit me back. I didn't expect him to just fall over.'

Martin Sanger shook his head vigorously at this example of victim-blaming, but DI Murphy just looked interested.

'I think I get it,' she said. 'Supposed to be like Fight Club, was it?' A faint smile spread across her face. 'With you as Brad Pitt?'

Justin felt himself about to erupt. The young police officer was having trouble keeping a straight face. Martin

Sanger had obviously decided that this was his cue to intervene. He grabbed Justin's arm.

'My client has nothing further to say. If you're not proposing to charge him, we're leaving.'

'We won't be charging you until we've heard from the victim, Mr Beattie,' said the young officer. 'We'd like you to make a statement and then you can leave. We know where to find you.'

Chapter Six

FRANCINE HAD BEEN DREADING Monday morning. Justin had come home in the early hours of Sunday and told her what had happened. He had looked completely wrecked and seemed genuinely contrite but Francine was too shocked to offer him any kind of absolution. She had discovered pretty early on that he had something of a violent streak, but he had not tried anything with her since she had become pregnant with Tommy -and since she had told him that she would leave immediately if he ever hit her again. So, she had thought that maybe that was all over. Violence within the home was awful, but at least it was within the home. If you could deal with it, nobody else needed to know. But to attack somebody else, whatever the provocation, made you a criminal, or at the very least a public nuisance. It brought shame on them all. Louise would have told everybody, all the other mothers. But that's not what really matters. What matters is whether Tom is OK. And how Louise feels. How will she ever be able to face Louise again? What can she say to her?

28

Justin had gone off to work early but Stanley was still there, holding the baby and eating cereal with Danny. 'I think I'll take Danny to school today,' he announced. 'It will be my morning exercise.'

'Yes!' shouted Danny. 'You come, Grandad.'

Francine felt the same, the temptation to send them off together and hide at home was definitely there. But it had to be faced sometime. 'Maybe we'll all go' she said.

The walk to the school seemed to take no time at all. It was always like that when you really didn't want to arrive somewhere. As they went through the gates a few people looked at them, several others smiled. Francine could see that they all knew, they were all complicit. They were talking about her already. And there, coming towards her, was Louise. It was too late to retreat.

But Louise was smiling. She grasped Francine's arm.

Francine stared at her. 'How is he?'

'He's fine. A bit of concussion, a lump on the head, bit of a bruise on the neck. They sent him home yesterday. No lasting damage. It looked more serious than it was. So don't worry.'

'I'm so sorry. I don't know what to say.'

Louise shook her head. 'You don't have to be sorry. You didn't do it. And I think probably Justin didn't really mean to hurt him. Tom and I have discussed it, he agreed with me in the end and he's not going to press charges. We're neighbours, after all.'

Francine let out the breath she had been holding. 'Thank you so much.'

Louise smiled. 'De nada. And, in case you're wondering, we haven't said anything to anybody else. Whoops, there's the bell, catch you later.' She ran off to retrieve Sally and Danny waved and made his way in.

'See?' said Stanley. 'Nothing to worry about. Sensible woman, not making a fuss.'

'I can't believe it' said Francine, as they went out through the gate. 'I really wasn't expecting that.'

If Louise was offering to forget the whole thing, Francine was going to take it and run. But it was a bit surprising. She and Louise were not close friends and what Justin had done was appalling. Why was Louise being so decent about it?

Chapter Seven

TED APPEARED SOON after they arrived home and Stanley remembered that he had invited Ted round to see the van. He collected the keys and they made their way out.

'It's brilliant' said Ted as Stanley showed off the shower and the waste disposal. 'The stuff you can have these days. I remember going to a pop festival once in one of these vans. Somewhere up North. No furniture, no mod cons. And six of us sleeping on the floor, just on the corrugated metal floor, no carpets. Don't think we even had sleeping bags. Never been so cold in my life. But this is something else. Going off in this will be an adventure.'

'That's what I'm hoping,' said Stanley. 'I didn't really do enough travelling when I was young. There was always something else to worry about, first the kids of course and then when Angela died, I thought about taking off. But then I met Shirley. Now I've lost Shirley, that was a terrible blow and, at my age, there's nothing left worth worrying about.'

'That's true enough,' said Ted. 'I did a bit of travelling in the army, and Molly came too, but she won't be travelling any more now. But, you know, we've had our differences over the years, like any couple, but our relationship now, for the short time we have left, is better than it's ever been. We can really appreciate each other in a way that's completely honest. There are no agendas, nothing hidden, neither of us has anything to gain from the other, anything we may have disagreed about in the past is of no importance now. I know it has to end, but I don't want it to. I used to think it must be easier if the other person just dies suddenly, and then it's all over. But now I know I would have hated that, because all the things we want to say to each other, we can say them now. It's a very precious time.'

'That's how it was with me and Shirley,' said Stanley. 'We were very close at the end. You do get a bit isolated 'though. What are your neighbours like?'

'I used to have lovely neighbours,' said Ted. 'Dorothy and Tony. They would come in and sit with Molly so that I could go shopping. Now I get it all delivered, of course. I miss Dorothy and Tony. They sold up and moved into one of those retirement villages. The new neighbours are a young couple. I've seen them around, they were at your party, but I haven't been introduced to them yet. Hope they don't have noisy parties.'

Chapter Eight

ADAM FOUND himself staring out of the window at the house opposite. He needed to formulate an approach and it now looked like it wouldn't be that easy. She hadn't looked too pleased to see him the other night, she'd looked shocked more than anything. She would need time to think about it, come to terms with the idea. He'd have to be patient. Maybe there were just a few things that couldn't be handled with money.

She was back from the school run now and the two old guys had gone off in the van, so this was his chance. He had to start somewhere. He cast a cursory glance in the mirror, not looking too bad, straightened his collar and let himself out of the front door. He couldn't see any movement in the house opposite, but she must be in there somewhere. Time to man up. He walked up the path and rang the bell. No time to think about it, that was best.

Francine opened the door and looked at him with what he could only describe as a mixture of shock and distress. This wasn't a good start.

'I'm not here to cause any trouble,' he began. No, that was a mistake. Start again. Smile for God's sake. 'What I mean is, this is just a social call. It's so lovely to see you again. I thought we could have a chat. We are neighbours, after all.'

The last bit was a low blow, reminding her that she couldn't avoid him anyway. He saw that register on her face. She stood aside.

'You'd better come in.'

Adam shut the front door behind him and followed her into the kitchen. She turned around to look at him.

'Now that you're here, I guess I should offer you coffee. That's what neighbours do, isn't it?'

He nodded. 'Coffee. Yes, I'd like that.' He looked around. The kitchen looked bigger than the last time he was in here – more space without all the bodies. One wall had a corkboard with children's drawings.

Francine brought over the cups and the coffee pot and sat down. She had one of those boiling water taps, so the process took seconds.

'Tell me how you came to be here, Adam. It can't just be a coincidence.'

'You're thinking I went looking for you?'

'Well, did you? Is that what you did?'

He nodded. 'Yes.'

She sat back and looked hard at him. 'Let me get this straight. You found out where I was and bought the house opposite. You actually bought a house for that purpose?'

'Yes. I did.'

'That's creepy. I won't have you stalking me like that.'

He sighed. This was going all wrong. 'I'm not going to stalk you. I just wanted to see you again. How can that be so wrong?'

Francine poured the coffee and pushed a cup across to him.

'It can be so wrong because we were finished years ago. Finished by you, as far as I remember. And now you think you can walk back in again and I'll be pleased to see you?'

'No, I'm not expecting you to be pleased. And I can see that it's been a shock to see me again. I was young and stupid, Francine. I didn't realise what I had. I'm different now. I've grown up. If you knew how many times I've regretted what I did. I accepted for years that there was no way back. Then I had a ...change of circumstances ... and I thought maybe...'

'You thought maybe that I would take you back now that you had money? You really haven't grown up at all, have you? But I have. I am all grown up. I have a family now and a life that doesn't include you.'

'The thing is,' he hesitated, 'when I left, you were pregnant.'

She sat back and crossed her arms. 'And?'

'And your son...'

'You want to know if he's yours? Well fuck you.'

'Francine, I know he's mine. You probably gave birth about six months after I took off. There's no way he's not my son. I'm not asking for custody. I just wanted the chance to meet him, to see both of you again.'

'You are not going to have anything to do with him. And you have a wife of your own now. Go and have your own babies.'

'Rebecca doesn't want children.' There. He'd said it.

'She doesn't want children, so you think you can help yourself to my child? Seriously?'

'No, of course not.' This was really going badly. 'I just

wanted to see you both. I'm not about to cause any trouble, or upset your life.'

'Don't you think you've already upset my life by turning up here? If you want to not upset my life, put that house back on the market and go somewhere else. You'll probably still make money on it.'

'Listen.' He sat forward and concentrated on engaging her attention. 'If you want me to go away, I will. It might take a while to sell the house, but I'll do it. All I wanted was to see you again, see how you were, see – OK, I'll admit it – if there was any chance of us getting back together. I wanted to see my child.' She opened her mouth to protest, but he carried on. 'But I'm not going to make a problem of myself. I'd like us to be friends, we could be old friends, we are old friends. What would be wrong with that?'

'Adam.' She was looking a bit more friendly, that was good. 'You have a wife now. You have to think about her. How would she feel about you sitting here saying all this stuff to me?'

He sighed. 'To be honest, I don't think she'd be too bothered. Sometimes I'm not too sure what goes on in Rebecca's head. Anyway, I'm not here to talk about her.'

'But it is about her. It intimately concerns her. She's your wife. You're here proposing to re-establish some kind of relationship with me, how can that not affect her?'

'It would affect her, of course, but I'd make sure she was OK.'

'You mean you'd pay her off? Adam, listen to yourself. You're no more responsible now than you were back then. This is all bonkers.'

He stood up. 'You're right. We need to deal with this in a grown-up fashion. I don't want there to be any awkwardness. Surely, it's OK for people to know that we're old friends from college? It seems preferable to trying to hide it.'

She nodded. 'OK, I'll go along with that, but that's all. And you're not getting access to Danny.'

'Oh, is that his name? That's a good name. Maybe I could help out, do some babysitting, take him out places. Boys need men in their lives.'

'He actually has a lot of men in his life. He has Justin and Stanley, who's his grandad and Ron, our neighbour, who takes him out walking the dog. So, no, we don't need you. We're managing fine. Get on and live your own life.'

Adam cast around for something else to say. Nothing came to mind.

Francine stood up. 'I'd like you to leave now Adam.' She led the way to the front door and opened it. Adam found himself standing on the other side of it faster than he had anticipated.

'I'm glad we had this chat…' he began, but she had already shut the door. Well, it could have gone worse. It could have gone better, that was for sure, but it could have gone a lot worse.

Adam made his way back, feeling slightly optimistic. She'd come round in time. That husband of hers, he was definitely flaky. He'd looked right at home chatting up the women at that party - Rebecca included. Maybe they could swap? No, that was stupid. He was getting ahead of himself. But if that husband was out of the picture, if anything happened to him, if he ran off with someone else, then he, Adam would be there to pick up the pieces. No doubt about it.

Chapter Nine

REBECCA REACHED ACROSS and topped up their wine glasses. This place had been a mistake, that was for sure. If there was any vibe at all it was a middle-aged one. They should have gone back to Notting Hill, met up somewhere there. It wasn't the East End, but at least there were young people. She was going to die of boredom living round here.

'It's not so bad,' said Ruby, looking around at the decidedly 90's décor. 'I don't see any fanciable blokes, so maybe it's not so good either, but it's definitely what they call a well-heeled area. Actually, the barman is quite cute.'

'I don't think that really makes up for the lack of edge,' said Rebecca. 'Hackney or Stoke Newington would have been more like the right area. I wouldn't have chosen to live round here. It's all a bit...settled.'

'But you're settled now,' said Ruby, 'so maybe this is the right area to be living in. It will be a good place to bring up kids. Plenty of green space, probably good schools. Isn't that what you moved for, now that you're married?'

Rebecca set her glass down. 'Moving here wasn't my

idea, I'm not thinking of kids and schools. It was Adam, I don't know what came over him. He put in an offer for the house without even consulting me. He's really changed since he became rich.'

'But Rebecca, let's be honest, you weren't married to him before he became rich. Maybe being married has changed him.' Ruby laughed. 'Maybe he wants to settle down now and have a family. And you said yourself, it's a pretty nice house.'

'Yes, the house is fine. It's a bloody expensive house in fact, better than I ever thought I'd find myself living in. The area's boring and the neighbours are boring, but there's not much I can do about that. And Adam has made noises about children, but I've made it pretty clear to him that it's off the table, for the foreseeable future at any rate. Can't see me breastfeeding and changing nappies. I've seen those women pushing buggies in the rain – that's not for me. And anyway, my job's important, the charity is really going places and I'm due a substantial pay rise next year.'

'I was a bit surprised, to be honest, when you got married. Just like that, as it were.' Ruby sat back and took a sip of her drink.

'You're thinking I married him for his money?'

'Well, didn't you?'

Rebecca shrugged. 'Maybe that was part of it. Not so much the money itself, although that's kind of nice, but he somehow became more attractive. Once he had the money, he was more confident, I could see myself staying with him.'

'And now you're not so sure?'

'Oh, I'm definitely staying for the ride. I just need to get him back under control. At the moment he never seems to hear a word I say. Either he thinks he can ignore me or he's losing his hearing – all those years of listening to loud bands.' She laughed suddenly. 'If he ends up needing hearing aids, I really will be leaving him.'

'It's weird, marrying for money,' said Ruby. 'I thought that only happened in books.'

'It happens a lot more often than you think. Not of course that it's true in my case.'

'But if you left him, you wouldn't get much. Not with no kids. So maybe you need to rethink that.'

Rebecca smiled and shook her head. 'Any rethinking I do won't be in that direction. You can bet on that.'

Chapter Ten

STANLEY CHECKED and double-checked Danny's seat belt. Maybe he should get new ones fitted, these were a bit old and stiff.

'It's alright, grandad. I told you I fastened it.'

'So you did. You were quite right.'

Stanley put it in first gear and eased gently away from the kerb. Francine was bound to be looking out of the window and he didn't want her worrying.

'We could probably go faster,' said Danny.

Stanley nodded. 'We could. But this is not a fast vehicle with a powerful engine. Not like your dad's car. And we have plenty of time, we don't have to be anywhere.'

'My dad never takes us anywhere in his car anyway,' said Danny. 'We always go in mum's car, that's where the car seats are. Not that I need a car seat anymore,' he added hurriedly.

'No, of course you don't. You're a big guy now.' Stanley eased his way past a removal van. 'What do you like doing at school Danny?'

Danny shrugged. 'Football, I guess. But I'm not one of the best. A lot of guys are taller than me.'

'I don't think being tall is the most important thing,' said Stanley, while admitting to himself that he had no idea whether that was true or not. 'Basketball players need to be tall. Footballers need to be fast runners.'

At that moment a woman went past being pulled along the pavement by four dogs and Danny burst out laughing. Football was forgotten. Stanley thought about the fact that he had never been a football 'dad'. The children of his first marriage had been Jess and Amy, and that was in the days when girls didn't play football, though he was sure he could remember both of them being good at netball. And by the time he had met and married Shirley, Justin was past the football stage, so there had been no Saturday mornings shouting encouragement from the side of a muddy field. Maybe that was what had always been wrong. They had never had anything much to bond over. Looking at it now, he and Justin had been disappointed in each other. He had looked forward to having a stepson to do things with, maybe woodwork and fishing. Justin wasn't interested in any of these sorts of pursuits. Maybe Justin had hoped to have a stepdad with a posh job, somebody with influence. Maybe he was being unfair. Actually, no he wasn't. He could remember Shirley introducing them and the look on Justin's face as he turned to Shirley.

'A postman? You're marrying a postman?'

Really, it was downhill from there. They cohabited in peace for Shirley's sake, but Stanley couldn't hide his relief when Justin went off to university and showed no inclination to come home for the holidays. The good thing was that Justin was clever, so Stanley had always known that he would be successful, financially at least. He'd make his own way. And now he had a good job and a big salary. The only problem was the fatal flaw. It had probably never gone away and now it was coming up again. Stanley circled the park and found a space big enough for the van. He pulled forward and put it into reverse. If what he thought was correct, something would have to be done.

Chapter Eleven

FRANCINE HAD TRIED hard to avoid Adam and Rebecca's housewarming party, suggesting that Justin should go and say she wasn't well.

'That's not like you,' said Justin. 'You always used to be up for a party. Or is there some reason you don't want to go?'

'I'm just tired,' she said. 'Tommy woke me up three times last night and I'll have to get Danny up for school tomorrow.'

'You'll be fine after a drink,' he replied. 'Sunday's an unusual night for a shindig, but maybe it stops people staying too late, although I guess these people don't have to worry too much about getting up in the morning. Aren't you going to wear a dress? This guy Adam is interesting, I'd like the chance to talk to him.'

'What, because he has money?'

'Partly, yes. I'm interested to see how he is investing. Offer him my expertise.'

'I think offering your expertise to the neighbours is not a good idea,' said Francine. 'Bit close to home.'

'Well anyway, we'll go and put in an appearance. Wilma's already coming to babysit. And it might give me a chance to smooth things over with Tom.'

That last point she couldn't argue with. Justin definitely needed to make things right with Tom. And maybe she'd just have to get used to seeing Adam around. He was unlikely to do as she suggested and move out.

They could hear the music from across the road, a heavy bass with an electronic undertone. Sounded a bit rough. Francine was glad she'd stuck with the jeans.

'Christ,' said Justin. 'They'd better have invited all the neighbours or the calls to the council will be flooding in.'

The door was opened by a young man in a faded T-shirt and tangled hair brandishing a beer bottle. He looked them up and down, said 'Hi' and wandered off leaving them to close the door. Francine smiled to herself. This was more like the sort of party she used to go to when she was young. Perhaps she could just head straight for the kitchen and get away from the mingling. Then she remembered that the person she had most often been accompanied by in those days was Adam. Best not think about that.

The kitchen was not the dropout bolthole that Francine was looking for. Two young women in long black aprons were arranging canapés and they looked at her in a way that was definitely unwelcoming. So much for that. Professional caterers. Who knew? She went back into the long knocked-through sitting room and looked for Stanley. Justin hadn't wanted Stanley to come, in fact he had tried to persuade her that Stanley should be babysitting, but Francine had made Stanley's attendance a condition of her own. She spotted Stanley in the corner talking to Ted and was about to make her way over there when Louise appeared in front of her and started relaying the latest happenings at the school. Francine wasn't too interested in school politics, but she did owe Louise a debt of gratitude, so she stood and listened and made what she hoped were the right noises and wondered how soon she could make her escape from this party. At least they were only across the road. If she got out without anybody seeing, she could be home drinking hot chocolate with Wilma in five minutes.

Sometime afterwards, Stanley joined them and she noticed that Ted had gone. 'He had to get back to Molly,' said Stanley, seeing her looking around. 'It's good that he looked in at all really.'

'Poor Ted,' said Louise. 'It's a hard situation to cope with.' She took a cracker with something on it from a passing tray.

Stanley nodded. 'Yes, it is hard,' he said, 'but he's making a good job of it. I've told young Adam that he should maybe turn the music down a bit, I'm sure it must be loud next door, but he looked at me like he didn't understand what I was on about.'

Ron and Wendy appeared at that moment, Ron with his fingers poised dramatically in his ears. Wendy cuffed him on the elbow and he took them out.

'This one of those moments,' he said, 'when one wishes one had hearing aids. Then you could just take them out. Never mind' he added, noticing the long black aprons circulating, 'perhaps the food will make up for it.'

'Don't wish hearing aids on yourself,' said Stanley. 'They'll arrive soon enough.'

'It is a bit loud,' said Louise. 'My boiler's making noises a bit like that at the moment. I'm just waiting for it to clap out.

'Probably trapped air,' said Stanley. 'Easy enough to fix.'

Francine spotted Adam heading in their direction, but he was headed off by Justin, who seemed eager to engage him in conversation. They took up a position behind her and she tried to keep one ear on their conversation while attending to Stanley's explanation of boilers.

'I've been looking been looking into your firm' she heard Adam say. 'Some people seem to be getting very high returns – well above the market average.'

Justin's reply was drowned out by a burst of laughter on the other side of the room and two young men, one of whom she recognised as the man who had opened the door to them, waved to Adam and headed for the front door. Rebecca appeared behind them, wearing what Francine recognised as a very fashionable dress, and one of them threw an arm round her shoulder and kissed her cheek. Then they were gone. So, people had started to leave. Francine was cheered by this and, when Justin joined her looking less than animated, she realised that he had, amazingly, had the same thought.

'It's been a long day' she told the others. 'I think I'm done.' Stanley nodded but showed no sign of accompanying them. Ron said 'Good idea. We'll be doing the same just as soon as I've had one of those shellfish things.' Louise smiled and said 'See you tomorrow' to Francine.

'I don't think we need to say goodbye to Adam,' Francine told Justin and, to her surprise, he agreed. 'I've pretty much said goodbye to him anyway,' he said.

Francine felt a powerful sense of relief as they pulled the door shut behind them. 'A French exit. I think that's the earliest we've ever extricated ourselves from a party,' she told Justin.

He was looking less pleased. 'I don't think he's somebody I can do business with,' he said. 'Plenty of money but no idea what to do with it.'

'He probably has his own financial advisors anyway,' said Francine. It was good that this possible connection was not going to come to anything. There was already too much connection between them.

Chapter Twelve

JUSTIN EMERGED from the shower and was surprised to find Louise already dressed.

'I thought we'd be staying for a bit longer,' he said. 'I usually take more than an hour for lunch.'

'I'm thinking,' said Louise, 'that we've outstayed our welcome with this.'

He took a minute to digest this as he towelled his hair. 'OK, what are you saying exactly?'

Louise straightened the sheets and sat down on the bed. 'I'm saying that it's been a pleasant diversion, Justin, but I think this is a good time to end it. You have a lovely wife that you should pay more attention to and me – well, I've realised that I really do care about Tom. I guess him being… injured…made that clear to me.'

Justin threw his towel down and retrieved his underpants from the floor.

'I see. So, what we've just had was a last fling, was it? Have you just made this decision or had you made it before you arrived?'

'It's been something I've been feeling for a few days,' she said. 'But I'm making the decision now.'

'My performance this lunchtime was not up to scratch, is that it? You weren't too bothered about Tom at the outset, were you? Now that I've decked him, you've decided you love him after all. And don't you dare weigh in with observations about me and Francine. Our relationship is nothing to do with you.'

'OK, that's fair enough,' said Louise. 'It's none of my business. The relationship I have to think about now is my relationship with Tom. That's what I need to repair.'

'I don't know what you need to repair, seeing as he doesn't even know about this.' He stopped. 'Or does he?'

'No.' She shook her head. 'I've made sure of that.'

'That's alright then,' he said savagely. 'You can concentrate on rekindling your romance. Maybe you can have one of those creepy ceremonies where you renew your vows, and we'll all come along and congratulate you.'

She sighed. 'Justin, we need to be grown up about this, I think. Our families are neighbours, we'll still be seeing each other. I'd like us to be friends. And I'd like to be able to talk to Francine without wondering at the back of my mind whether she knows anything.'

'She doesn't know anything' he shouted. 'I've told you that before. Actually,' he lowered his voice, 'I'm not sure she'd be that bothered. She's more interested in bloody Stanley than me. And possibly that Adam guy.'

Louise smiled. 'I love Stanley,' she said. 'Do you know, he came round and fixed my boiler.'

'Well, I'm glad he was of some use to you,' said Justin. 'Because as far as I'm concerned, he's someone who's really outstayed his welcome. I'm getting rid of the bugger, one way or another.'

Chapter Thirteen

'I'VE NEVER BEEN one for fishing,' said Ted, stretching out on the grass, 'but now I can see the attraction. I'd heard of Syon Park of course, but I had no idea it was like this.'

'Two hundred acres of parkland,' said Stanley. 'To just sit here for an afternoon on a lovely day is all you need. What other activity gives you the excuse to do that?'

'I'd have loved to bring Molly here,' said Ted. 'So beautiful and peaceful. But it's not really feasible.'

'I don't think the trip out here in the van would do her much good, unfortunately,' said Stanley. 'There's a lot of rocking around. You'd have to hire a very comfortable vehicle.'

'Even then it wouldn't work,' said Ted. 'She's not even strong enough to get out of bed now. But she was determined that I should come. She phoned Wilma up herself. She doesn't want me to be tied down, she says. What I'm dreading is the moment when I won't be tied down. Even the way she is, I want to hang onto her. I kid myself that a cure is just round the corner, maybe it will arrive in time. But that's not fair on her of course.'

'No, it's not,' said Stanley. 'But I understand how you feel. I felt the same way about Shirley. And the good thing is, we have no decision to make. Nature takes its course and there's nothing we can do about it. All we can do is make it as bearable as possible for them.'

'I'll be glad when Stevie gets here,' said Ted. 'You must have found it a comfort, having Justin there.'

Stanley attached a lure to the end of his line. 'Not so much, to be honest' he said. 'I'm not actually Justin's dad of course and we never managed to establish any kind of father-son or rather stepfather-stepson relationship. It was sad for Shirley, because she really wanted that. I guess he loved his mum, but it was never much in evidence. He didn't seem that bothered when she died. And now of course he's as mad as a sack full of rattlesnakes, because Shirley didn't make a will so, as her husband, everything has come to me.'

Ted raised his eyebrows. 'Yes, I can imagine that causing some upset.'

Stanley smiled. 'Obviously there's plenty of money and I'm not going to spend it all. Most of it will come to him when I die and I've made a will to that effect. But he wants to get his hands on the money now and I'm holding off on that, because I think he has a gambling problem.'

'I associate gambling more with chaps at the bottom end of the income ladder,' said Ted. 'Not people with nice houses and good jobs.'

'It's a bit like drugs,' said Stanley. 'You associate drugs with rough estates, but lots of smart, wealthy people enjoy having a sniff. And nowadays gambling's online so nobody knows you're doing it. And there are exclusive gambling clubs too, if you want to do it in a bit of style.'

'And you think Justin's involved in all this?'

'The fact that he's desperate for money makes me think he must be. Nobody in his position should be desperate for money. And it's not fair on Francine and the kids. How he hangs onto her, I don't know.'

At that moment Stanley's rod started to bend and he passed it to Ted.

'Here, grab hold of this, I'm going to make a quick video. Brilliant, now wind it in slowly…'

———

TED HAD BEEN BACK HOME for a couple of hours when he heard the screaming from next door. He ran round and knocked on the front door but it wasn't opened. The screaming was now interspersed with sobs. He ran back into his own house, through to the garden and climbed over the fence. The back door wasn't locked.

In the kitchen Rebecca was kneeling over Adam who was lying flat on the floor. There was a small pool of blood around his head. He was very dead. Ted clapped a hand to his pocket and discovered he hadn't brought his phone. He squatted down next to Rebecca.

'Where's your phone? We need to call the ambulance.'

Rebecca looked wildly at him and began to scrabble in her handbag. Ted took the phone from her and called the emergency services. Then he sat on the floor next to her and put an arm round her. There was nothing much else he could do.

Chapter Fourteen

'WELL, there's not much doubt about how he died.'

Detective Inspector Miranda Murphy looked down at the body on the floor. A man in his mid-thirties, in T-shirt, jeans and socks. Probably had the sort of wife who made him take his shoes off in the house. 'And we won't have any problem identifying him. Poor chap.'

'Still with the headphones round his neck. He must have been playing music or recording something.' Detective Constable Kevin Wilcox walked around the body. 'It's possible he could have tripped over the flex.'

The paramedics had pronounced life extinct and left. Noises at the front door announced the arrival of the pathologist. It was Frank, already togged up, dropping his bag on the floor and pulling out his gloves.

'Massive trauma to the back of the head,' he announced a few minutes later. 'And there's a bruise to the jaw just coming up. Looks like somebody punched him and he fell backwards and hit his head – on that.' He pointed to the corner of a granite worktop.

Murphy nodded. 'We'll get SOCO to swab that area. What about time of death?'

Frank ran a finger down the jaw. 'First signs of rigor are appearing now. So probably one to two hours ago. That's as close as you're going to get. PM might tell you a bit more. I'll book it in now.'

He stripped off his gloves, picked up his bag and made his way out. Murphy gave the signal to the mortuary attendants.

'OK,' she said, 'let's make room for SOCO. Time to talk to his wife. What's her name?'

'Rebecca.'

Rebecca was sitting on a sofa in the room next door with her head in her hands. A female PC sat with her, passing tissues. Murphy took a seat opposite.

'Mrs Bryce, I'm Detective Inspector Miranda Murphy and this is my colleague Detective Constable Kevin Wilcox. We're very sorry for your loss and we don't want to intrude more than necessary, but I'm sure you can appreciate how important it is for us to get an investigation underway quickly. If you feel up to answering a few questions, that would be very helpful.'

Rebecca looked up, blew her nose and nodded briefly.

'You arrived home at what time?'

Rebecca frowned. 'Just before seven o'clock. I noticed the clock in the kitchen before...' She mopped at her eyes.

'Yes, I understand. And where had you come home from?'

'From work. Just off the Strand. I came home on the Northern Line. Then I got off the tube and walked.'

'And can you tell us exactly what you found when you came home?'

'I walked into the kitchen and there he was. I just

screamed, I guess it must have been loud because one of the neighbours came in.'

'That was Ted Yardley,' said Wilcox, looking at his notes. 'Did you know Mr Yardley well?'

Rachel looked confused for a moment. 'No. I didn't know him at all. Well, I'd seen him before but never spoken to him.'

'And you opened the door to him?'

'No, he came in the back. The back door must have been unlocked. Adam was always leaving it open.' She began crying again.

'Mrs Bryce,' said Murphy. 'Just one more question and we'll leave you in peace. Did your husband have any enemies, anybody he was in dispute with, anybody who had threatened him with harm.'

She shook her head. 'No, of course not. We'd only been living here a fortnight.'

Murphy stood up. 'Thank you. That's all we need to know for the moment. Is there somebody we can call to come and be with you?'

'I don't know... My sister.'

'That's good. And is there somewhere you can go and stay? With your sister maybe? We'll need you to leave the house for the time being. Diana here will stay with you until that's arranged.' Murphy nodded at the PC and they let themselves out, skirting around the SOCOs going in and out of the front door.

'Next stop next door,' said Wilcox and Murphy nodded.

Ted Yardley opened the door and admitted them silently. They followed him into the kitchen.

'My wife's asleep,' he said. 'We'll go in here and she won't be disturbed.'

'Is your wife ill, Mr Yardley?' asked Wilcox.

Ted Yardley nodded. 'Yes. Terminally.'

'We're sorry to hear that,' said Murphy. 'Can you tell us exactly what happened this evening?'

'I was in here and I heard screaming. It was really loud, coming from next door. There was no answer at the front door, so I climbed over the back fence. The back door was open. Then I saw him – and his wife.'

'And you were the one who called the emergency services.'

'Yes, I called them from her phone.'

'Did you know the Bryces well?'

He shook his head. 'No, hardly at all. They only moved in about two weeks ago.'

'But you knew you could get in round the back.'

'Yes, because Tony and I – Tony used to live there – often climbed into each other's gardens to share a beer. We built a stile over the fence and it's still there. And Ron could get over from his side because the fence there is quite low with trees on both sides. Ancient history, sorry.'

'So you'd been in this house before?'

'Yes, many times when Tony and Dorothy lived here, and again yesterday. These young people had a house-warming party and I went along for a while.'

'Can you tell us who else was at this party?' said Murphy.

He sighed. 'I probably didn't know everybody there – only the neighbours.'

'We can start with those' said Wilcox, getting out his notebook.

Chapter Fifteen

THEY RETURNED to No.17 just as Rebecca Bryce was getting into a car driven by a woman who looked just a bit older than her.

'That's her sister – Angela' said PC Diana Short. 'Lives in Streatham. So that's where she'll be staying until we've finished with the house. I've got the details.'

'Well, she's not far away, so that's good' said Murphy. 'We'll probably have more questions for her. In the meantime, we can have a look around.'

SOCO were packing up, evidence of their work left all around the kitchen and a few dustings up the stairs.

'We've concentrated on the surfaces in the kitchen,' the chief SOCO told Murphy. 'Loads of fingermarks layered over each other in there – not so much upstairs. It will be difficult to distinguish them.'

Murphy nodded. 'They had a party here last night, so most of our suspects will have been here. Fingerprint evidence probably won't get us far.'

Wilcox walked around the kitchen which ran almost the length of the house. 'They've knocked a wall through here,' he said. 'And it's like this is where they lived most of the time.'

'Probably hadn't fully unpacked,' said Murphy. 'It's a big house for two people. So many speakers – reminds me of when Ben was living at home. Such unwieldy bloody things – you'd think these days they'd make them smaller.'

'No,' said Wilcox. 'You still need the big ones for the real sound. And three guitars – two of them electric. And that bloody great amp. They were seriously into music. He looked like somebody into music, didn't he?'

Murphy nodded. 'Yes, he did. He looked like a student who'd never grown up. Because he must have been at least in his mid-thirties. Let's have a look upstairs.'

Two of the bedrooms upstairs were full of boxes, another seemed to be functioning as an office, and the last one had a double bed and assortments of clothes strewn around.

'Looking at this, they were sleeping together,' said Murphy. 'They weren't estranged. Maybe that makes it less likely that she killed him.'

'She didn't look strong enough to kill him.'

'She's not big, that's for sure, but she might be strong. She might be lifting weights at the gym. And it may not have taken much force to knock him over.'

'Well, my money's on the next-door neighbour,' said Wilcox, as he headed into the bathroom. 'He's elderly but he looks tough enough. And he managed to get back in afterwards, so he knows he doesn't have to worry about DNA or prints. OK, here's something.'

It was a small tightly-wrapped foil package at the back of the bathroom cabinet. Murphy unwrapped it and sniffed.

'Cannabis. Not much, to be honest. They weren't dealing. But this warrants a really good search.'

Two hours later a peanut butter jar at the back of one of the kitchen cupboards was found containing a small amount of a white powder. Murphy took a sample and bagged it. 'Probably baking powder,' she said, 'but we'll check it out.'

'That office upstairs is a bit surprising,' said Wilcox. 'It's pretty professional looking. There were even tax manuals on the shelf. Maybe he's more establishment than he looks.'

'Or it could be her office,' said Murphy. 'His phone and laptop will probably make things a bit clearer. OK, not much more we can do tonight. I'll drop you at home.'

'Thanks.' Wilcox gritted his teeth and got into the passenger seat.

———

CLIVE AND JAMES were just finishing dinner when Murphy let herself in.

'Grab a seat Murph,' said James. 'There's some left and we'll make you a salad.'

She sank into a chair and rested her elbows on the table. 'No, you carry on eating. I'll make myself something in a minute.'

'Oh, will you?' said Clive. 'And what will you be making yourself?'

She shrugged. 'I dunno, just something easy. Maybe a boiled egg.'

Clive burst out laughing. 'I don't know why the boiled egg has a reputation as the thing everybody should be able to make. It's the most difficult thing there is to cook. Everybody has their own timing, depending on how hot the water is, anything from cold to boiling, and whether you start it off in cold water or put it in when the water boils and then you have to adjust for whether or not the egg has been in the fridge, and how fresh the egg is, and of course whether you like the yolk runny or not.'

'And' finished James, 'you don't know what state it's in until you take the top off, by which time it's too late to do anything. And you can bet your arse it's either runny all the way through or hard-boiled. All in all, I think you have to be a pretty adventurous cook to attempt the boiled egg.'

'Well, as you know, that's certainly not me,' said Murphy. 'Adventurous cook, that is.'

'It certainly isn't,' said James. 'You're the intrepid crime fighter. Leave the cooking to us.' He stood up and started doing something with lettuce leaves. Murphy relaxed into her chair and let her arms flop. Barney padded over and she fondled his ears.

'You were meant to be going out for dinner tonight, weren't you?' said Clive. 'I've just remembered. With your new mystery man.'

'Enough with the 'new mystery man',' said Murphy. 'He's just a colleague. We worked a case together and decided we'd have a decent meal when it was over, having spent weeks living on coffee and crisps. But now I'm involved in another one – case I mean.'

'Back to the coffee and crisps, then?'

She nodded. 'Looks like it.'

Clive tutted. 'I'm sure that's not good for your long-term health. Maybe we should be making you packed lunches.'

'That probably wouldn't fit in with her tough CID persona' said James, putting a bowl of salad on the table.

'It's true' said Murphy regretfully. 'Real women don't have lunchboxes. And that's not a euphemism.'

Chapter Sixteen

ADAM BRYCE'S parents lived in Luton and had been contacted by the uniformed branch. Rebecca had already identified the body, but his parents wanted to see him, and Murphy could see from their tight nods that they had already prepared themselves for the news that there would be a post-mortem.

David Bryce was a large man with a strong handshake and a grim expression. His wife was clutching his arm and looked in danger of falling over.

'So do we know how it happened?' he asked as they walked away from the morgue.

'We won't know anything definite until after the post-mortem,' said Murphy. 'He suffered a serious head injury, but that's all we can say at the moment.'

'He was a good lad, really,' said David, his expression softening. 'If he hadn't come by all that money, he'd have stayed near home and this wouldn't have happened.'

Hi wife gave a sob and seemed to stumble.

'Money?' said Murphy.

David nodded. 'He got an inheritance. From a bat-shit crazy old aunt. Her way of sticking up two fingers at the rest of us. Well, the old baggage has had the last laugh now.'

Their taxi drew up at that moment and Murphy had to regretfully let them depart. There was a lot more she'd have liked to ask, but probably best to let them recover a bit. They weren't suspects, after all. Which was more than could be said for the wife.

———

REBECCA BRYCE WAS SITTING in an armchair nursing a mug of herbal tea when her sister showed them in.

'I'm Angela Parrish' she said. 'I work from home, so I'll just be next door if you need me.' She went into an adjoining room and shut the door.

Rebecca didn't look pleased to see them, but Murphy could understand that. She'd been hit with the loss and now she'd be hit with the questions.

'Thank you for seeing us again Mrs Bryce,' she said. 'As you can imagine, there's a lot we still have to find out and we're hoping you can help us.'

Rebecca nodded.

'So can I begin by asking how long you had been married?'

Rebecca looked momentarily surprised at this. 'Almost a year,' she said.

'But you had known Adam for some time before that?'

'Well, yes. We'd lived together for two years.'

'And you'd both decided it was time to settle down, something like that?'

'Something like that.' She was looking a bit more belligerent now. 'But I don't see...'

'Helps us to get a fuller picture of Adam, what was going on in his life, that sort of thing,' said Murphy. 'And I gather you had only recently moved into this house.'

'Yes.'

'And you had a housewarming party on Sunday?'

'Yes.' Rebecca shrugged. 'Probably waste of time and money, but Adam thought it was important to build relationships with the neighbours.'

'And you didn't?'

She sighed. 'Well to be honest most of them are a different generation from us, so we can hardly be expected to have much in common with them.'

'Can you tell us who was at this party?'

Rachel appeared to be taking time to think. 'OK, there was Bert and Lennie, and my friend Ruby and Adam invited two people from Starswipe Records, but I don't think they turned up. If they did, I never saw them. And the rest of them were neighbours, a couple called Tom and Louise and another couple from across the road and the old guy from next door, and another elderly couple from the other side. And a slightly younger couple who didn't stay long – she was called Sandra.'

'It's a big house,' said Murphy. 'You must have been very pleased with it.'

Rebecca was looking anything but pleased. She shrugged. 'It's OK. Not my choice really, but Adam liked it.'

'You mean you'd rather have lived somewhere else?'

'I'd rather have stayed in Notting Hill, where we were before. In the flat. We were quite happy there.'

'But Adam wanted a house?'

'Yes. He said he wanted more space to store his equipment.'

'He was in a band, was he?' asked Wilcox.

She nodded. 'Dead Cells,' she said. 'That's what they're called. Sort of heavy metal, rock, bit of pop. Indie of course.'

'Of course,' said Wilcox. 'And who else was in this band?'

'Bert and Lennie. Bert Wilson and Lennie Bright.'

'And do you have contact details for them?'

She picked up her phone. 'I have Bert's number. He'll know where to find Lennie.'

She read it out and Wilcox copied it into his phone.

'Adam had three guitars,' he said, putting his phone back in his pocket. 'What did he play? Bass guitar?'

'Lead guitar,' she said. 'Bert played rhythm and Lennie played drums.'

'And did they get many gigs?'

'Usually about once a week they'd go somewhere. Pubs, whatever.'

'Got it. And did Adam have a day job?'

Rebecca shrugged. 'No, that was all he did. He didn't need a day job.'

'Because of the money,' said Murphy.

Rebecca looked taken aback. 'Well, yes. Adam had inherited quite a lot of money, so he didn't need to do a job.'

'And did he have a job before that?' asked Murphy.

'He worked in IT,' said Rebecca. 'But he didn't like it much.'

'And then about a year ago he got the inheritance and he left.'

'That's right.' She put the cup down and folded her

arms. Murphy could see her coming to the point of refusing to answer any more questions. Wilcox ploughed on regardless.

'And since then, he had been...working on music?'

'Yes.' She sighed. 'Writing songs, organising recording venues, doing gigs. All that sort of thing.'

'And is the band doing well?'

She hesitated. 'Well, it hasn't had much of a chance yet. They were about to bring out an album and that would really have boosted their profile, but it's not ready.' She shrugged. 'Don't know what will happen now.'

'So, Adam was mainly spending money, rather than making it.'

'Investing,' she said. 'That's what he called it.'

———

'INVESTING, MY ARSE' said Murphy as they got back into the car. 'He was squandering all the money, so she decided to top him while there was still some left.'

'We need to find out how much he inherited,' said Wilcox, putting his phone back in his pocket and climbing gingerly back into the passenger seat. 'It might have been some vast sum which he hadn't even made a dent in. But I think it's hard to make money in the music business now, what with streaming and all. This Bert Wilson lives in Kentish Town and he says he's in all day. Shall we go round there now?'

Murphy nodded and pulled away, narrowly missing a cyclist. 'Yes. We'll see what he's got to say. Maybe they had a bust-up in the band. Like Pink Floyd.'

Wilcox shook his head. 'Somehow I don't think they were in the same league as Pink Floyd.'

Chapter Seventeen

BERT WILSON LIVED in a top-floor flat in one of a row of Victorian houses leading off from the high street. The hallway was littered with junk mail and the stair carpet was worn thin. His living quarters looked like what had originally been just two bedrooms, with the internal walls reconfigured to fit in a tiny kitchen and shower room.

The man himself was just over six foot to Murphy's eye, with longish hair and two-day stubble. He smiled briefly and his whole face seemed to light up. Definitely a man the groupies would be keen on – if they had any groupies. She stole a glance into the bedroom as he led the way in. No sign of female occupation

'Thank you for seeing us at short notice,' she said, settling herself on the sofa and motioning the other two to sit. 'This must have been a dreadful shock for you. When did you hear about it?'

'Rebecca called yesterday and I called Lennie.' He shook his head. 'We don't know what to think.'

'When was the last time you saw Adam?'

'We saw him that afternoon. All three of us were together at his house. We were trying out some new songs.'

'What time did you leave?'

'About four thirty. Lennie and I thought we'd get ahead of the rush hour. I got back here on my motorbike and he took the bus.'

'You and Lennie left together?'

'That's right.'

'And how was he when you left?'

He shook his head slowly. 'He was fine. We were quite pleased with the songs. He was still playing them back when we shut the door. Was it just an accident?'

'We can't say for certain until the post mortem is done,' said Wilcox. 'But for now, it's a suspicious death. How was the band doing?'

He hesitated. 'To be honest, it hadn't really gotten off the ground. I mean, we were getting gigs, but not well-paid or high-profile ones. That was why we were working on the album. It was the important next step.'

'And you played bass guitar?'

Bert Wilson looked surprised. 'That's right.'

'Who wrote the songs?'

He thought for a moment. 'I wrote some of them, Lennie wrote some and some of them we all collaborated on.'

'Adam didn't write any on his own?'

'No, he didn't. Not ones that we decided to perform or record.'

'Would you say Adam was a good musician?'

He sighed. 'He could do the basics. And his singing voice wasn't bad.'

'You mean you were probably a better guitarist.'

'I didn't say that...'

'So why was he the lead guitar?'

Bert threw his arms up. 'Because he had the fucking money. That's what you want to hear isn't it? Well, it's true. Travelling around to gigs, getting into recording studios, having good equipment – it all costs money. We couldn't really have done it without Adam. I think he knew he wasn't the best, but he put in the finance, so that was his contribution.'

'How did you guys get together?' asked Murphy.

'Adam and I were at college together. He wasn't particularly into music then, as I remember, but I was. I didn't hear from him for few years after that but then he looked me up about a year ago, wanting to get into a band. I was doing some session work with Lennie and we had a meetup.'

'And he told you that he now had money.'

'No, that was before the money. All he had to offer was enthusiasm, but Lennie and I were willing to give it a go because we were fed up of session work. To be honest, being an unsuccessful band is not much better. You're not being ordered around, but you're not making much money either. At the point where Adam suddenly came into the money we were just about to give up.'

'And what happens now?'

He shrugged. 'Who knows? We have a few gigs lined up, but we'll need to find another guitarist. We haven't even talked about it yet.'

'And of course, you won't have any money.' She looked closely at him. 'Unless he's left you some.'

Bert shook his head. 'I don't think so.'

LENNIE BRIGHT LIVED in a top-floor flat in a council block in Bethnal Green. The lift was small and pungent and seemed to take forever to inch its way up fifteen floors.

He was a small, muscular man with a full beard, who waved them in with what looked like a gesture of defeat. 'It's not council anymore' he said. 'We have a private landlord and they charge what they like.'

'You live here with your wife?' said Murphy

He nodded. 'Wife and son. Although they're not here at the moment.' He wiped a hand across his face. 'Visiting her mum.'

Murphy sat down and motioned Wilcox to do the same. Lennie switched off the TV and joined them.

'This must be a terrible shock for you,' said Murphy.

He sighed. 'You bet. Just when we were putting the album together. Can't believe it.'

'We know you saw him that afternoon,' said Wilcox. 'Can you tell us about that.'

'Nothing much to tell. We were there for a couple of hours – the three of us – going over song lyrics and a couple of the chord changes. Getting final versions ready. We had a slot booked in a studio – for today actually. So much for that.'

'How did Adam seem that afternoon.'

'Fine. He was fine, normal. Better than normal, actually. He said he'd finally made it to the top of that tree in the garden and he was really pleased with himself. He liked climbing up things.'

'And you left at what time?'

'Bert and I left together about two-thirty.'

'And how did you travel?'

'He had his motorbike and I got on the bus.'

'You saw Bert head off before you got on the bus?'

'That's right. I was still at the bus stop.'

'What was your route home?'

'Bus to Warren Street, walked down to Tottenham Court Road station, Central line back here.'

'And you got back at what time?'

'I dunno. About four o'clock, maybe four-thirty.'

'Was anybody here when you arrived?'

'No.'

Looking around Murphy got the impression that nobody else had been here for some time. At least nobody else who bothered with clearing up.

'Can I ask you about the financial structure of the band,' said Wilcox. 'Is it a limited company?'

Lennie shook his head. 'Partnership.'

'So do you all get equal shares?'

'That's right.'

'But we've been told that you write most of the songs. Do you get a salary?'

'No.' Lennie's shoulders stiffened. He didn't seem to like this line of questioning. Wilcox pushed on.

'Bit unfair that, isn't it?'

Lennie shrugged. 'Whatever.'

'And Adam was putting money into the business?'

'He was, yes.'

'And was he paid interest on that?'

'I think so. Accountant deals with that.'

'Who is the accountant?' asked Murphy.

He shook his head. 'I don't know. Adam dealt with all of that.'

'And before he came into the money, did you have an accountant then?'

'Course not. Or maybe we did. I think Adam already

had the accountant, but he didn't have much to do at first as we weren't making much money.'

'And now you are?'

'Not yet. Might have done when the album came out.'

Murphy levered herself off the sofa. 'Can you think of anybody who had any disagreement with Adam, any enemies that he had?'

He shook his head. 'Couldn't it just have been an accident?'

'We're still looking into it,' said Murphy.

'I can't face that lift again,' she said when the door had closed behind them. 'Let's take the stairs.'

'Looks like his wife's left him,' said Wilcox as they headed down.

'I would say so. Can't blame her. I'd leave him if I had to lug my shopping up all those stairs, or get in that lift. It's an interesting scenario, don't you think? Here's this band – three guys – and you would somehow expect them to be all in the same boat. But they're not. One of them lived in an Edwardian house worth about two mil and the other two live in places like this.'

'And if he was getting interest on his loans to the partnership,' added Wilcox, 'that has to come off before the profit shares are calculated, leaving maybe even a loss for Bert and Lennie.'

'That's right,' said Murphy. 'We'll need to track down that accountant.'

Chapter Eighteen

WILCOX HAD BEEN QUITE keen to attend the post-mortem, but Murphy decided to send him off to do something else. Having initially worried that he would find the whole dissection business difficult to confront, both of them had been surprised when he had found his first post-mortem fascinating rather than upsetting. Murphy had now decided that this fascination needed nipping in the bud, before he became completely intolerable, so he went off to look up the names of everybody who had been at the housewarming party, while she climbed into the plastic suit and prepared to look at the body. So here she was now, togged up in protective garments and breathing through her mouth. Linda Fleming was checking the recording equipment while the morgue attendants brought in the body.

Murphy had never seen Adam Bryce in life, and it was hard to discern much about him from looking at his body, at the thing he had left behind when he went. When she had attended the scene, she had seen signs of distress – probably pain and shock – on his face. Now all that was wiped away, smoothed over. Expressionless from here on out.

Murphy had her own set of procedures for coping with post-mortems. She was happy to look at the body before the dissection began, but always had to look away as the scalpel went in. At that point she would turn her attention to the room. Counting the ceiling tiles. Tracing all the pipework. Estimating how many litres of paint would be needed to coat the walls (that was a new one). She could tell by the sequence of sounds how far the process had advanced and of course she was alert to any pronouncements from the pathologist.

Linda Fleming began with the usual description. Male, about thirty-five, thirty-six, bruise in area of lower jaw, no other marks. Generally good health but slightly undernourished and arms showed some slight evidence of drug use.

'He played in a band,' Murphy contributed.

Linda nodded and grunted. She ran a finger over the jaw, where an area of bruising could be seen.

'Strange,' said Murphy. 'I don't remember that being so noticeable when we first saw him. Although Frank did say there was something there.'

'It started to darken soon after he arrived here,' said Linda. 'It's a bony area so bruises appear quite quickly.'

'So how long before death…?'

'Probably concurrent with death, although we'll need to be sure about that.'

'If somebody punched him, might there be any DNA traces?'

'Touch DNA. It's possible. I'll swab for it and we'll see what comes up.'

Heart, lungs and liver were pronounced healthy. 'I'd say no heavy drinking,' Linda said, pouring out the stomach contents and sniffing. 'And I can't smell any alcohol, although we won't be sure until it's all analysed. In fact, not much in the stomach at all,' she added, looking at the contents in the bowl. 'Doesn't look like he had any lunch.'

Murphy felt that she, too, would not be having any lunch. The morgue attendant helped Linda turn the body over. Murphy knew what was coming next and decided to take an interest in the x-ray slides pinned up on the wall. She stole a glance to see Linda peeling back the scalp. This, after all, was the most important area for this autopsy. The wound at the base of the skull had been cleaned but still looked catastrophic.

'Traumatic brain injury,' said Linda. 'The brain stem is severely damaged. And I wouldn't say the skull is danger-ously thin, but it's on the thin side, which is unlucky in this case. Death would have been instantaneous.'

'What we're thinking,' said Murphy, 'is a blow to the jaw which toppled him backwards. Looks like he hit his head on the granite work surface on the way down.'

'I would agree with that,' said Linda. 'These high-end kitchens can be dangerous places. Can't get much harder than granite.'

'That means whoever hit him,' Murphy said, 'may not have intended to kill him. They weren't to know he'd hit his head and die.'

'That's true.' Linda dropped her instruments into the tray with a clatter. 'But it was a decent punch. Somebody knew what they were doing.'

———

WILCOX WAS on the Police National Computer when Murphy arrived back in the CID room.

'I've been checking into the Adam Bryce's neighbours. And,' he clicked on the screen, 'look what I found.'

Murphy pulled up a seat. 'Justin Beattie,' she said. 'Actual bodily harm. Just a week ago. We remember him, don't we? Let off with a caution. Victim declined to press charges. I wonder why? I'm interested already. OK. Let's start with him. Ideally, I'd like to get him in here.'

'He says he'll be home about six' said Wilcox putting the phone down.

'Good enough,' said Murphy. 'We can go now, have a chat with his wife before he gets in. That might be useful.'

Chapter Nineteen

THE POLICE TAPE had gone from number 17, Murphy noticed, as they pulled up across the road in front of number 22. There was a camper van parked in the driveway and an older man emerging from the back door carrying a large plastic water carrier. He stopped and looked questioningly at them.

'Police,' said Murphy, reaching for her badge. 'We're here to talk to Mr Beattie.'

The man nodded. 'I've seen you before, over the road,' he said. 'Justin's not home yet.'

'Well perhaps we can have a word with his wife in the meantime,' said Murphy. 'And you are?'

'Stanley Farrow' he said. 'I'm Justin's stepfather.'

'This yours?' asked Wilcox, nodding at the van.

Stanley smiled. 'That's right. My current project.'

Murphy carried on ahead to the front door and rang the bell. After a few seconds the door was opened by a woman with striking blue eyes, a baby in her arms and an anxious expression.

'Mrs Beattie?' Murphy held out her badge.

'It's the police, Francine' said a voice behind her. 'About young Adam. Terrible business.'

'Yes, well, thank you, Mr…Farrow.' Murphy drew a deep breath and addressed the woman at the door. 'Detective Inspector Murphy and Detective Constable Wilcox, Mrs Beattie. We arranged to speak to your husband, but perhaps we can have a word with you in the meantime.'

Francine Beattie nodded. 'Yes, of course.' She stood aside to let them enter.

It was a spacious sitting room with two large sofas, a marble fireplace and a couple of expensive-looking rugs. Just like her sitting room ought to look, thought Murphy, not that she got the chance to sit in it much. In this case the furnishings were overlaid with a layer of baby and young person detritus and, looking closely at Francine Beattie, Murphy wondered if what looked like stress was simply tiredness.

Stanley Farrow had followed them in and now seated himself next to Francine.

'Can I start by asking you if you knew Adam and Rebecca Bryce?'

Francine swallowed. 'Adam and Rebecca. Yes.'

'And how long did you know them for?'

'Well … since they moved in.'

'They came to Justin's birthday party,' Stanley supplied. He tapped on his phone. 'Ten days ago. First time we met them.'

'Was that the first time you met either of them, Mrs Beattie?' Murphy asked pointedly, wondering how she could usefully get rid of Stanley.

Francine blinked. 'Me? Yes, of course.'

'And you then attended this party at their house on Sunday?'

'Yes, we did.' Francine was looking slightly more relaxed now. 'We left quite early, to let the babysitter get home. I don't know if anything happened after that.'

'I stayed a bit later,' Stanley volunteered.

'You weren't babysitting then?' Murphy turned her attention to him.

He smiled and shook his head. 'I've become something of a party animal in my old age.'

'Have you indeed?' said Murphy. 'Excellent. And do you have any observations you'd like to share with us?'

He leaned towards them. 'Well, as it happens...'

There was a slam from the vicinity of the hall and a man strode into the room, looking profoundly displeased.

'Our appointment was for six,' he began, 'and now I find you here already, harassing my wife.' He stopped and looked at them. 'Oh,' he said. 'It's you.'

Murphy smiled. 'Hello again, Mr Beattie.'

'There is no harassment going on, Justin,' said Francine, now definitely more into her stride. 'We were just having a chat while we waited for you. We'll leave you to it now.'

Francine and Stanley left the room and Justin threw himself onto the empty sofa.

'OK, so what can I help you with this time?'

Murphy sat back and looked more closely at him. Definitely a man on the edge.

'As you will know,' she said, 'we are investigating the death of Adam Bryce.'

He nodded. 'Yes, of course. Shocking.'

'And we would like you to come down to the station for a chat, just a voluntary interview.'

His face froze. 'On what basis?'

'On the basis,' said Wilcox, 'that you were detained a week ago for an assault on one of your neighbours, and now another neighbour has been attacked. That being the case, we would like to talk to you.'

'So that puts me in the frame for murder, does it? You're planning to fit me up. And if I refuse?'

'You're entitled to refuse of course,' said Murphy. 'In which case we can have our chat here, but I think that might be more disruptive for your family. You can have a lawyer present if you like, but it wouldn't be strictly necessary. You are not under arrest. You are simply assisting in our enquiry.'

'You bet I'm going to have a lawyer present,' he said, grabbing his phone. 'And I'll drive myself.'

Chapter Twenty

IT WAS PROBABLY UNFORTUNATE, Murphy thought afterwards, that Rebecca had appeared at the end of the street just as they came out of the house with Justin. Well, unfortunate for Justin anyway. But at least Rebecca didn't see him being manoeuvred into a police car like last time he had been taken away. Justin ignored Rebecca, slid into his car and slammed the door. The convoy set off.

'Good job you're driving,' said Murphy as Wilcox accelerated smoothly away. 'You can set a good example of driving within speed limits. It might be a new experience for that powerful motor of his.'

Martin Sanger was waiting when they arrived at the station, sighing and looking pointedly at his watch. Murphy led the way to the least dismal of the interview rooms and they seated themselves.

'We're recording this, as we have to record all interviews' said Wilcox, pressing the button.

'Is that switched on now?' asked Martin Sanger. 'Good. In that case, the first thing you can record is my absolute amazement that you have dragged my client down here, for no good reason whatsoever. Are you going to charge him with an offense? If not, we're out of here.'

'Thank you for sharing that with us,' said Murphy. 'We have asked your client to come here for a voluntary interview. We are investigating a murder and we owe it to the victim's family to pursue our enquiries in any direction that appears relevant. There is a reason why we wanted to interview Mr Beattie in a more formal environment and you both know what that reason is. If you let us get on and ask our questions, this will be over more quickly.'

Sanger sat back and folded his arms. 'OK. Let's get on with it.'

Murphy addressed Justin. 'Mr Beattie, can you start by telling us how you spent yesterday afternoon.'

Justin looked at Martin Sanger, who nodded. 'I was in my office in Canary Wharf until about two o'clock, then I went to visit a client in King's Cross and after that I came home.'

'What time did you arrive home?'

He shrugged. 'About six o' clock.'

'And can we have the name of this client?'

Sanger nodded again. 'Seymour. Richard Seymour. Seymour Properties, Caledonian Road.'

'And you left there at what time?'

'About four.'

'It took you two hours to get home from King's Cross?'

'OK, not exactly. I wandered into St Pancras on the way home and had a drink at the Booking Office.'

'The booking office?' said Murphy.

Justin rolled his eyes. 'It's a bar. That's what it's called.'

'And did you see anybody you knew there?'

He shook his head. 'No.'

'I'd like to ask you what dealings you have had with Adam Bryce.'

'Dealings?' His face seemed to freeze for a moment. Then his expression relaxed. 'I hardly knew him. He's lived round here less than a fortnight. None of us had time to get to know him.'

'You didn't know him before he moved into the area?'

He shook his head. 'No. Not at all.'

'How did you get on with him when you did meet him.'

He shrugged. 'Pleasant enough chap. He came to the party we had here and then we went to their party. Sounds like it's all parties, doesn't it? It's not usually like that. Well, anyway, don't think I exchanged more than a few words with him.'

'About what?'

'Oh, I dunno.' He waved a hand. 'Football probably.'

'What team did he support?' Wilcox asked.

Justin sighed. 'Not sure I can remember. Arsenal, I think, or Spurs.'

'Is this relevant?' Martin Sanger interjected.

'Possibly not' Murphy conceded. 'We'll move on. How about Mr Bryce's wife, Mr Beattie? How did you get on with her?'

'I didn't get on with her. I never spoke to her.'

'What, not at all? She's a new neighbour, she came to your birthday party, you went to her housewarming, and you never spoke to her?'

'OK.' He held his hands up in the time-honoured gesture of frustration. 'I never spoke to her beyond the normal polite exchanges that take place between neighbours.'

'Adam Bryce was wealthy, wasn't he?' said Wilcox.

'Maybe. I don't know.'

'And your business is wealth management, isn't that right?'

'OK, that's it.' Sanger stood up. 'This is just a fishing expedition. We're leaving right now.'

'Thank you for coming,' Murphy said, opening the door for them.

'He's right of course,' she said to Wilcox, sitting back down. 'It was just a fishing expedition. But it was interesting in lots of ways. Did you notice that he looked shocked for a moment when I said 'dealings'? And then he claimed to have exchanged hardly a word with Rebecca. I don't believe that. I think he's the sort of guy who will always have plenty to say to a good-looking woman. And I think he'll always be able to sniff out money. He's a person of interest in so many ways. Unfortunately, I can't immediately think of any reason for him to want to dispose of Adam Bryce.'

'Whoever killed Adam Bryce may not have wanted to dispose of him, of course' said Wilcox. 'It could have been an assault that went too far. Like the assault on Thomas Fraser.'

'Yes, that makes him look likely again. But we'll need a bit more to go on. And we have to explore all other avenues. Justin Beattie might have nothing to do with it, but we'll dig a little deeper.'

Chapter Twenty-One

MURPHY WAS in the office early next morning. Early in, and then get out before Bellweather arrived. It usually worked well. But they did need somewhere to get out to, they needed to grasp some link in the chain.

'Justin Beattie's a broker at Watson Fullerton' said Wilcox, scanning LinkedIn. 'They're a pretty substantial firm. I don't think there's any information we can get from them – client confidentiality and all that. He's on Facebook, but we can't get access unless we arrest him. And we're not proposing to do that, are we?'

Murphy shook her head. 'No. We have no evidence against him or anybody else. We'll have to proceed the old-fashioned way. Have we checked all the neighbours on that street.'

He scrolled up. 'Yes. Nobody saw anything. One neighbour said she thought she heard a scream, but the timing of that fits in with Rebecca Bryce arriving home. We've checked them all.'

'OK, let's go back to the ones who might have something to tell us. That stepfather of Justin's, what was his name?'

Wilcox consulted his notes 'Stanley Farrow.'

'Yes. Stanley. He looked like a chap who takes notice of what goes on, and probably draws his own conclusions. Let's start with him. Hopefully he hasn't yet packed up his motorhome and swanned off.'

———

STANLEY HIMSELF OPENED the door and, if he was surprised to see them, he hid it well.

'Hello again,' he said.

'Mr Farrow,' said Murphy. 'We'd like to have a chat with you.'

'You'd better come in,' he said. 'Teacher inset day today and Danny and I are in charge of the house. We're Minecrafting.'

Danny was sitting in front of a coffee table, clicking away at a mouse.

'Keep going on your own for a bit, Danny,' said Stanley. 'I'll be in the kitchen,' and he led the way next door.

Murphy took a seat at the kitchen table and the men followed.

'We didn't really have a chance to talk to you the other night,' she began.

'Before you hauled my stepson away,' he finished. 'No, I guess you didn't.'

'I'm sure you understand why we took him away for questioning,' said Murphy.

Stanley nodded. 'I understand alright. Really, it was my fault.'

'In what way?'

He sighed. 'I wound him up, told him I'd lost money that he thinks belongs to him. That's why he went and hit Tom.'

Murphy stared at him. 'Why didn't he just hit you?'

'That would have been a much better idea. I would have hit him back and it would have been a fair fight, not a one-sided attack. Obviously, I wasn't expecting him to hit anybody, but I told him that I was acting on financial advice obtained from Tom. All very unfortunate.'

'How did you lose money that he thinks belongs to him?' asked Wilcox.

'It was money left to me by his mother. If she hadn't married me, the money would have come to Justin, so he's angry about that. Of course, he'll get it when I go, but he's now getting a bit impatient.'

'And now it's all gone?'

He shook his head. 'Actually no, it isn't. Justin has had one substantial amount of money from me and now he's after more, so I told him that just to put a stop to it. I knew he'd be angry, but I didn't think he'd go nuts.'

'He doesn't look like he's short of money,' said Murphy. 'And if he's going to get it in the end, why not give him some of it now?'

He shrugged. 'I have my reasons. I'm not going to discuss Justin's business, but I'm biding my time on the money. What I can tell you, for what it's worth, is that he would never kill anybody. I know him well enough to say that.'

'How does he feel about you staying in his house, if he's so mad at you?' asked Wilcox.

'He's not happy about it, and I'm planning to leave in

the next few days. I'm just helping Francine out for a bit, then I'll be off.'

'And where were you yesterday afternoon?'

'Ah, the question. I was just here, cleaning my roof. So much stuff comes off these trees. Francine got back with Danny from school at about four o'clock and then I watched TV with him while she went to collect something from the drycleaners or whatever. Then we were both here for the rest of the day. Justin came home a bit later and we had dinner.'

'What time did Justin get in?'

'Probably just after six. The news had been on.'

'OK.' Murphy stretched her legs. 'I wanted to ask you, as somebody who doesn't live here, what you can tell me about the neighbours at this end of the street – apart from your stepson and his wife of course.'

'You're looking for scurrilous gossip, are you?'

'Yes. That's exactly what I'm looking for.'

'I've only seen them at these various social occasions, when people are probably on their best behaviour.'

'Understood,' said Murphy. 'We're investigating a murder here so we're grateful for any insights – or impressions – that come our way.'

'Impressions is all it will be,' he said. 'OK. On one side of the Bryce house are Ray and Wendy. He's a retired estate agent and still-practising hypochondriac and she's a nurse who still works part-time at the doctor's surgery – probably so she doesn't have to stay at home all day with him. That said, they are decent, pleasant people. I met them at Christmas and again at Justin's party, and then at the Bryces' party. And Ron helps out a lot with Danny. He has a new puppy that Danny really likes, so they go for walks together. Yesterday he picked Danny up from school and kept him until Justin went over to get him. That meant Francine was able to do a full afternoon's work – subject to the baby, that is. The people next door to Ron and Wendy I don't know. Never met them. Next door here there's Eddie and Sandra. They're a bit younger, they have teenage children. They run a cleaning business – office cleaning – seems to be doing quite well from what they say. I saw them at Christmas and then again briefly at that housewarming party, but they didn't stay all that long because they said they were off on holiday the next day – Greece, I think. They're probably still away.'

'Yes,' said Wilcox. 'We haven't been able to contact them yet.'

'On the other side of us – well, I say us, but of course that doesn't include me – are Tom and Louise. You'll have spoken to them. I like Louise. I've only had one conversation with Tom, which was a bit ill-advised considering the repercussion. On the other side of the Bryce house are Ted and Molly. Sad situation, but it comes to us all. You'll have spoken to Ted, I'm sure.'

'Yes, we've spoken to Ted,' said Murphy. 'How do you think he got on with his new neighbours?'

'He didn't have much chance to get to know them,' said Stanley. 'Justin's party was when they put in their first appearance and then their party. But Ted doesn't tend to stay that long at these things. He doesn't like to leave Molly. I think he misses Tony and Dorothy, who lived there before. These new people are a different generation, of course, but he would probably have got on fine with them.'

'And how about the new people, the Bryces?'

Stanley sat back and crossed his arms. 'Well now you're

asking. I was briefly introduced to both of them at Justin's party and I had a bit of a chat with him at that house-warming do.'

'What did you talk about?'

'Fishing.'

'Really? He was interested in fishing?'

Stanley looked momentarily offended. 'Lots of people are, you know. Millions of them worldwide. Anyway, he told me he doesn't fish now, but he used to go when he was young with his dad, that and birdwatching, and he really liked it. Said he'd spotted me on Instagram.'

'You have an Instagram page?' said Wilcox.

'Yes. You've heard of wild fishing, I'm sure? Oh well, never mind. I travel around and post about my fishing experiences.'

'In the van.' Wilcox seemed to be getting the hang of this now. Murphy was glad about that, because it was well outside her experience.

'That's right,' Stanley smiled. 'I'm setting off soon on a tour of Europe.'

'I could fancy that,' said Murphy. 'But maybe without the fishing.'

Stanley shook his head. 'It's the fishing that makes it worthwhile' he said.

'What surprises me,' Murphy said, 'is Adam Bryce being interested in fishing. I never met him in life, of course, but what I've heard so far is that he was into rock music, bands and all that. Fishing seems like a much more ... peaceful occupation. Although I guess it's not peaceful for the fish...' She left the sentence trailing, aware somewhere in her brain that she probably shouldn't have started it.

Stanley wagged a finger. 'Just goes to show,' he said. 'People are more complex than we think. I told young

Adam that fishing is a good occupation for escaping from the wife and I think he liked that idea.'

'You think he wanted to escape from his wife?'

'He didn't say as much, obviously, but they weren't exactly presenting a united front, if you know what I mean.'

'You mean they were ignoring each other?'

'I wouldn't say that, but I just noticed, at that party of theirs, that they were never in the same group. He seemed to be mostly talking to the neighbours and she spent her time with the younger crowd. None of that PDA between them, as they call it now.'

'Who was in the younger crowd?' asked Murphy.

'I didn't get to talk to any of them, but there was a young woman who seemed like a good friend of the wife's – Rebecca, I should call her – and two young men who floated between Adam and the two young women. They were a bit separate from the rest of us. Not surprising really, they probably thought we were all a bit old – me especially.'

'Adam Bryce wasn't that young,' said Murphy. 'Mid to late thirties. I think she's a bit younger.'

'In that case he wasn't much younger than Justin,' said Stanley. 'He just seemed less grown-up somehow. I'd say she seemed more grown-up than him, even if she was younger.'

'That's interesting,' said Murphy. 'Grown up in what way?'

'It's a bit hard to describe,' he said, 'but she looked to me like a young woman who knew what she wanted and was confident of getting it. Maybe confident is the word. He looked much less confident. He wanted to be friends. He was really making an effort to talk to everybody whereas she didn't bother at all. She'd decided that there was no mileage in it.'

'How about the other young people?'

'That young female friend of hers looked a bit friendlier. She exchanged a few words with me when we were fetching drinks, but I can't remember what we said and I didn't catch her name. The chaps were probably in his band with him – that's what they looked like. They looked like they'd ended up at the wrong party. Like they were wondering what they were doing at this bash with old people, some of us older than others. Don't blame them – I'd have thought the same at their age.'

'Me too, to be honest,' said Murphy, just as they heard the front door opening, followed a few minutes later by the kitchen door. Francine's face registered shock, then resignation when she saw them.

'Hello, Mrs Beattie,' said Murphy. 'We've just been having a chat with Stanley here and we'd like to talk to you if that's OK.'

'I'll get back to Minecraft,' said Stanley, rising from the table.

Francine deposited the baby in a high chair with a banana and began to unpack her shopping. 'I don't think I've got anything useful to tell you, apart from the fact that my husband hasn't killed anybody.'

'In that case you should be happy to assist us,' said Murphy. 'Because somebody did kill Adam Bryce and, the sooner we find out who it was, the better for everybody. For instance, when did you first meet Adam?'

Francine immediately swung round and began putting stuff in the fridge. 'Same time as everybody else,' she said. 'Tom and Louise brought them to our party.'

'And what did you think about him?'

'Nothing. I thought nothing about him. I hardly spoke to him.'

'You mean he came to your party and you went to his party and you hardly spoke to him?'

She pulled out a chair and sat down. 'What I mean is nothing beyond the usual polite chitchat, what a nice area this is, something or other about his house, where he works, things like that. All pretty meaningless.'

'So where does he work?' asked Murphy.

Francine waved a hand. 'I don't know. I don't think he does. Something in the music business.'

'And how about his wife?'

'Rebecca. Yes, I exchanged a few words with her,' said Francine. 'She works for a charity located somewhere in the City or the West End and she told me about the changes she wants to make to the house. Awful for her. I don't know what she'll be doing now.'

Francine's eyes were looking suspiciously bright, Murphy thought. Francine reached behind her for a tissue and blew her nose. The baby had massaged the banana into a paste and now started dropping bits on the floor.

'Before we leave,' Murphy said, noticing a look of relief spreading across Francine's face, 'can I just ask you where you were yesterday afternoon. We have to ask everybody this.'

'Yes, of course you do. I was here until just after three, then I went up to the school to collect Danny and we got back here about four.'

'And did you leave the house again?'

'No. Oh, actually I did. I went up to the drycleaners and picked up a few bits and pieces at the shop at about four-thirty. Stanley was here.'

'OK, we'll leave it at that,' said Murphy, standing up. 'Thank you for your help, Mrs Beattie.'

They were escorted to the door in record time. Wilcox craned his neck as they walked down the path.

'What are you doing?'

'Getting a look at his roof. It does look like it was recently cleaned, but he could have done that any time.'

'That's right,' said Murphy, as they reached the car, 'but she's the one I'm more interested in. What was she not telling us do you think?'

Chapter Twenty-Two

RUBY FOSTER WORKED in a bank in Cheapside and had agreed to see them in her lunch hour. She was a plump, smiling girl who looked quite unfazed by the idea of talking to the police. The best sort of witness, Murphy thought. Whether she would have anything useful to say was another matter. They walked down to the river and sat on a bench.

'I couldn't believe it when Rebecca called and told me,' Ruby said. 'So shocking. But I don't know how I can help.'

'We're talking to everybody who was at that house-warming party,' said Murphy. 'You might have seen or heard something that might lead to useful information. To start with, can you tell us a bit about Adam and Rebecca, how long you've known them, that sort of thing.'

'OK,' Ruby began, settling herself more comfortably on the bench. 'I met Rebecca when we were both working in telesales – just temporarily, you understand, we were on our way to better things, as it were, although sometimes I think all jobs are basically the same, once you've been there long enough it all gets boring and then you're back to square one, looking for the next step. After that, Rebecca went off to work for the charity, which surprised me a bit, because I said her, you won't be earning much there, but I was wrong, wasn't I? She said no, the salary is really good, and it was. You think that everybody who works in the charity sector doesn't earn very much, but that's not true. In fact, I have another friend, she's been working...'

'So what happened after Rebecca changed jobs?' asked Murphy.

'Nothing really happened as such, I wouldn't say that. I mean we stayed in touch and sometimes we'd go out for a drink together and things like that, but she didn't really change. She was doing quite well at her new job and I was doing well here, well I got promoted to team leader after the first month, so you can't say fairer than that.'

'No indeed,' said Murphy. 'And when did Adam come on the scene?'

'I think it was about six months after Rebecca started at the charity. Or perhaps it was seven months. Let me think. No, I was right the first time, it must have been six months, because it was just after my birthday and that's in March. We went to a gig one night, in a pub. There weren't many people there and the gig wasn't great, but we liked the band. Well, to be honest, we liked Bert, so we started hanging round with them. But Bert had a girlfriend and Lennie was married, so Rebecca started going out with Adam. I was surprised when they got engaged. Then Rebecca told me that Adam was getting an inheritance – a big one, millions. They got married soon after that. Not a big wedding. Rebecca didn't really have much family. Her mother is dead and her father lives in Canada, so there's just her and her sister living here. But her dad did fly over for the wedding – registry office, it was – and he gave her away. She had a really great outfit, not like a traditional white wedding dress, but a sort of pale linen suit. Looked very classy, I thought, and with an outfit like that you can wear it again. You can even dye it. I think linen dyes quite well. The reception was at a really nice restaurant, no expense spared, but not a lot of fuss, if you know what I mean. Adam's parents were there, of course, and they didn't look all that happy over the whole thing. As far as I remember, they left pretty soon after the meal. I think they thought it was a bit sudden, the marriage, that is. But what could they say?'

Ruby paused for breath and Murphy got in quickly.

'And did anything change after they got married?'

'They moved into a really nice flat in Notting Hill. I used to go and meet Rebecca there and we'd go out for drinks, such a great place to live. But then they moved to Muswell Hill. Very respectable area, very expensive, but not exactly cool, is it?'

'So why do you think they moved?'

'Beats me. I can tell you one thing – it was not Rebecca's idea, no way. She was definitely not in favour. But she said that Adam had changed since he inherited the money. It was like he was calling the shots now. Before that, it had really been her, I think. She said he was now getting into finances and investments and all that kind of thing. Well of course I know all about that sort of thing, with my job, but it was hardly the sort of thing you could have imagined him being interested in – an IT guy who was into indie music. Though I suppose he was right, because if you have access to a lot of money, there's lots of people who would like to con you out of it, so you have to learn what you can, safe-guard your assets. We've had a lot of in-house learning about that at work. There are so many scams around and some of them are really clever. I guess Adam was probably aware of that. I think Rebecca found him a bit harder to deal with at that point. She told him what she thought, she said she didn't want to move from Notting Hill, but he pushed it through anyway and what could she do? She was hardly going to leave him, was she?'

'No, indeed. And can you tell us a bit about this party. I guess that was the last time you saw Adam?'

'Yes.' Ruby looked mournful for a moment. 'Just shows, doesn't it? You never know what's going to happen. He looked happy and full of life. It was a strange party though. I mean, the sort of parties I would normally go to, would be all people like me, young people, loud music, all of that. This one, well there was loud music, but otherwise it was like going to one of your parents' parties. There was a couple of us – me, Rebecca and the guys from the band that is - then there were a few couples about ten years older than us and then there were a few people who were really old – so like three generations really. But I guess that's how it is in that sort of neighbourhood. I think only older people can afford to live there.'

'So why do you think Adam wanted to move there?'

She shrugged. 'Search me. Maybe now he had money, he wanted to live near people who had money, but there are plenty of them in Notting Hill. Probably more of them, actually. Rebecca asked him why, but she never got any answer that made sense. He must have had some reason, but he wasn't telling her what it was.'

'Did you see who he was talking to at the party?'

Ruby frowned. 'He seemed to be talking to everybody. He spent quite a long time talking to one old bloke, he was quite a nice old bloke actually. I heard one of them mention 'trout', don't know what that was about, maybe it's the name of an app. He introduced me to one couple, he was called Tom, quite an attractive guy and I don't remember her name, but she wasn't bad-looking, for an older woman. There was another couple and I saw him talking to the guy, quite a good-looking guy to be honest. That guy's wife – actually she was pretty good-looking too – was giving them a wide berth. Maybe she'd had a row with her husband. And that's all I can tell you because Bert and Lennie left soon after that and I went with them. And,' she looked at her phone 'I have to go now. I can't be late back.'

'Thank you very much for your help, Ruby,' said Murphy. Ruby raised a hand and set off along Upper Thames Street.

Murphy sat back down. 'I'm exhausted' she said. 'We should have recorded all that, then we could sit quietly and sift through it.'

'It's right what she says,' said Wilcox. 'It is a mystery why Adam Bryce was determined to move to Muswell Hill. It's a nice place, and very expensive, but not up-and-coming. Not cool like Notting Hill. More a place for families.'

'Maybe that was what he wanted,' said Murphy. 'A family.'

Chapter Twenty-Three

ADAM BRYCE'S mother opened the door without looking at them, like she no longer cared who she was admitting. Murphy could understand that. There was no good news they could bring her. Even finding who had killed her son wouldn't bring him back.

They followed her into the sitting room, where her husband rose to meet them, looking utterly defeated. The loss had really sunk in now.

'I'm afraid we have no particular progress that we can yet report, but we are following a number of lines of enquiry and you will be first to know when we have a result,' said Murphy. 'I wanted just to have a proper talk to you, about Adam and what was going on in his life. You might have some information that would be helpful.'

Alan Bryce nodded wordlessly. His wife just shrugged.

'So can we start with the point at which Adam left home?'

Alan sighed. 'Adam wasn't what you call a high-achiever.

He was a good lad, an outdoors sort of person and we loved him, but he was never going to make a million or anything like that. He worked for a few years at fairly boring jobs. But he saved his money and then he went to art college. When he was there, he probably hung out with the wrong crowd, but he had left home at that point, he was living in some shared house in Hackney, so it was none of our business. He still came to visit every few months. He never brought any of his girlfriends home. I think he was playing the field. When college was over, he realised he'd have to get some sort of a job. I think he'd done quite a lot of digital artwork as part of his degree, so he moved into IT, some telesales firm. He said it was very boring, but it paid the bills and he enjoyed playing in the band with his mates. I don't know how good they were, but they were doing what they wanted to do. He had a few girlfriends and this Rebecca was just the latest. It didn't look like anything serious, as far as we knew. Then this silly old baggage, Nora's sister Daphne, pops her clogs and leaves him all her money – roughly six million.'

Murphy shook her head. 'That's an awful lot of money.'

'It's a disgraceful amount of money.' Nora Bryce now joined in, looking suddenly more animated. 'Daphne was my older sister and God forgive me, but she was a hard-faced old cow. Used to push me around all the time. She wasn't interested in men until this rich old guy, Arthur, comes along. He's the heir to a string of shoe shops – all up and down the country. She married him like a shot, they sold all the shops and invested the proceeds. Five years later he's dead and she's sitting on a fortune, so she spends the next twenty years travelling the world, hanging out in flesh-pots, or whatever, going to ashrams in India to 'find herself' – all that kind of thing. Trying to recapture the youth she never had, pathetic at that age. Meanwhile, despite all her attempts to spend it, the money keeps growing. Old Arthur had a good investment manager, he knew what funds to put it in. She contacted me out of the blue a few years back and asked how the kids were doing. I told her David was a teacher and doing well and Adam had just finished art college and was hanging round with a crowd we didn't know much about, but we hoped drugs weren't involved. I think that must have been when she was finalising her will. And apparently what I had said about Adam led to her deciding that he should be her heir. She saw herself as some kind of 'free spirit', not part of the establishment, despite all her money. We were just too boring, so she left the money to him.'

'And it's not that we wanted her money,' said Alan. 'Adam has tried to give us some of it, but we're not short of money. He's going – he was going' his face fell suddenly, 'to give some to David, but we don't need it.'

'And at what point did Rebecca come on the scene?' asked Murphy.

'About the same time as the money,' said Nora. 'I'm sorry to say it, but there it is. All of a sudden, he wants us to meet his fiancée and next thing you know they're getting married. If she had been pregnant, I would have understood, it would have made sense, but that wasn't it.'

'Where was the wedding?' asked Murphy.

'Chelsea registry office,' said Nora. 'Rebecca didn't want a church wedding, but she wanted to get married somewhere fashionable, so that's where it was. Where pop singers used to get married when we were young. Her dad gave her away, that's the only time we've met either of her parents and there was a reception in some expensive restaurant, can't even remember the name of it now.'

'Did you see much of him after he got married?'

'Not really,' said Alan. 'They had a honeymoon in the Seychelles and we got a visit after they got back, but I don't think we've seen Rebecca since then. Adam used to come on his own when he visited.'

'Was there anybody you knew about that Adam had problems or disagreements with?'

Nora shook her head. 'He just wasn't that sort of person. I don't remember him ever being in any fights at school, there was never any trouble. How could anybody want to do this?'

'It's some nutter,' said Alan. 'Obviously. I hope you catch him.'

'Oh, I intend to,' said Murphy. 'However long it takes.' She stood up. 'We'll leave you in peace now. Thank you for talking to us. We'll be in touch.'

'I wonder if he did give his brother any money?' said Wilcox as they walked down the path. 'I don't imagine he'll get anything from Rebecca.'

'We'll go and see him and find out,' said Murphy. 'Next stop.'

———

DAVID BRYCE HAD JUST FINISHED COACHING a girls' basketball team when they arrived. He was taller and broader than his brother, with a tattoo snaking up his arm and a firm handshake. If Aunt Daphne saw him now, Murphy decided, she wouldn't think him too 'establishment'.

'We're very sorry for your loss,' said Murphy 'and we don't have any news for you, but we did want to talk to you and see if you have any information that you can give us.'

'I don't honestly think I'll be able to help,' he said, leading the way to a bench outside the court. 'I haven't actually spent much time with Adam over the past few years, so I don't know much about what was going on with him.'

'You weren't close as brothers?'

'When we were young, we were close. There was scrapping of course, but we also did a lot of things together. And we used to go out with dad – fishing and hiking. Dad was big on the outdoors in those days, he was a bit of a birdwatcher. Then we got older and became kind of different. Adam got in with an arty crowd and later he went to art college. We went to his final exhibition, but I haven't seen anything he did after that. And he was into music, he was in a band. I didn't think they were that good to be honest, but Adam was very enthusiastic about it all. I was more interested in sport, so I did sports science. We moved in very different crowds, but we'd occasionally have family gettogethers. If I'd known we were going to lose him, I'd have seen more of him. People always say that don't they?'

Murphy nodded. 'Yes. They do. At what point did Rebecca come on the scene?'

'I'm not sure. He had a fairly long-term relationship at art college, another art student, but that ended for some reason and after college he got jobs in IT, that sort of thing, nothing artistic. The first time I met Rebecca was some gig of theirs that I went along to. She was sitting with the wife and girlfriend of the other two band members – WAGs we'd call them now – and I got introduced.'

'What did you think of her?'

He drew a deep breath. 'Difficult to say. Very attractive and he was obviously very keen, hugging her all the time, all that. She was a little bit more distant and I thought at the time that he was probably punching above his weight. I thought she was going to dump him at some point, when someone else came along. But that didn't happen. Maybe it would have done, if the money hadn't appeared.'

'Is that what you think?'

'It sounds pretty uncharitable, doesn't it? Maybe she was in love with him and I just read the signals wrong.'

'Did the money change Adam in some way?'

'He certainly changed at about that time, but it could have been the money or it could have been that he was older now. It's funny really. Aunt Daphne left him the money because she thought he wasn't 'establishment' and he then became as establishment as you can get, hiring an accountant, getting into tax matters, looking at investments. It's like all those celebrities, music business people, all the rest, they might act very wild in public, but behind the scenes they're concerned about their money and their assets.'

'One thing that we wondered about' said Wilcox, 'is why he moved to Muswell Hill. And he moved from Notting Hill, which is a much cooler, wealthier area.'

'I don't know,' said David. 'Mum and dad thought it was a good sign. They thought he was going to settle down and start a family, I think he'd even said something to them about wanting children. I don't know whether Rebecca was keen, but that's something else that didn't happen.'

'We have to ask everybody where they were on Monday afternoon,' said Murphy.

'Yes, of course you do. It was a Monday, so I had a free period from lunchtime until three thirty, which I spent going for a walk and doing some paperwork and then I was coaching football teams until five thirty. Then I went home, which is a flat in Ealing which I share with my girlfriend, Lesley.'

'What time did you get home?'

'About six thirty. Trains were messed up as usual.'

'We'll need your girlfriend's details,' said Wilcox.

David Bryce sighed, scrolled on his phone and showed them the screen.

'When we spoke to your parents,' said Murphy, 'they thought Adam was intending to give you some of the money he had inherited. Did that happen?'

He shook his head. 'We did talk about it, he was insisting on giving me some, but it hadn't yet happened?'

'How did you feel about him having all that money?'

'I dunno. Envious, a bit, to start with. Then worried.'

'Worried?'

'Well, yes. Getting a lot of money that you've worked hard for is one thing. Getting a big sum of money just gifted to you like that, well it often doesn't end well. I worried that he'd just spend his time sitting around getting high. It was probably a good thing that he was so tied up with the band. It was money down the drain as far as I could see, but at least it was something to be invested in.'

Murphy nodded and rose from the bench. 'Thank you for talking to us, David' she said. 'We may need to talk to you again. We'll be in touch.'

'That's no problem' he said. 'I want whoever did this to face justice. We may not have been all that close over the last few years, but he was still my brother.'

'Just one more question,' said Wilcox. 'Which team did he support?'

'Football? Newcastle. Always.'

Wilcox had got through to Lesley Franks by the time

they reached the car. 'She confirms he got home about six thirty' he said.

'He's not a prime suspect,' said Murphy. 'He might have received a substantial sum of money if Adam had not died. On the other hand, maybe that's not true. We only have his word for it. Maybe Adam wasn't going to give him anything.'

Chapter Twenty-Four

THE NEXT TIME Murphy saw David Bryce was at the inquest into Adam's death. From her seat in the back row, she watched him escort his parents to seats near the front. All three of them looked as if they were bracing themselves for an ordeal, which was really the only way to describe it, Murphy thought. At least there were, as far as she knew, no terrible details. It had been a quick death. And the lack of press interest was a blessing, indicative of the fact that Dead Cells had not had time to make much impact in the music business.

Rebecca arrived at the last minute, wearing dark colours and supported by Bert, and sat a few rows behind Adam's family. The lone reporter from the local paper suddenly looked interested. Rebecca had her head down and was not making eye contact with anybody.

The pathologist's evidence, given by Frank, accorded with what Murphy had already been told. A punch to the jaw and contact with a granite surface, leading to a catastrophic skull fracture. Death would have been instantaneous. Murphy saw Adam's mother bury her face in her hands when the detail about his thin skull emerged.

Frank's evidence made it clear that another party was involved in the death. Murphy stated that the police were following a number of lines of enquiry and the inquest was adjourned to allow the police to continue their enquiries.

Murphy was able to get out of the building ahead of the main players and saw David Bryce approach Rebecca. They exchanged a few words but there were no hugs or hand clasps. At that moment a car sped into view and Rebecca and Bert got in and were carried off. An Uber, Murphy realised. They had called an Uber before they were even out of the building. She approached Adam's parents, who were looking around as if wondering where they were. David was busy on his phone. Another Uber on the way.

David's mother looked up.

'This has been very upsetting for you' Murphy said. 'But I want you to know we are doing our very best to find out exactly what happened.'

Mrs Bryce shook her head. 'It won't make any difference. He'll still be dead.'

'It will make a difference as far as I'm concerned,' said her husband. 'If somebody was responsible for this, I want them to pay for it.'

Murphy nodded. 'I'll be in touch' she told them as the car arrived and David ushered them into it.

———

WILMA FOSTER AGREED to meet them that afternoon at four-thirty. 'I have to pick my granddaughter up from school and keep her till five-thirty, so I'll be at home doing nothing else for that hour.'

'Hard-working woman,' said Murphy. 'But she's going to fit us in.'

Wilma lived in a spacious flat round the corner from her clients. 'We bought this place thirty years ago,' she said. 'I'd be too embarrassed to tell you what it cost, but we couldn't buy it now, that's for sure.'

They followed her into a sitting room where a girl of about five was watching TV, a small dog sitting next to her.

'I'll just be in the kitchen, Isobel' said Wilma and they followed her through.

'Thank you for seeing us, Mrs Foster,' said Murphy. 'As you know, we are looking into the death of Adam Bryce and we'll be grateful for any insights you can offer.'

'Insights,' said Wilma Foster. 'Is that what they call it? I think what you're after is gossip, isn't it?'

'Yes,' said Murphy. 'That's definitely what I'm after. I'm not asking for confidential information about your clients, but I'd like to know those facts which are common knowledge and I'd be interested in your personal impressions. And I have to start by asking you where you were on Monday afternoon. We're asking everybody that.'

Wilma narrowed her eyes. 'OK. Let me see, I was cleaning for one of my other clients, about a mile from here, until two-thirty. Here's her details.' She scrolled on her phone and showed it to Wilcox. 'I came back here on the bus, tidied myself up a bit, and then went with Jimbo to collect Isobel from the school at three-thirty. So, I guess there's a small window during which I could have killed that poor chap, but I never even met him, so you'll have to come up with a motive.'

'That's alright, Mrs Foster,' said Murphy. 'You're not a serious contender.'

'You can call me Wilma. And as for the rest... I clean

for four families in that street. There's the Beatties –
Francine and Justin, the Frasers – Tom and Louise, the
Yardleys – that's Ted and Molly and the Warners – Wendy
and Ron. And I used to clean for Tony and Dorothy Parker
until they moved. They've gone into sheltered accommodation – rather them than me. I was expecting to be asked to
clean for the new people who moved into their house, but I
don't think that's going to happen now. I clean for the
Baileys – Eddie and Sandra – just once in a while. For
instance, now while they're on holiday I'll go in and clean
the place, water the plants, all that.'

'You really do know them all,' said Murphy. 'Can you
tell us a bit about each of them?'

'I wouldn't want my clients to think I go round talking
about them,' said Wilma. 'Because I don't.'

'I appreciate that,' said Murphy. 'But we are investigating an unexplained death, and you may have information that allows us to rule people out.'

'OK.' Wilma sat back and folded her arms. 'Francine
Beattie has two children. The older one – Danny - is hers
from a previous relationship and the baby is her husband's.
That's no secret. Justin works in the City somewhere doing
something, probably involving other people's money.
Francine does artwork and she's hoping to get back to work
when Tommy – that's the baby – is a bit bigger. I like her a
lot, him not so much. Stanley, who seems to be around a lot
at the moment, is Justin's stepfather. I'm not sure he and
Justin are all that close, but Francine likes him. He's a
friendly enough chap, but don't get him started on fishing.'

'Why don't you like Justin?' asked Murphy.

'I don't know, really. He's always friendly to me. But I
think he's friendly to everybody, especially women – it
doesn't mean much. I think underneath it all he might be a

bit different. That's just one of my, probably totally mistaken, impressions.'

'OK,' said Murphy. 'How about the Frasers?'

'They're next door to the Beatties, kids go to the same school, so they're good friends. He's another of these finance people and she manages a couple of properties. I know that because I've cleaned them for her when tenants move out. And you should see the mess they leave, but that's another story.'

'Do you like them?'

'Yes. Especially Louise, I think she's the one who calls the shots in that house. Just looks that way to me. He's not at home much. On the other side of the Beatties are Eddie and Sandra – nice people, two teenagers. He's mad about golf, but they're otherwise good people.'

'And your other clients are on the opposite side of the road?' Murphy was feeling the urge to scribble a diagram.

Wilma nodded. 'Poor Ted and Molly. They're my oldest clients. She's never going to get out of that bed.' She lowered her voice 'Cancer. And he's like a lost child. I take him some dinner over sometimes, because I know he's not eating properly. Will be better for them both when it's over, I think, but he wouldn't agree with that. Life can be very hard.'

'True enough,' said Murphy. 'And next to Ted and Molly are the Bryces.'

'That's the new people, isn't it? Yes, that used to be Tony and Dorothy. And on the other side of what was Tony and Dorothy's house there's Wendy and Ron. I think Wendy is a bit strict with Ron, he's not allowed to make a mess anywhere. Well apart from the back bedroom upstairs which is his kind of den, or where he escapes to. She's a nurse, very capable. If you had an accident, Wendy would be your best person to have around. Ron is one of those people always talking about their health, but she takes no notice. Although he does have excema, looks painful sometimes. He says it's caused by the stress of living with her. She says he has third-year medical student syndrome. Apparently in their third year they start thinking they have all the diseases they're learning about. He's not a medical person, but he's had a lot of doctor's appointments, so maybe that's where it comes from. Probably where he met Wendy. They don't have any children, so I guess that's why she keeps working. She wouldn't want to be at home all day and them both just sitting there looking at each other, would she?'

'I guess not,' said Murphy. 'Are you aware of any problems or disagreements among any of these people?'

Wilma shook her head. 'No, nothing. And I haven't heard anybody say anything about these new people. Although I do think the neighbours miss Tony and Dorothy. They always used to host drinks at Christmas and the three men – that's Ted, Tony and Ron – used to get together in the back gardens, have a beer or whatever. Now Tony's gone and Ted's become a full-time carer, so that's all gone. Life moves on, doesn't it?'

'It certainly does.' Murphy stood up and Wilma escorted them to the front door.

'Thank you, Wilma. I hope we won't have to bother you again.'

'No problem.' She shut the door.

'She had plenty to say,' said Wilcox, 'but I'm not sure how useful any of it was.'

'I was more interested in what she didn't say,' said Murphy. 'There were definitely things she was keeping back. I'd like to know what they were.'

Chapter Twenty-Five

WENDY WARNER WHIPPED the door open and regarded them belligerently. She was a comfortably-sized person lightly dusted in flour. Murphy held out her badge and introduced herself.

'Come in then' said Wendy, 'I'm doing something complicated in the kitchen, so you'll have to wait a few minutes – unless you want to talk to my husband.'

'That would be fine,' said Murphy.

'Straight ahead up the stairs' said Wendy, waving them away as if she was swatting flies.

Murphy shouted a greeting as she opened the door and a man sitting at an outsize desk with his back to a large window pushed his laptop to one side and rose hurriedly. He was a plump man, probably in his early sixties, with unruly hair and a neatly trimmed beard

'Dear me,' he said. 'I think I was dropping off. Just as well you arrived. Didn't get my nap this afternoon.'

He waved them to seats and came to join them.

'We're talking to everybody living round here, because we're investigating the death of Adam Bryce,' said Murphy.

He nodded. 'Of course. Shocking. Ted Yardley told me what happened.'

'Did you know Adam Bryce at all?'

'I can't say I knew him. I saw him at Justin's and then we went to his party – well, you have to as neighbours. It's important to get on. That said, I think I only exchanged a few words with him. He admired my garden; said he liked all the trees round here. And that was it.'

'And can you tell us where you were Monday afternoon?'

'I was just here, I don't tend to go out in the afternoons. Having my nap.'

'And how long would that have been for, sir?' asked Wilcox.

Ron Warner seemed to be giving this some consideration. 'About three hours. I think I went down about three o'clock and I got woken up by Wendy at about six when she came in.'

'And did you hear any noises from next door at all?'

He shook his head. 'No, nothing. I was asleep. We heard noises later on of course, while we were having dinner and Wendy was about to go round, but then it stopped.'

The woman herself appeared at that moment. She had dusted herself down and taken off her apron. Ron swivelled in her direction

'I was just saying dear, we heard the screaming from next door, but that was the first we knew of it.'

She nodded. 'Awful, such a shock. That poor young man. There's so little you can do for a head injury. Or was it a head injury? That's what Ted seemed to think.'

'Yes. It was a serious head injury', said Murphy. 'Were you at work on Monday afternoon?'

Wendy nodded. 'Yes. We were rammed at the surgery. It's like that every day now. I guess you'll want to check my alibi. It's the surgery in Mount Crescent.'

'Thank you,' said Murphy. 'Did you get much chance to speak to Adam Bryce or his wife?'

'Justin Beattie introduced me to the wife – Rebecca – at his party. And she invited me to their party, so of course we went along. They seemed like nice young people. She's very pretty, told me she works in the charity sector. I'm not sure what he does - did.'

'I don't think he had to do much,' said Ron. 'I heard he had lots of money. I think he was mostly into music. He seemed a decent young man. Surely it was just a tragic accident.'

'We haven't established exactly what happened yet,' said Murphy. 'But thank you for your time. We'll let you get on now.'

Wendy accompanied them down to the front door and shut it behind them.

'Well, that's it,' said Murphy. 'None of the neighbours saw or heard anything. Or so they say.'

Chapter Twenty-Six

'FRANCINE BELLING' said Wilcox, looking up from the laptop, which Murphy recognised as belonging to Adam Bryce. 'That's who he was googling. Then he found her on Facebook and eventually tracked down her address. She was promoting herself under her maiden name — she's an illustrator, isn't she? Looks like Francine Beattie.'

Murphy frowned. 'When was this?'

'Just over six months ago.'

'So he was looking for her before he moved into that house. He bought the house to be near her?'

Wilcox shrugged. 'I guess that's what you can do when you have lots of money.'

'What else have you come across?'

'Nothing else of interest. He seems to have been quite into the natural environment — not very rock 'n roll. Lots of shots of birds — with their names. Who the hell knows the names of birds? And landscape shots taken from high up. He was into climbing. And lots of stuff about the band — dates and venues where they were playing. Photos of them posing together - for promotional material by the look of it. The other two look properly languid and Adam looks dreadfully enthusiastic. Not the right music business image at all. It's like, he had the money but they look like pros and he looks like the amateur.'

'What about his wedding?'

'Yes. There are a few shots here – look.'

Murphy bent to look. The unmistakeable façade of Chelsea registry office and the sun was shining for it. Adam looked shellshocked and Rebecca, resplendent in an ivory linen suit, looked like a woman who had sealed a deal. Which of course she had. A small wedding party. His parents and a few other people. Murphy checked the date.

'About a year ago. And six months later he's trying to re-establish contact with another woman. That's a bad sign. OK, let's go and have a chat with her.'

———

'WE WERE STUDENTS, just silly kids. No, maybe that's not quite right. Adam wasn't really a kid; he was five years older than me. He'd worked at different things and then decided on art college. We were in love, or I thought we were. We took risks a few times but I thought it didn't matter. When I got pregnant, I found out that it did matter. Our time at college came to an end and Adam took off.'

Francine rubbed her fingers over her eyes. 'I really don't want to have to talk about this. It was so long ago.'

'What happened after he left?' asked Murphy. 'What did you do?'

Francine sighed. 'I moved into a flat with two of my girl-friends – Cheryl and Liz. They saved my life really. I knew I wasn't going to give up the baby, even if I couldn't give him a father. He was born and he was wonderful. I managed to get some freelance illustration work, enough to pay our share of the rent and life went on. I thought that was how it would be for the next few years. Then Liz got married and I met Justin at the wedding.'

'And then you got married.'

'Yes. Not a big wedding. I didn't want anything like that. I was pretty estranged from my parents and I didn't have any brothers or sisters. A few friends came and I met Shirley and Stanley and they were so kind to me. Shirley is dead now, which is sad.'

'Justin was already quite wealthy when you met him?'

She shrugged. 'I suppose so. He made it clear that he wanted to provide for me and Danny.' She looked up. 'But that's not why I married him. I wouldn't have married anybody just for money and a roof over my head. He was charming and fun and I loved him.'

'And then Adam tracked you down.'

'That was such a shock. I never expected to see him again. I still don't understand why he did it.'

'Didn't he tell you why he came back?'

'He gave me some spiel about how he had been young and made a mistake and he should never have left me and now he realised that I was the one. He wanted access to Danny. It was just deluded, especially as he's now married to somebody else.'

'What did you say?'

'I tried to tell him that Danny wasn't his, but that didn't really work. I told him I wouldn't allow access. I said I wasn't happy about him coming after me and that he should put his house back on the market and move somewhere else. He said he wanted to provide support for Danny, maybe take him out sometimes, and I said I had Ron and Stanley for that, so I didn't need him.'

'Bit like an alternative ending to Madame Butterfly, isn't it?' said Murphy. Wilcox rolled his eyes.

Francine smiled. 'Yes, I suppose it is. Pinkerton comes back and she tells him to piss off.'

'And did Justin know about this? About the relationship between you?'

'No, definitely not. I certainly never told him. When I told Adam that I wasn't interested in having a relationship with him, he suggested that we could tell people we were old friends, and I half agreed, but really, I didn't even want that, and I never mentioned him to Justin.'

'You weren't at all tempted?'

'Not at all. For the first few months after he left, I really wanted him back. But then Danny was born and he immediately became all I cared about. After that, I never thought much about Adam. Having a child makes you kind of grow up and, if I ever thought about Adam, I just thought about somebody a bit juvenile. He was fun to be with and I was in love with him at the time, but I could see that he would never have been able to be responsible for a child. That's probably something of what I saw in Justin. He probably had his faults, but he was an adult.'

'And what did Justin think about Adam. Did he say anything about him?'

'Justin discovered quite quickly that Adam had money, so he was interested in him. Justin makes his money by managing other people's money and he seemed to think Adam could be a potential new client. Then he found out that Adam didn't need anybody's financial services, he had all of that already arranged. At that point he lost interest. I hope you're not thinking,' she stared hard at Murphy, 'that

Justin had anything to do with what happened to Adam. Justin would never hurt anybody.'

'Our attention was drawn to Justin because of his previous skirmish,' said Murphy. 'But that was the only reason. We're not pursuing him particularly; we're still investigating all leads. So, tell me, what were your thoughts when you heard the news?'

She shook her head. 'Shock. I was just shocked. I'd been thinking of him as a problem and wanting him to go away, but I certainly never wanted him to be dead. He's Danny's father after all. And I feel responsible, because if he hadn't come here looking for me, he'd probably still be alive.'

'Did you see much of his wife?'

'No, I only met her briefly when they came here and then later at their house. She seemed very nice, very attractive. I don't think moving here had been her idea, she didn't seem all that pleased about it. I think she's usually part of a younger crowd.'

'OK, we'll leave it at that,' said Murphy. 'What's happening with Stanley? Has he gone off on his travels?'

'He was supposed to have gone, but he's still here.'

'That's good. We might have a few more questions for him at some point and we don't want to be scouring the autobahns.'

Francine smiled. 'I'll tell him not to leave town.'

'I'M NOT sure that got us any further forward,' said Wilcox as he climbed gingerly into the car.

'Oh, I don't know', said Murphy, as she swerved out of the parking space. 'Despite her protestations, I wonder if Justin did suspect something. After all, I've only seen Danny once, but I can see a resemblance to Adam. I wonder if anybody else has spotted it. And it did make me think rather better of Justin. He took on a woman with a child that wasn't his and he's the one who's been a father to Danny. Then Adam turns up threatening to upset everything. He could have insisted on a DNA test and demanded access. I wonder if he did that.'

'Francine's also in the frame,' said Wilcox. 'She couldn't deny that he was Danny's father and eventually she'd probably have had to tell Justin. It would have been easier for her if he'd just taken off, but he wasn't proposing to do that. She would have been afraid that, if Justin found out, there would be another fight, just like with the guy next door. And maybe that is what happened, after all.'

'Money seems to be a big issue for Justin,' said Murphy. 'The original fight was over money. And Francine says he considered Adam as another possible source of income. He has an expensive house and an expensive car, but maybe he has money problems. I think we need to investigate him a bit further. Stanley might be the person to talk to. We'll do that tomorrow. I'll drop you off here. I'm having a night off.'

Wilcox climbed gratefully out of the car and headed for the tube station.

Chapter Twenty-Seven

SIMON RAYMOND, the DI that Murphy had worked her last case with, was already at the pub when she arrived, nursing a pint and reading the evening paper. He looked up and smiled. 'What can I get you?'

'A gin and tonic please.' Murphy sat down on the padded bench and stretched her legs luxuriously. It was much less comfortable than her ergonomically-designed seat in the CID room, but somehow more relaxing.

'You weren't in the station this afternoon, were you?' Raymond said, putting her drink on the table.

'No. Why? Did something happen?'

'Certainly did. Bellweather's in hospital.'

Murphy stopped with the glass halfway to her mouth. 'What? Really? What happened?'

'He just collapsed. He was in the middle of tearing one of the PCs off a strip and suddenly he was on the floor. Avril did mouth to mouth and chest pumps, for which she should really be nominated for an award, and then the paramedics took over and carted him off.'

'Blimey' said Murphy. 'I don't know what to say. I've said so many uncharitable things about him for so long and now…'

Raymond laughed. 'Exactly. That's what we encounter all the time isn't it? Misfortune and death ennoble anybody, even Bellweather, in the eyes of all their detractors.'

'I wonder which hospital he's in?'

'St Thomas's. Don't even think of turning up there, not unless you want to give him a relapse.'

'No, I don't suppose the sight of me would do much for his recovery. But I hope he does recover. He's an annoying bastard, but I don't want him to be a dead bastard. Do you think it was a stroke?'

He nodded. 'Looked like that, not that I would particularly know.'

'I wonder who takes over?'

'DCI Millbrook. Ernie. Although he's still covering his existing cases, so I don't think we'll see much of him.'

'So, things are going to be a bit different?'

'Yes, for as long as he's away. We'll be able to get on with things without having to deal with his temper tantrums. Anyway, how's your case going?'

Murphy sighed. 'Slowly. There are a number of people who could be responsible, like they could have been in the right place at the right time, but I can't see any reason for any of them to want to harm him.'

He nodded. 'Motive's not really what we look at though, is it? All we're interested in is evidence.'

'Well, there's precious little of that. He was punched on the jaw, then fell backwards and hit his head. I was hoping the punch on the jaw might have left some trace.'

He nodded. 'Touch DNA.'

'Exactly. But Linda called me just before I left and said no, no DNA traces. How can that be?'

He shrugged. 'Maybe a very fast, light punch, maybe it got brushed off when the body was moved, maybe whoever punched him wore gloves, but that seems a bit unlikely.'

'It's very strange. We have a suspect who committed a similar assault a week ago, so he's the most likely perp, but no evidence so far. Nobody saw him in the vicinity, no fingermarks, no DNA. I could hazard a motive, but that won't get me far.'

'Sometimes,' said Simon Raymond, 'it's just a matter of perseverance, just doggedly going through the motions. There are no sudden insights, the facts just gradually emerge. Easier said than done, I know.'

'It would be good to get it wrapped up before Bell-weather gets back,' said Murphy.

'Now you're assuming he'll be back. That's good. That's the vote of confidence he probably needs.'

Murphy laughed. 'And how about your domestic?'

'We're not supposed to be talking shop, are we? Anyway, it's an interesting one. I think she's been beating him up for some time and he finally hit back. Of course, now he's over-come with remorse and when she gets out of hospital, she'll definitely make him pay for it. She's adamant that she's not pressing charges. She'll have much better ways of punishing him. So, we're taking no further action.'

Murphy shook her head. 'Why couldn't he just leave her? Alright, I know, that's the question we don't ask women in that position, so we can't ask men either. Relationships can be very complicated.'

He nodded. 'That's the truth. In his case, I don't think he would want to leave. They've been together for so many decades and he's a bit scared of her, but he wouldn't really want to be on his own. Unfathomable to me, but there it is. So shall we go and find something to eat?'

'Yes, let's do that. I missed lunch, so I won't be fussy.'

'There's the Thai place next door.'

'That sounds good.' Murphy reached down to pick up her bag and heard the buzz. 'Just a minute.' She swiped and listened. 'OK, call DC Wilcox. I'll get along there.' She looked up and sighed. 'Well so much for my dinner. That was Avril. She's having a busy day. She was one of the first responders. It's my prime suspect. He's dead.'

Chapter Twenty-Eight

PROBABLY JUST AS WELL SHE'D missed dinner, Murphy thought, as she exited Tower Hill station and set off round the Tower, along East Smithfield and into St Katharine's Dock. Looking at bodies always felt worse on a full stomach. The site was a patch of rough ground at the back of some sort of old industrial building. The area was partly walled, with access on two sides, and a fire escape snaked up the back of the building with a balcony at each level.

Wilcox was already there. Presumably he hadn't been drinking, so he'd been able to drive. A tent had been set up over the body and a length of police tape further out. Avril Duffy and another PC were keeping interested onlookers away and two other officers had been deployed to question people in the bar three floors up.

Murphy put on the protective suit she was handed and joined Wilcox at the entrance to the tent. Frank was bending over the body. He looked up and saw her. 'Pretty instantaneous' he said. 'Looks like he fell from quite a height so there will be a lot of broken bones and internal injuries. Head and spine injuries will have done for him, poor chap. Do you know who he is?'

Murphy nodded. 'Yes, we know who he is alright. We were talking to him yesterday.' She sighed. 'This is not what I was expecting.'

Frank came out to join them. 'Not much more I can do here' he said. 'Pm should be tomorrow, I'll get it in early as possible, and we'll know more after that.' He snapped his case shut and began to strip off his suit. 'We'll have to see if any drugs or alcohol were involved.'

'Thanks Frank.' Murphy raised a hand as he walked back to his car. Murphy rubbed her eyes. 'I don't know what to say about this' she told Wilcox.

'It could be suicide,' he said, 'but I wouldn't think so. Not how I'd choose to do it. His phone was right beside his hand, like he'd been holding it when he fell. Torch switched on. Wanted to have a last look around him.'

Murphy signalled to the morgue attendants that they could pick up the body and stood there as it was carried out. Justin Beattie was unrecognisable. His arms and legs hung limply. His head was tilted at an unnatural angle. Frank had thankfully closed the eyes. The confident demeanour and the ready smile were gone. Death had knocked everything out of him.

'I've sent the uniforms to his home,' said Wilcox and Murphy nodded, thinking of Francine Beattie being woken with the news.

Avril came over. 'Who called it in?' asked Murphy. Avril pointed behind her. 'A passing cyclist. He's over there. I've got his details.'

Murphy was expecting a young man in Lycra wearing a skid lid. What she saw instead was a late middle-aged man with an upright bicycle and one of those helmets that look like casserole dishes.

'Thank you for calling this in, Mr Granger, and for staying behind to talk to us,' she said. 'This was a late cycle ride you were doing.'

He nodded. 'I go for a ride before I turn in at night' he said. 'Good for helping me get to sleep. And there are never many people around, so I can ride mostly on the pavement. If I'd been riding on the road, I wouldn't have seen…' He shook his head as if trying to dislodge the image. 'I suppose the poor man's dead?'

'Yes, he is,' said Murphy. 'I suppose you didn't see anybody else around?'

'No, nobody.'

'And you didn't hear anything.'

He shook his head and pointed to the ear buds draped around his neck. 'I'm afraid I was listening to a novel.'

'Not a good idea, sir, when riding on the public highway,' Wilcox chipped in.

Murphy rolled her eyes. 'We're grateful to you for helping and we'll let you get home now.'

He nodded, fastened his helmet and set off.

'That was a bit unnecessary,' she told Wilcox.

'It's part of our job to keep people safe,' he said. 'He looks harmless enough, but he's a potential public menace.'

'OK. The fire escape is part of the crime scene, so nobody uses it until SOCO have finished' said Murphy and Wilcox signalled to a uniformed officer, who arrived with a roll of tape.

'The only occupied bit is that bar on the top floor,' said Wilcox. The floors below were in darkness. Each floor had a wrap-around balcony leading off from the fire escape.

'Let's go up and see who we have in there,' said Murphy and they made their way round to the front of the building, where a door opened onto an internal staircase. The ground floor looked as if it housed some kind of industrial unit, the next two floors were offices and the bar was on the third floor

'We call it the third floor,' said Wilcox, 'but if you fall it's four floors down.'

Illuminated arrows at each floor pointed the way up to Bennie's Bar and a final illumination told them they had arrived.

'I suppose this is how the punters work up a thirst,' said Murphy, as they pushed open the door.

The premises was bigger than it looked from down below, with an assortment of tables, sofas and bar stools and a big circular bar at one end. The back door leading to the fire escape was on the opposite side of the room. Two police constables stood just inside the door. Murphy showed her badge and they stood aside. The staff, a man with a pony tail and multiple piercings who seemed to be in charge and two younger women, stood silently behind the bar. Murphy estimated that there were about fifty people inside. She approached the bar.

'Do you have CCTV?'

The barman nodded.

'We'll need the footage from tonight. My colleague here will deal with that.' She indicated Wilcox. Good job he was here. She was crap at all this technical stuff. Now to deal with the clientele.

'Thank you all for waiting,' she shouted, hoping they could all hear. 'As you will have realised, there has been a serious incident. If anybody here saw anybody enter or leave by that back door, please come and talk to us. Or if you noticed a man, probably early forties, in a navy-blue suit and pale blue shirt, dark blond hair. Or if you saw anybody on the fire escape. Otherwise, if you will just leave your details with the officers by the door, you are free to go.'

There was muttering and a general movement towards the door. Murphy turned back to the bar staff.

'Was it busier than this earlier on?'

'You bet,' said one of the women. 'Lots of people having a quick drink at the end of work and a couple of big groups. They've all gone now.'

'How about any of you here? Did you see anybody leave by the back door?'

They all shook their heads. 'It was rammed in here earlier tonight,' said the barman. 'We wouldn't even have been able to see that door.'

'Do you normally have people going in and out there?'

He shook his head. 'Most people probably don't even know it's open. They leave by the same door they came in by. We leave it unlocked to comply with the fire regulations. If a fire broke out up here, we'd need more than one exit, and that's the fire exit.'

'It's a bit cold out there tonight,' said Wilcox.

The barman nodded. 'In the summer we leave that fire door open and we have tables out on the balcony. Nobody would want to be out there at this time of year.'

'Did you notice this man, early forties, slim, blondish hair, navy-blue suit? I don't have a photo at the moment, but we'll come back with one.'

The barman shook his head. 'We get a lot of people in here look like that. I don't remember him.'

'I think I do,' said one of the girls. 'He had a nice smile, if it's the same guy.'

'That sounds like him,' said Murphy. Justin would definitely be a man who smiled at barmaids. 'So, he didn't look at all depressed?'

She shook her head. 'If it's him, no, not at all.'

'And how many drinks was he buying?'

She thought for a minute. 'He bought a bottle of wine,' she said suddenly. 'Shiraz. And two glasses.'

'At what time was that?'

She shrugged. 'About two hours ago, say 7.30.'

'Any idea where he was sitting?'

She shook her head. 'I didn't see him after he moved away from the bar.'

'That's very helpful,' said Murphy. 'We'll definitely want you to see the photo and confirm it's him. Just give your details to DC Wilcox here.'

'How often do you collect the glasses?' she asked the barman.

'It's continuous,' he said. 'It's not a good look, empty glasses sitting around.'

'Who collects them?'

'We all do. Soon as there's not a rush at the bar, one of us will go out and collect them.'

'So do any of you remember collecting an empty red wine bottle and two glasses?'

They all shook their heads.

'Where do empty bottles go?'

They barman indicated a cardboard box at his feet.

'And what about the glasses?'

'Straight in the dishwasher.'

'Any here now that haven't made it into the dishwasher?'

He shook his head. 'We've just put a load in. They're about to come out.'

Murphy sighed. 'OK. We'll need to get somebody up here to examine all these bottles and we'll need to take all your fingerprints for elimination. I'll send somebody up to do that now and then we'll let you get on and close up. Nobody is to touch that door or use the fire escape.'

They made their way back out through the front door and walked round to look at the fire escape. 'He probably didn't fall from the top,' said Wilcox. 'Somebody in the bar would have seen something, although the bar is lit up and the fire escape is in darkness, so they wouldn't have seen very clearly. But the next level down, nobody from the bar could have seen anything and that floor of the building was deserted, so nobody to look out and see. The fall would still have been three floors, so quite enough.'

Murphy nodded. 'Yes, that makes sense. SOCO will have to check the whole of this fire escape, but floor two looks the likeliest.' She pulled her coat more tightly around her. 'I just can't see Justin Beattie killing himself. I can see him getting himself into trouble, but he's – or he was – the sort of chap who tells himself that things will be OK, that he'll get away with whatever it is. But maybe I'm wrong, I often am.'

'If he killed Adam Bryce, he might have felt that murder was something he wasn't going to get away with,' said Wilcox.

'But somebody else was with him,' said Murphy. 'Maybe the other person left and then Justin went out the back way and chucked himself off the fire escape, but I don't find that very convincing.'

'You think somebody chucked him off the fire escape?'

'I think, whether they did or they didn't, we need to find that person as fast as possible.'

Chapter Twenty-Nine

FRANCINE AND STANLEY were sitting together in the kitchen when they arrived. They both looked as if they had been up all night, which they probably had, and Francine's eyes were red and swollen.

'We're very sorry for your loss,' said Murphy. 'We're not yet sure exactly what happened but we will find out. Did you have any reason to think that Justin was depressed at all?'

They both shook their heads. 'Justin's never been depressed in his life,' Stanley declared. 'He's just not that sort of person.'

'He did seem like he had something on his mind,' said Francine, 'but I never asked him about it.' A tear ran down her cheek. 'I wish I had.'

'Can you think of anybody who would have wished him harm, anybody he had a dispute with, anything like that?'

'No,' said Francine.

'You mean somebody else could have been involved?' asked Stanley. 'I thought we were looking at suicide.'

'We have to consider all possibilities,' said Murphy. 'We can't rule anything out at this stage.'

'I should have given him the bloody money,' said Stanley. 'It's all my fault.'

'I wouldn't assume that,' said Murphy. 'It may have had nothing to do with money. We just don't know enough yet. We will need somebody to identify the body. Will you be able to do that, Mr Farrow?'

Stanley nodded. 'You want me to come now?'

'That would be best.'

Stanley stood and put a hand on Francine's shoulder. 'Get some rest love. I'll be back in time to take Danny out for a bit.' He put his jacket on and followed them out.

Wilcox held the back door of the car open for Stanley. 'Make sure you put your seatbelt on,' he said.

Murphy started the engine and they set off, narrowly missing a double-parked taxi.

Stanley whistled through his teeth. 'I'm not sure my life insurance will cover this,' he said.

'Brace position is a good idea,' said Wilcox.

They reached the morgue without further mishap and Stanley climbed stiffly out. 'It's a funny thing' he said to Wilcox, 'but having your life endangered really perks you up. I'm feeling much better now than I was back at the house.'

Wilcox nodded and escorted him inside. Murphy, who had also been up most of the night, was tempted to climb back into the car and have a nap, but decided she wouldn't get away with it, so she locked up and set off after them.

Stanley nodded tersely when the sheet was raised. Murphy was glad that one side of Justin's face was undamaged. She wouldn't have wanted him to see the other side.

The attendant covered the face up again and Stanley took a step back. His eyes were watering.

'He wasn't a bad lad, I don't think' he said. 'He was just a weak character. And I was probably the wrong sort of stepfather, so I never had a good relationship with him.'

Murphy led the way outside. 'Let's get coffee' she said. 'I need some and you probably do too.'

They crossed the road to a café with tables outside. It was cold, but a weak sun was breaking through and sitting outside allowed more privacy. Murphy rewrapped her scarf and warmed her hands gratefully on the cardboard cup Wilcox put in front of her.

'In what ways was he a weak character?' she asked Stanley. He was silent. 'Anything you say about him now won't do him any harm,' she said 'and it might give us some insight into what was going on.'

Stanley swallowed a sip of coffee and sat back in his chair. 'He was easily led' he said. 'Any silly scheme that somebody else came up with, Justin would join in. Selling stolen cigarettes at school – nearly got expelled for that one. He wasn't stupid. He got into university, although I know that doesn't take much, as long as you can pay the fees. Shirley paid the fees and gave him money for whatever else he needed. But it wasn't enough, he always wanted more money. She had it and she didn't mind giving it to him but, when I came along, I persuaded her that giving him money wasn't really doing him any good. So, I was the wicked stepfather from that point on. Then I discovered that he was gambling. These online sites, they should be bloody closed down. We had a lot of words about that and he said he'd stopped. Then he went back to university and we kind of forgot about him for a while, as you do.

He came back after his three years and got a job, which we thought was a great thing. Not so great that it was financial services. I'd rather have seen him doing something decent and practical, rather than playing with money, but that was his business. The problem was that he still seemed to need more money, even though he must have been earning a good salary, or maybe most of it was on commission, I don't know. That made me wonder if he was gambling again. He'd had various girlfriends, most of them we never met, then he took up with Francine. She was different. Shirley and I thought Francine would be the making of him. And she had a child, so he had to start being responsible. Then Shirley got ill and the cancer was diagnosed. It moved very fast. She was in a hospice at the end and I spent most of my time there. It was heartbreaking. Justin would call in from time to time, he never stayed long, usually just long enough for me to have a break. Shirley was on a high dose of morphine and slept most of the time. The day she died, Justin came in for one of his flying visits and, after he had gone, the nurse looked at the drip and said the level had gone down too quickly. An hour later she was dead. It's true that she was already dying and it may have been nothing to do with Justin, but I always wondered. Then, when he discovered there was no will and the money was all coming to me, he hit the roof, and I wondered a lot more. I'm probably doing Justin a massive disservice here.'

'The truth just is what it is,' said Murphy. 'The character of the victim is one of the first things we want to know about when we begin an investigation. Warts and all. That's what points us in the direction of what may have taken place. So, thank you for being frank about it.'

They stood up and walked back to the car. 'I'm staying

here for a while,' said Murphy. 'DC Wilcox will drive you home.'

Stanley shook his head. 'No need' he said. 'I don't have to be back for hours yet and a bit of walking will do me good.' He raised a hand and walked away.

'OK, so it's the PM for both of us' said Murphy and they walked back inside.

Chapter Thirty

LINDA FLEMING WAS LOOKING at X-rays when they shuffled in, rustling in their plastic suits.

'Is that his?' asked Murphy.

Linda nodded. 'Yes. The usual breakages we'd expect from a fall. What was the height?'

'Roughly thirty feet,' said Wilcox.

'That looks about right,' said Linda. 'OK, let's get him in.'

The attendants wheeled the trolley in and transferred the body to the table. Justin's face had been cleaned up but it was still hard to look at. Murphy kept her attention on the unmarked side. Linda switched on her microphone.

'Male, early forties, well nourished, no scars or tattoos. Extensive bruising.' She lifted up an arm. 'Rigor still present.'

She picked up the scalpel and Murphy braced herself. Wilcox, by contrast, looked perfectly relaxed. How did he do it? Lack of imagination, she thought savagely.

Linda made the Y incision and peeled back the muscles.

'Not much damage to the heart' she said, lifting it out carefully. 'One lung punctured by broken ribs. Damage to the spleen. The lower part of the spine is undamaged, but fractures in the neck area. I think we'll find the catastrophic damage when we look inside the skull.'

She picked up the saw and Murphy forced herself to look as the top of the skull came away. 'OK, so this is the cause of death,' said Linda. 'Subarachnoid haemorrhage.'

'Bleeding on the brain?' asked Wilcox.

'That's right. It's a leading cause of death following car accidents or falls. The head is the heaviest part of the body so it tends to hit the ground first. There may be drugs or alcohol involved but I won't know until the toxicology report comes back.'

'We know he was drinking red wine,' said Murphy.

'In that case he may have been inebriated,' said Linda. 'Or there may have been something else in the wine. We'll have to wait and see. But it was definitely the fall that was fatal.'

'And it's just a matter of did he fall or was he pushed,' said Murphy.

'I can't see any pressure marks that would indicate a push,' said Linda. 'But it may not have needed to be a hard push. What did he fall from?'

'A balcony, part of a fire escape.'

'That means he had to be tipped over the balcony,' said Linda. 'It wasn't just a straight push.'

'It would be possible to do that if he was leaning over the balcony' said Murphy, 'but it was dark, there was nothing to see.'

'You'd need to be quite strong to heave somebody over a balcony,' said Wilcox.

Linda moved towards the other end of the body and

looked at the legs. She raised one of them. 'There is a pressure mark here around the ankle. It's quite faint and I took it to be from his socks, the top where they are a bit elasticated. But it's more noticeable on one ankle than the other, so there was some additional pressure on one leg.'

'That would be the way to do it,' said Wilcox. 'Get at least one of the legs off the ground. Would it take a lot of strength?'

Linda shrugged. 'Depends whether he realised what was happening and fought back and also on whether he was drunk or drugged. That would have made it a lot easier.'

'So, a woman could have done it?' said Murphy. 'If anybody did it.'

'It's possible. A strong woman taking him unawares. He's not a heavily-built man. But, if he was drunk or drugged, it could have been accidental. He could have lost his bearings and climbed over, not realising where he was.'

'Lot of questions to be answered,' said Murphy.

Chapter Thirty-One

FRANCINE OPENED the door to let them in and led the way back to the kitchen where an iron was steaming.

'Don't ask me why,' she said, bending down to pull out the plug. 'I just needed something mindless to do. Otherwise, I'll sit here and think.'

'How's Danny?' asked Murphy.

'He's very upset. It's hard to know what to say to him. We told him daddy had an accident. Stanley's taken him out to the park.'

'Good thing you have Stanley.'

'He's been wonderful. Without him and Ron, I don't know how I'd have coped…'

'We need to ask you where you were last night. It's just something we have to ask everybody.'

'Of course. I understand.' Francine drew a deep breath. 'I had a night off last night. I went to meet a friend in the West End. We did a bit of shopping in Bond Street, wandered around Selfridges, had early supper in an Italian restaurant and then I got back here about nine thirty. I paid

Wilma and went straight to bed. Justin had phoned earlier to say he had a meeting with a client, so not to wait up for him. I didn't realise he wasn't there until the early hours when the police arrived.'

'Can we have the details for your friend?'

She nodded and scrolled down on her phone.

'OK, so you and …Fiona … both set off for home at the same time?' said Murphy.

'No, she left before me, about six thirty, because she had to get a train back to Maidenhead. I didn't feel like going straight home so I went and had a look at some of the galleries. I like looking at the artwork in the windows and that would have been a bit boring for Fiona.'

'You didn't go into any of these galleries.'

'No, they were all closed. I just like to look in the windows. We did visit most of them when I was at art college, but that was all pre-arranged. Now I wouldn't find them so easy to just walk into. They can be snobby places.'

'Stanley wasn't around last night?' said Murphy.

'No, that's why I got Wilma to babysit. Stanley was away somewhere. He probably told me about it, but I've forgotten.'

'That's fine,' said Murphy 'we'll catch up with him at some point. It would be helpful if we could establish Justin's state of mind yesterday. Did you have any reason to think he was worried or depressed? Was there anything making him angry?'

Francine seemed to hesitate. 'Justin was quite a … volatile character. In some ways, it made him a lot of fun, but his mood could change very quickly. He has been preoccupied with something but I don't know what. If I asked, he would snap at me. And he's been angry with Stanley. Mainly about money. But also wanting Stanley to leave.'

'Why didn't Stanley just leave?' asked Wilcox.

'Because I asked him not to. I like having Stanley around. It's someone to talk to and Danny likes him. Bit selfish of me, I suppose.'

'You think Justin was having problems with money?'

'It seemed that way. I don't know why, because he was on a good salary and commission and our mortgage is not that ruinous. I'm not a big spender and Danny's not at a private school, so it shouldn't really have been a problem. Unless he'd lost his job and not told me – you do hear of cases like that.'

Murphy nodded. 'Yes. They carry on commuting and hope nobody will notice. It all comes out in the end, because there's no salary. I'm sure that wasn't the case with Justin, but it's something we'll look into.'

They heard the front door opening at that moment and Stanley appeared, followed by Danny, who was uncharacteristically quiet.

'Let's go and put that video on for you Danny,' he said 'and then I'll come and join you in a bit.' They disappeared next door into the sitting room and then Stanley came back into the kitchen and closed the door.

'Thanks Stanley,' said Francine. She stood up. 'I'll go and get Danny's bath ready.'

'Glad you're here, Stanley,' said Murphy. 'I didn't get round to asking you where you were last night, so I can ask you now.'

He smiled grimly. 'Alibi time, is it? Thought it wouldn't be long. Mine's not going to hold up, I'm afraid. I went down to Brighton. Yes, I know it's not the right time of year for Brighton, but I wanted to give the old bus a decent run and I felt like a bit of sea air.'

'What time did you leave and get back?' asked Wilcox.

'I left about two thirty, got there about three thirty. Lot of traffic even in the afternoon and took a while to get parked. Walked around the Lanes, lovely shops but not my sort of thing, most of them. Then I did a long walk along the beach, well not that long, just as far as Hove. Nice place, Hove. Used to be a fishing village, but it's very upmarket now. Fishing's still probably very good.'

'What did you do after that?' asked Wilcox.

'Let me see. I walked back to Brighton. Then I bought some fish and chips and a bottle of water for my dinner and ate them on the seafront. That would be about six thirty, maybe seven. It was getting dark but the sea air was still good. Then I just sat facing out to sea, like a bloody pensioner, just thinking about things, until it got really cold. I don't know what time I left, could have been eight o'clock, maybe a bit after. Traffic was really slow on the way back, roadworks and all sorts. Not actual work going on, not at that time, but all the lanes were still closed. I got back here about nine thirty. Everybody else was in bed.'

'What was the name of the fish and chip shop?' asked Wilcox.

Stanley looked at him. 'I don't know. I didn't even look. It was down on the seafront. There's several of them there.'

'Thank you for that, Stanley,' said Murphy. 'We'll let you get on now.'

They made their way out and Stanley shut the door behind them.

'Sounded bloody fishy to me,' said Wilcox. 'Excuse the pun.'

'Sounds like neither of them has an alibi,' said Murphy, as she climbed into the passenger seat.

'That's right,' said Wilcox, accelerating away smoothly. 'Do you think they were in it together?'

Chapter Thirty-Two

'SO HOW DID your hot date go?' asked Clive. 'We were expecting to see him down here for breakfast, looking exhausted.'

'Very funny. It wasn't a hot date, as you very well know, it was just dinner with a colleague. Anyway, I got called out before I got to eat anything, so it finished pretty sharpish.'

'So when's the last time you ate dinner?'

'I dunno. It's faded from my memory.'

Clive tutted. 'That's appalling. We're making wild mushroom risotto and you're to stay and eat it no matter who phones up.'

'Believe me, I will. If I wasn't on a case, I'd switch the phone off. I'm going to have a quick shower.'

Half an hour later Murphy sat down to eat. It tasted wonderful.

'What do you guys know about fishing?' she asked.

'Nothing' said James. 'We like eating fish so I'm glad somebody catches it, but I wouldn't be able to.'

'I mean, more in terms of the pursuit of fishing. Are people very keen on it?'

'Some people are mad about it,' said Clive. 'There are all these extreme fishing sites.'

'Extreme fishing? What's that – catching sharks?'

'Something like that. They parade around in their waterproofs and waders and display these thrashing monsters. Then they chuck them back in for somebody else to haul them out.'

'Sounds a bit hard on the fish.'

'The fish might enjoy it, for all we know. They get to eat whatever the bait is and after a few times they're pretty sure they'll get chucked back in.'

Murphy shook her head. 'It's all a mystery to me. I've met someone who has moved into a van, one that's all fitted out, and he plans to travel the world doing fishing, probably posting pictures online, I don't know.'

'There's a number of people doing that,' said James. 'There's a lot of money in it.'

'Advertising?'

'That's right. What's this guy's name?'

'Stanley. Stanley Farrow.'

He did some clicking and scrolling. 'Is this him? Fishing the World?'

Murphy stared. There he was, on video, talking to the camera, demonstrating something intricate with nylon thread. He looked and sounded like a confident performer.

She pointed. 'Try that one.'

James clicked another link and Stanley was now giving a tour of the interior of his van, showing the storage facilities, where he kept his rods and his wellingtons, and his sleeping and cooking arrangements.

'What's the most recent one?'

'Looks like this one. Trout fishing in Walthamstow', said James. 'Funny, I never associate Walthamstow with fishing. Just shows – you never know half of what goes on.'

'I find that all the time,' said Murphy. 'This video was posted the day before the day I'm interested in. I wonder why he didn't post one the next day?'

'Maybe he's got another one to post,' said James.

'"Tell you what I notice,' said Clive. 'This guy has 500,000 followers. He's fishing royalty. He'll be making serious money.'

'Will he?'

'Of course. Affiliate links to all sorts of stuff – rods, nets, flies, stuff for carrying your equipment, bait, boots, raincoats. And all the stuff he's done his van out with. His curtains and cushions, his waste disposal, his gas and electric setup. Plus, he's got advertisers paying to be on his site. That one there, for instance – Outdoor Online – they'll be paying him good money.'

'And I thought he was just an eccentric old man,' said Murphy.

'Eccentric old millionaire probably,' said Clive.

Chapter Thirty-Three

WILCOX WAS ALREADY in the office when she arrived, sorting through a pile of reports. It was a Saturday, so they had the office pretty much to themselves.

'These are the interviews with the people in Bennie's Bar,' he said. 'We got a picture of Justin off his laptop and printed it off. That barmaid who served him confirmed it was him. And one of the people drinking in there told our chaps that he'd seen him before. He left a mobile number, so I gave him a ring. He works at a hotel in Bloomsbury, sounds like one of those little boutique places. He's there all day.

'Good job.' Murphy put her coat back on. 'Let's get down there. Probably quicker on the tube.'

It wasn't quicker on the tube, as it turned out, because there was a hold-up of some sort. Their train came to a grinding halt in the tunnel and after ten minutes those who had been staring at their phones were blearily surfacing, wondering what was going on.

Wilcox looked up, shrugged and went back to whatever

game he was playing. Murphy disposed of anything readable in that day's newspaper, and then she sat and looked around at her fellow passengers. Nobody was panicking yet. It had only been twenty minutes so far. Give it an hour and things would start happening.

Just as she was trying to predict who would crack first, there was a sudden lurch and they were on the move. There was an audible collective sigh of relief. At the next station there was an enthusiastic rush for the doors.

'It would be an interesting experiment,' she told Wilcox. 'Stuck on a motionless tube. Then you'd find out how people react under pressure.'

He snorted. 'Sounds like one of those crap team-building things.'

'That's right,' said Murphy. 'But sometimes people under pressure commit crimes. If they can't think what else to do.'

———

LOUISE FRASER HAD BEEN SITTING at her kitchen table surrounded by paperwork when Murphy and Wilcox turned up.

'You've caught me doing my tax return,' she said, leading the way in.

'We'll be quick then,' said Murphy. 'I wouldn't like to keep anybody from their tax return.'

'Have a seat,' said Louise. 'Would you like coffee?'

'Yes please,' said Murphy immediately. Louise looked like a woman who would provide proper coffee.

'You'll know why we're here,' she said. 'Two of your neighbours dead in less than ten days.'

Louise was silent for a few moments. Then she came

back with the coffee pot and sat down. 'I can't believe it,' she said. 'Poor Francine. I went round to see her, but I just didn't know what to say. It's good that she has Stanley.'

'Stanley, yes.' Murphy took a sip of coffee. It was good. 'Can we just start by asking you where you were on Friday evening?'

Louise looked surprised at this. 'Well … I was just here. Sally was off at a sleepover so I didn't have to pick her up, so I was here doing some work. Tom had dinner with a client, so he wasn't in until late. I'd gone to bed by then.'

'Are you saying you didn't see Tom all evening?'

Louise shook her head slowly. 'But you're surely not thinking…'

Murphy shook her head. 'We're not drawing any conclusions at the moment, but we have to establish where everybody was, although most of them will have had nothing to do with the event.'

'I see.' Louise frowned. It looked like either she didn't see or she saw all too well.

'How well did you know Justin Beattie?' asked Wilcox.

'I … not at all. Not really. Well, I know Francine of course and we're neighbours but I wouldn't really say I knew him.'

'That's surprising,' said Murphy. 'I only spoke to him a few times, but Justin Beattie struck me as a man who probably liked women, and you were just next door. And how many years were you neighbours?'

'I don't know – maybe four years.'

'There you are, then. I would say you probably did know him a bit. Did you like him?'

Louise got up from the table and returned with a piece of kitchen paper. She blew her nose and wiped her eyes.

'I think you liked him quite a lot,' said Murphy.

Louise brushed a tear away from her cheek. 'Yes, I did. He made me laugh. He probably had all sorts of faults, but he was good company.'

'I understand,' said Murphy. 'Did your husband know that you were …close… to Justin.'

Louise shook her head. 'No, not at all.'

'So the fight they had was nothing to do with you?'

'No, of course not. That was about financial advice that he said Tom had given to Stanley, although Tom said he couldn't remember much about it. I don't think it was serious, professional advice, just a passing suggestion.'

'And you called the police and reported Justin.'

'Actually, it was the paramedics who called the police, although I did describe it as an assault. I was very shocked. But Tom agreed not to press charges.'

'Justin took money very seriously, didn't he?'

Louise shrugged. 'His business was all about money. That's what financial services is all about – moving money around, mostly other people's money.'

'But he seemed to have had a strong personal need for money.'

'He may have done. I don't know anything about that.'

'So how long had you had a relationship with Justin?'

'It wasn't …'

'A woman who matches your description was seen at the Havisham Hotel with Justin. It's a nice hotel, not one of the ones that lets rooms by the hour. But you never actually stayed the night, did you?'

'No,' Louise whispered. 'We didn't.'

'OK, tell us about it.'

She bit her lip. 'It was a bit of fun. That's all it was. Justin said Francine didn't have much time for him and it seemed like Tom didn't have much time for me. That's no excuse, but that's how it started.'

'And when did it start?'

She drew a deep breath. 'About two months ago. And I finished it over a week ago – last Monday.'

'The day after the housewarming party. The same day that Adam Bryce died,' said Wilcox.

Louise looked shocked. 'But it had nothing to do with his death.'

'Probably not', said Murphy. 'But we like to get a feel for the chronology of events. What was happening when, all that sort of thing. How did Justin react when you finished it?'

Louise sighed. 'Predictable really – he was quite offended. Or maybe it wasn't predictable, because we had agreed at the beginning that it wasn't anything serious, so I thought we should have been able to part as friends.'

'And he didn't feel that way.'

'No, he was quite put out, but I think he was angry that I had finished it, rather than him. I don't think that it was because it was any great loss to him.'

'Do you think Francine or Tom knew about it?'

She shook her head. 'No, I'm sure they didn't. We were very careful. We wouldn't have wanted either of them to know. It certainly wasn't worth destroying a marriage for.'

'And you were with Justin on Thursday evening. Was that just a signing off meeting?' said Wilcox.

Louise looked confused. 'No, that's not right. I told you where I was Thursday evening. I was here.'

'You didn't go along that evening to meet Justin for a drink?'

'No, of course not. We'd hardly spoken to each other since that last occasion.'

'So, after you broke up with him, do you think Justin was seeing anybody else?'

'No, not that I know about. I'm sure he was just concentrating on his relationship with Francine.'

'Things were not going well between him and Francine?'

Louise sighed. 'I think Justin felt that Francine didn't have much time for him anymore. I'd say he's – he was – a man who likes to have attention. But Francine had Danny and now the baby, so I told him he should show some patience.'

'And how about your husband?' said Murphy. 'How had he been getting on with Justin following that bust-up?'

She was silent for a moment. 'I don't think they had much to do with each other for a few days after that. But then I saw them talking together at the housewarming party and it looked friendly enough. So, I think it blew over quite quickly.'

'That was very forgiving of Tom, don't you think?'

Louise looked intently at them. 'Tom's a peaceable sort of person and I think he realised that Justin hadn't really intended to hurt him. It was just a stupid thing.'

'Well thank you for your help, Mrs Fraser,' said Murphy, rising from the table. 'And thank you for the coffee. What will be a good time to catch your husband?'

Louise rubbed her arms. 'He's usually home by seven during the week,' she said. 'He's playing golf today, so I'm not sure what time he'll be back.'

'We'll catch him at some point,' said Murphy, recognising the double meaning as she said it.

Chapter Thirty-Four

WATSON FULLERTON HAD an office in One Canada Square, Murphy was pleased to see.

'Lovely' she said. 'Good way to start the week. Let's go and inspect the working conditions of the wealthy.'

'Half of them are probably working from home' said Wilcox.

'Oh, I don't think so,' said Murphy. 'If my company was based in there, I'd be happy to spend the day at work, using all their facilities rather than my own.'

In the event, it was impossible to know how many people worked in the building because the lobby was open to the public and also acted as an entrance to a mall. It was clad in marble and the proportions were so large that the humans in it were dwarfed. They showed their badges at the reception desk and headed for one of the lifts.

'Floor thirty-six,' Murphy said as the doors closed. 'Should be a good view.'

The receptionist had rung through to Watson Fullerton and a man who introduced himself as David

Cargill was waiting for them when the lift arrived. He had a brisk manner, a firm handshake and a very expensive suit and they were immediately ushered into a small unoccupied office.

'We heard about what had happened to Justin. His wife called earlier. We're all very shocked.'

'Indeed,' said Murphy, sitting down. 'We haven't yet uncovered exactly what happened, so we are interviewing all of his friends and associates – and that will include business associates.'

He nodded. 'Quite. Well, everybody here will cooperate, of course, but I don't know how much help we will be.'

'Oh, I think you can give us lots of help,' said Murphy brightly. 'We'll want to talk to everybody who worked with him and we'll need to take possession of his company laptop.'

His face fell. 'There's confidential, sensitive information…'

'I'm sure,' said Murphy. 'But this is a possible murder investigation. Perhaps we can start with you. You are – were – Justin's boss?'

He nodded. 'That's right. He's been here about three years and he reported in to me in that time.'

'Good. And what can you tell us about his work?'

He hesitated. 'His work was good to begin with. He is – was – good at dealing with clients. He inspired a lot of confidence. And he always had a good understanding of the market.'

'Alright, he talked the talk,' said Murphy. 'But what?'

He sighed. 'But lately we – I – had begun to suspect that he may have been trading on his own account.'

'How could that happen?'

'It's not a very common fraud, because it's not easy to

pull off, but a broker can divert the client's money to an account that they control and simply pay the returns. We charge 3% of funds under management, so the client will be directed to pay the charges to the same account. The client thinks their investment is held by the brokerage and it can go on for some time – until the client wants to withdraw some or all of their money, when everything unravels.'

'And you think Justin is – was – doing this?'

He sighed. 'I was at a party a week ago and I got talking to somebody who told me he had just invested quite a large sum with us. He spoke highly of his broker – Justin. I had never heard this man's name, so I went through the files and there was no record of him.'

'Did you ask Justin about it?'

'Yes, and he apologised for his poor admin. He told me he would look into it and later that day the funds arrived in the correct account and the files were updated.'

'But you still thought he was up to something.'

'Yes, I did. Because if I hadn't run across that client, would the money ever have been transferred? I was afraid that there could be other cases, but it's a difficult thing to investigate. After all, if there's no record of something, how do you know it exists? I had a meeting with HR to try and see a way forward and we agreed that we would just keep a close eye on Justin for the moment. It's a very serious matter for us, because it involves misappropriation of people's money. We would have our licence to trade withdrawn.'

'That was a difficult situation,' said Wilcox. 'You couldn't accuse him without evidence.'

'Exactly. And it would have been difficult to fire him. Or certainly not without paying him a large sum of money. Or indeed making public what had been going on – which would have been even worse. We were holding our fire on it.'

'Do you think he needed money?'

He shrugged. 'He must have done, to take such an appalling risk. If it had come out, that would have been the end of his career. No other firm would have looked at him. And he might have gone to prison.'

'This has solved a problem for you, then,' said Murphy. Wilcox drew in a breath and stared intently at David Cargill, who was looking shocked.

'I don't know what you are suggesting…' he began.

'No suggestion, just a remark,' said Murphy. 'But we will have to ask everybody where they were on Thursday evening.'

'You want to know…? OK, well I was here until about 9.30. Then I left for home – Holland Park – and arrived about 10.30. My wife had gone to bed but my teenage children were still up. You can interrogate them if you want to.'

'Well, it might not come to that. Perhaps we can just take your wife's details,' said Wilcox and David Cargill tapped on his phone and showed him the number.

'I imagine you have already looked through his work laptop,' said Murphy.

He nodded. 'Yes, we have. We haven't found anything so far.'

'OK. Maybe we won't either. Do let us know if you turn anything else up. In the meantime, can we talk to those colleagues who worked closely with him?'

He was silent for a moment. 'Justin wasn't part of any team. The brokers tend to work individually. But the person who knew him best was probably Jim – Jim Saxon. If you want to use this office, I'll send him along.'

'How about the women? Did any of them have much to do with him?'

'There's Melanie. Melanie Fisher. She did the back-office work for Justin and Jim. You can see her after Jim.'

'Perfect,' said Murphy and gave him her best smile.

It seemed to work. 'Coffee?' he enquired.

'That would be lovely.'

'It definitely will be lovely,' she told Wilcox when Cargill had shut the door behind him. 'They won't be drinking instant in this building.'

The coffee arrived at the same time as Jim Saxon, a willowy man with spiky dark hair and a ready smile. Something of the same type as Justin Beattie, Murphy thought. Maybe that was just the broker persona.

Wilcox made the introductions while Murphy busied herself with the coffee.

'Thank you for agreeing to talk to us, Mr Saxon,' she said. 'This must all have come as rather a shock.'

'Absolutely. We don't know what to think. Poor Justin.'

'We're still looking into the circumstances of Justin Beattie's death,' said Murphy, 'so we're keeping a very open mind and we're grateful for any information or insight that you are able to offer.'

He nodded. 'Of course. Happy to help.'

'So can you begin by telling us how long you knew him for, what your working relationship was like, that sort of thing.'

He waited a moment before replying. 'Justin was already here when I arrived. That was about two years ago. He showed me the ropes and we shared an office. It's a bit quiet in there now.' He gestured vaguely behind him. 'Justin was good company, always on hand with a joke. 'Though I must say, the jokes have been few and far between this past few months.'

'You think he's had something on his mind?'

'Seemed that way to me. He started making mistakes, letting things slip, not really keeping up. You have to do a lot of keeping up in this industry, things are moving all the time and if you're not on top of them, somebody else will be. He was a really top-class operator when I first met him, but towards the end something had gone out of it.'

'Did you wonder if he was breaking the rules in any way?'

'Not at first. I thought he probably had trouble at home. But then I came into the office a few times and he immediately cut off the phone call he was making. And he wasn't bringing in the same amount of business as he used to. So yes, I wondered what was going on.'

'Did he ever talk about his home life?' asked Wilcox.

'Not much. He'd shown me photos of his beautiful wife and his baby, but he didn't really talk about home life. Mind you, I probably didn't talk much about mine either. Our conversations were all about work – the firm, the market, the clients. Everybody here is focussed on keeping up, not much time is spent talking about your family.'

'Do you know of anybody who had disagreements with Justin, didn't like him, might have wished him harm, anything like that?'

Jim Saxon slowly shook his head. 'There will always be people you rub up against, or people who lost out because you got to the deal first, but that's just business. I can't think of anybody who sustained losses because of Justin or who would have wanted to harm him. There may have been people who didn't like him, but he was a generally friendly, disarming sort of guy, so not the sort of person to be generally disliked. I liked him, I'll miss him quite a lot.'

'Did you ever go for drinks together?' asked Murphy.

He shrugged. 'Yes, of course. Often on Fridays.'

'And what did you drink?'

'Um – beer.'

'Not whiskey or gin or wine?'

He shook his head. 'If we went for dinner, maybe with a client, we'd have wine, but that's pretty rare. So mostly beer.'

Wilcox nodded. 'Did you see him on Thursday?'

'Yes, he was here all day. He left before me, around six thirty.'

'Did he say he had any plans for the evening?'

'No. I assumed he was going straight home.'

'And how did he seem?'

'A bit on edge, but then he'd been on edge for months. I was used to it.'

'And now,' said Murphy, 'the killer question. What were you doing on Thursday evening?'

'I was just at home with my girlfriend. I left here about quarter to seven, got home about seven thirty, then we were just in, eating dinner and watching TV.'

'Where's home?' asked Wilcox.

'Stratford. Not far from the stadium. I go home on the DLR.'

'Can I have your girlfriend's details?'

'I wasn't really expecting this – that I'd need an alibi.'

'Don't worry about it,' said Wilcox as he copied them down. 'We have to ask everybody the same thing – it's just procedure.'

'That's all from us,' said Murphy. 'Thank you for your

help, Mr Saxon. Can you ask Ms Fisher to come in and see us if she's free.'

Jim Saxon nodded and left the room, closing the door behind him. Melanie Fisher opened it a few seconds later. She was a large woman with grey hair – not quite what Murphy had been expecting.

'Come in Ms Fisher and grab a seat,' said Murphy. 'We're talking to everybody who knew Justin Beattie and I guess you've known him for some time.'

She nodded and Murphy noticed that her eyes were reddened. 'I've been here since the firm started up – over twenty years now – so I've known him since he arrived.'

'What did you think of him?'

She sighed deeply. 'To begin with, I thought him an arrogant young smartarse, but then he got his edges rubbed off – or maybe I got used to him. Justin always had plenty to say for himself, but he certainly livened the atmosphere. I think we'll all miss him.'

'Do you think he changed over the past year?' asked Murphy.

'He got quieter, he was definitely under stress.'

'You deal with the back-office functions, so you're probably best-placed to make a judgement about this. Do you think he may have been engaged in illicit trading?'

She hesitated for a moment, then seemed to come to a decision. 'Yes. He's no longer around, so it won't matter to him now. What I could see was quite a lot of frantic activity, but less money actually coming in. So, I started to wonder what was going on.'

'Did you mention that to anybody.'

'No, because it's not an accusation you make lightly, and I didn't want to think that of Justin. But Mr Cargill had evidently also started to wonder and he asked me about it. I couldn't say much but I agreed with him that there could be something wrong.'

'Did you know much about Justin's home life?'

She shook her head. 'Not really. He showed the photo around when his baby son was born. He was very happy about that. But he didn't talk that much about home life. To be honest, nobody here does. It's not that sort of environment.'

Melanie Fisher had nothing more to add. She had seen Justin in the office on Thursday but she had left early to visit the dentist. Murphy led the way out, down thirty-five floors in the high-speed lift and out into the vast reception area.

'So we know Justin was in trouble,' said Wilcox, as they emerged onto the street. 'Something was about to catch up with him.'

Murphy nodded. 'Makes suicide look a bit more believable, doesn't it?'

Chapter Thirty-Five

'TOM FRASER WORKS SOMEWHERE ROUND HERE,' said Wilcox. 'Perhaps we can arrange to have a chat with him.'

'Yes, give him a ring,' said Murphy. 'I'd rather see him without the wife in attendance, he might be a bit more forthcoming on his own.'

'He'll meet us in the reception at one pm,' said Wilcox, leading the way to another tall building just off Cabot Square.

Tom Fraser appeared at the appointed time with a ready smile and a firm handshake. Quite an attractive man, Murphy thought. So why had his wife been sleeping with Justin Beattie? He led the way to a cluster of seats situated at some distance from the reception desk. Probably didn't want to be overheard, Murphy decided, although in such a vast space there wasn't much danger of that.

'Thank you for seeing us, Mr Fraser,' she began. 'As you will know, we're talking to everybody who knew Justin Beattie.'

He nodded. 'Of course. Terrible shock.'

'Perhaps we can begin by asking you how long you knew him for?'

'About four years, I think. Since they moved in.'

'And relations have always been good?'

He hesitated. 'Of course, you'll know about our little fracas, won't you?'

'Bit more than a fracas, wasn't it?' said Wilcox. 'You ended up in hospital.'

'Well, yes, just for observation. Nothing serious.' He smiled.

'And can you tell us what brought it about?'

He sighed. 'Justin was under the impression that I had given Stanley – that's his stepfather – some dubious investment advice.'

'And had you?'

'Not as far as I was aware. It was at a party at Christmas. We'd all had a few drinks. I probably did make some observations to Stanley, but I never expected him to act upon them. It wasn't investment advice as far as I was concerned.'

'In that case, you must have been pretty angry when he attacked you.'

'I wasn't angry at the time because I was unconscious. When I came round, I was pretty shocked. My wife had witnessed the immediate aftermath and she was convinced that Justin had not intended to seriously injure me. So, I didn't press charges.'

'That was very magnanimous of you,' said Murphy. 'If somebody had put me in hospital, I would be tempted to press charges.'

'But these are my next-door neighbours. We have to go

on living next door to each other. And who the hell wants to get involved in litigation?'

'That makes sense,' Murphy conceded. 'But you must have harboured some sort of … residual grudge.'

'Which led me to kill him a couple of weeks later? No, absolutely not.'

Murphy looked at him for a moment. 'Did you know anything about Justin Beattie's financial situation?'

'No, none of my business. He was working for Watson Fullerton, so I assume he was well rewarded.'

'So, if a man in his position did have financial problems, what would that be due to?'

He shrugged. 'I don't know. An expensive mistress? A drug or gambling habit? Too many fast cars? Any of the above, or none of them, or something else entirely. None of those apply to Justin, by the way. Not as far as I know, anyway.'

'Thank you for talking to us,' said Murphy. 'If anything else occurs to you, please get in touch.'

'Certainly.' He raised a hand and made his way back to the escalators.

'If you think about it,' said Wilcox. 'Justin Beattie was screwing his wife and had assaulted him. That's two good reasons for disliking Justin. But would either of them have made him want to kill?'

'On paper he's a tempting suspect,' said Murphy, 'but I'm not really buying it. He just doesn't seem like the type. Of course, there isn't a type, we all know that. Ted Bundy never looked like the type either. But murder's a serious business. Some people don't need much provocation, but I don't think he's one of those people. He would need a really good reason to kill somebody and neither of those reasons are sufficient. If we believe what his wife says, she'd finished things with Justin some time before he was killed.'

'The thing is' said Wilcox, 'we haven't uncovered any reason for anybody to kill Justin. With Adam Bryce there's a lot of money involved, but who gains anything from killing Justin?'

'Maybe Justin knew something about whoever killed Adam. In that case, somebody gained security from killing him. If you were Justin Beattie and you had some urgent need for money and you happened to discover who had killed Adam Bryce, what would you do?'

'Blackmail them, no question,' said Wilcox immediately.

'Exactly. That's the most obvious way in which these deaths can be connected. So, if there's money involved, who is the most obvious suspect?'

'Rebecca.'

'That's right. We need to look much further into her alibi. What we have got so far is a bit sketchy. And we need to look into Adam's affairs. She might have arrived home if we head up there now.'

Chapter Thirty-Six

REBECCA OPENED the door when they arrived at 6.15pm and looked shocked to see them. She was still wearing what were probably her office clothes but her feet were bare.

'I don't think there's much I can help you with...' she began.

'Well, you never know,' said Murphy. 'Can we come in for a few minutes?'

Rebecca seemed about to argue, but then stood aside. A man rose from the sofa as they entered the room.

'Mr Wilson,' said Murphy. 'Sorry to intrude. Don't leave on our account.'

But Bert Wilson was already halfway to the door. 'I was just leaving anyway. See you soon, Rebecca.' And then he was gone.

'Oh dear,' said Murphy. 'Hope we didn't frighten him off.'

'Not at all,' said Rebecca. 'He was just here to discuss some of the finances.'

'Just what we wanted to ask you about. I assume Adam had an accountant?'

She nodded. 'You want his details?'

'Yes please,' said Wilcox. She crossed to a desk and took a card from the drawer. 'Excellent' he said, pocketing it. 'And how about his solicitor?'

'I don't have business cards for him, but there's some paperwork somewhere. I haven't been in touch with him yet.' She opened another drawer and flicked through a pile of papers. 'Here.'

'Thank you,' said Wilcox as he scribbled down the details.

'I guess there's a lot of administrative stuff to sort out' said Murphy, taking Bert's place on the sofa.

'A certain amount,' said Rebecca stiffly. She remained standing, as if hoping that Murphy would get up and leave.

'Do sit down, Kevin, you're making the place look untidy,' said Murphy.

Wilcox sat and Rebecca sighed and followed suit.

'You're here all on your own now, Mrs Bryce?'

'Yes.'

'No family to pitch in and support you.'

'My parents divorced years ago. My mother died and my father lives in Canada now. He came over for the wedding, but he can't afford another trip, so there's really only me and my sister. We both have busy jobs, so we see each other when we can.'

'Busy jobs. Of course. You work for a charity, isn't that right?'

'Yes, Energy Aid. It works to facilitate access to energy for global populations.'

'That sounds good,' said Wilcox. 'Green energy presumably.'

'Predominantly green energy. In some areas the right infrastructure has to be put in place before there is access to green energy.'

'And what is your role there?' asked Murphy.

Rebecca held her hands up. 'PR, publicity, lobbying, all that sort of thing.'

'That means you're out and about a lot.'

'Not really. I organise all these activities, other people carry them out.'

'And I guess you're paid below the going rate because it's a charity.'

Rebecca looked momentarily insulted. 'Not at all. It's a marketplace. Charities have to pay the same as anybody else to get access to talent. You're trying to assess how far I was dependent on Adam's money?'

'Not really,' said Murphy. 'I assumed you would have your own income. But I also wanted to ask you about Adam's state of mind in the few days before he died. Did you have any reason to think he had anything on his mind?'

Rebecca shook her head. 'Not that he discussed with me, and I didn't notice any signs of him being worried about anything.'

'How do you think he got on with the neighbours here?'

'Pretty well, as far as I'm aware. It was important to him to get on with the neighbours.'

'He wanted to fit into the community,' said Murphy.

Rebecca nodded. 'Something like that.'

'How did he get on with Justin Beattie?'

Rebecca stiffened. 'I really don't know anything specific. Adam seemed to get on with all the neighbours, so that would have included Justin Beattie.'

'What did you think of Justin Beattie?'

'I didn't think anything of him. I'd hardly ever spoken to him.'

Murphy smiled. 'Justin was a man who liked women. And he would have seen you at two parties. At one of them you were the hostess – can we say hostess these days? Maybe not. Anyway, you were responsible for welcoming all of your guests. And at the earlier one, he was the host, so he would have been welcoming you. So, I can't really believe that you didn't get to have a chat to Justin. He would have made it his business to get to know you.'

'I probably talked to a lot of people that night – both of those nights – but I can't remember Justin particularly.'

'How about his wife?'

'His wife? You mean Francine? Yes, I spoke to her at the first party. She seems a very nice person.'

'Yes, I'm sure she is,' said Murphy. 'Did Adam speak to her much?'

She shook her head. 'Not that I noticed.'

'I gather that Adam's family – his parents and brother – didn't come to your housewarming. Bit surprising that, isn't it?'

She shrugged. 'They were invited, naturally. But his parents are not really party people. We visited them when we got back from our honeymoon.'

Murphy nodded. 'Yes, they told me that. Have you heard from them since Adam died?'

Rebecca sighed. 'No, I haven't. I would imagine they are very upset. I wouldn't want to intrude on their grief and they probably don't want to intrude on mine.'

'Very sensible,' said Murphy. Rebecca flashed her a look. 'I think we've taken up enough of your time, Mrs Bryce. Thank you for seeing us. We'll keep you informed.'

Rebecca shot up and led the way to the door. It was closed as soon as they were through it.

'Interesting,' said Murphy, as they walked back to the car. 'I don't know whether she's involved or not, but she won't be easy to break. She's a worthy adversary. Not so Bert Wilson. Him we can definitely crack.'

Chapter Thirty-Seven

ADAM BRYCE'S funeral was a small, private affair at the crematorium. Made sense, thought Murphy. He was presumably not a churchgoer. She noted who went in. Rebecca and her sister. Adam's parents and his brother and a woman that was probably his partner - Lesley Franks, she reminded herself. Bert Wilson and Lennie Bright. A bunch of other people who could have been from one of the record companies. And several elderly couples who had arrived with Adam's parents– probably relatives of some description.

None of the neighbours were there. Maybe they didn't even know it was taking place. Adam and Rebecca had not been in the neighbourhood long enough to really cement any friendships, despite Adam's efforts. Francine Beattie might have wanted to come. She had known him a long time, after all. But Francine now had her own loss to deal with. Both of her lovers dead within a fortnight. And she didn't have a cast-iron alibi for either death. Rebecca seemed the more likely candidate, but logic dictated that they should be seriously looking at Francine.

The coffin was carried in by four young men and Murphy slipped in and stood at the back. Lennie Bright hadn't brought his wife, which was surprising as she had presumably known Adam well. His flat had looked as if no woman was in residence. Maybe she had left him? But what did that have to do with anything?

Bert and Lennie were sitting together with Rebecca and her sister on one side of the chapel, with the music business people (if that's what they were) arranged behind them. On the other side was Adam's family. No love lost, not even in death.

When it was over, she waited outside for a few moments. David Bryce and his partner were looking at the flowers and she noticed the pall bearers talking to his parents. She wandered over to David, who acknowledged her with a nod and introduced her to his partner.

'I suppose we still don't know anything,' he said.

'Not yet,' said Murphy. 'But we will. We're not going to be closing the case, nothing like that. Were those college friends of Adam's who carried his coffin?'

David looked across. 'Two of them were from college and the other two were guys he used to go climbing with. Adam had neglected his old friends over the past year, but when I put the message out on Facebook they came forward. That's proper friends.' He looked across at Rebecca, who was now leaving with Bert and Lennie. 'He wasn't always just a 'music business' type. He didn't always associate with people like them. He was into art and sport, all kinds of things. If it wasn't for the money, those types would never have pursued him – and he'd still be alive.'

Chapter Thirty-Eight

DCI ERNIE MILLBROOK was a more measured man than Bellweather, but even he was concerned about the apparent lack of progress in the two murders which had been assigned to Murphy.

'Surely you must have at least one realistic suspect.'

'Adam Bryce's wife is the only person who directly benefits from his death. If she wanted to get rid of him but get access to the money, killing him would have been her only option. She doesn't have an unbreakable alibi, but we don't have any evidence to tie her into it. The way he died suggests that whoever was responsible may not have intended to kill him. Justin Beattie was my preferred suspect on account of a previous attack on somebody else, but he is now also dead.'

'But if you accidentally kill somebody, surely most people would call an ambulance? Do we think that Justin Beattie's death could have been suicide?'

Murphy sighed. 'It would be neat, wouldn't it? It would tie everything up. But we haven't uncovered any real motive.

Justin Beattie had a need for money. It looks like he was committing fraud and probably needed money to cover his tracks. But killing Adam Bryce wouldn't have brought him any money, not unless he was going to be paid by Rebecca Bryce. If it was Justin, and it was an accident, he might have been scared to call an ambulance, because we'd already arrested him once. He might have thought that he wouldn't be believed.'

'Have you found any evidence of a connection between him and Rebecca Bryce.'

'No. As far as we can make out, they hardly knew each other. She'd only moved into the area two weeks earlier.'

Ernie Millbrook sat back and folded his arms. 'We're in the realm of speculation here, but if Justin Beattie had killed Adam Bryce as part of an agreement with Rebecca Bryce, would he then go on and commit suicide? Just when he's presumably about to get some money?'

Murphy shook her head. 'No. At that point it's easier to see him being murdered. He was in the bar with somebody that night. It could have been Rebecca Bryce.'

'Sounds like she's the person you need to take a closer look at. We need to show some progress on these cases. DCI Bellweather is apparently coming back next week. It would be good to be able to demonstrate that we haven't been slacking in his absence.'

'Understood, sir. I'll keep you posted.'

Wilcox was sorting paperwork when she arrived back at her desk. 'Results are back for the bottles at that bar,' he said. 'They found Justin's prints, but nobody else's.'

'That means he did the pouring,' said Murphy. 'That's believable enough. Does the fact that it was wine mean anything? Would two men out together for a drink choose wine?'

Wilcox shook his head. 'Beer.'

'That's my thought. Wine makes me think a woman was involved. How about the lab results on the blood?'

Wilcox scrolled up. 'Yes, they're here. They've just arrived.' He stared at the screen. 'GHB, how about that?'

Murphy raised her eyebrows. 'The party drug. What does it stand for?'

'Gamma-hydroxybutyrate is what it says here. It's a depressive, so combine it with alcohol and the effect is enhanced, or more dangerous, depending how you look at it.'

'I think dangerous is what we're looking at in this case,' said Murphy. 'What does it say here? Induces relaxation, euphoria, loss of inhibition, desire for sex. I suppose if it was self-administered, he might have felt weird and gone outside for air and fallen off the balcony. On the other hand, if somebody else put it in his drink and he felt weird, they could take him outside for air and probably heave him off the balcony without too much trouble. He wasn't a big, heavy person.'

'If it was a woman,' said Wilcox, 'they might have invited him outside for sex, quick knee-trembler on the balcony, and then heaved him over.'

Murphy nodded. 'Yes, that's a possible scenario. Perhaps he wasn't getting much sex at home. Ernie thinks we should be paying serious attention to Rebecca Bryce. We were thinking of her for Adam's murder, but maybe Justin's murder is the event to concentrate on. But it's hard to know where to look for evidence.'

'Can we find any link between Justin and Rebecca? There was nothing in his phone or laptop.'

'No. She'd be too clever for that. Justin had a well-paid

job, but he was possibly engaged in very risky, fraudulent activities. So where was the money going?'

Wilcox frowned. 'Didn't Stanley Farrow say something about gambling?'

Murphy sighed. 'That would certainly be a good way to burn through money. Let's go and have another chat with Stanley.'

Chapter Thirty-Nine

BUT STANLEY WAS NOT in evidence when they knocked on the door of number 22. The van was gone from the driveway and Francine answered the door. Her face was pale and drawn and she stared at them blankly.

'We wanted to have a chat with Stanley' Murphy said, 'but I guess he's not here?'

She shook her head. 'No, Stanley's gone for a drive. I don't know when he'll be back.'

'Well, as we're here, maybe we can come in and talk to you,' Murphy suggested.

Francine hesitated for a few seconds and then wordlessly stepped back and let them in.

'A cup of tea would be fabulous,' Murphy declared, pursuing Francine into the kitchen. Francine put got the teapot out and busied herself rattling with the cups.

'How have you been doing?' Murphy asked.

Francine shrugged. 'Oh, OK, fine.'

'You don't look fine. You look like somebody who hasn't been eating.'

Francine turned around. She opened her mouth but no sound emerged. 'Sit down,' said Murphy and Francine sat. 'I'm afraid I don't have any news for you' said Murphy, 'but we will find out what happened to Justin, however long it takes. And I think you need somebody here to support you.'

A tear slid down Francine's cheek and she smiled uncertainly. 'I have a lot of support' she said. 'I had the Family Liaison Officer for a few days. She was very nice. Stanley's still around and Ron's doing a lot of the school runs for me. Wendy keeps coming over with food. People are very decent.'

'I'm glad to hear it,' said Murphy. 'Two men you had relationships with have died within two weeks. That's a lot to cope with.' She put in the teabags in the pot, poured in the boiling water, fetched the milk from the fridge and brought it all over. 'I was at Adam's funeral yesterday. Four of his old friends carried his coffin. Two of them were from college, so you might have known them.'

'Adam had a lot of friends at college,' Francine said, wiping her eyes. 'He wasn't the most outgoing person, not one of your flamboyant artists, but he played a lot of football. That gets you mates better than anything else. I'm glad they turned out for him.'

'Did you ever meet his family?'

'No. I wanted to meet his family and I thought he would introduce me to them, but then I got pregnant and he took off.'

'So how did you cope, being pregnant at college?'

'Luckily it was near the end of our third year, we were just about to graduate. Adam didn't come back for graduation, but I'm pretty sure he got his degree. I found a flat with friends and worked at all sorts of jobs until Danny was born. Then I managed to find a bit of freelance design work – badly-paid, but at least I could do it from home. When Danny was old enough for a day nursery, I was able to work part-time. Then I went to a wedding and met Justin. I think I've told you all this before. I can't remember any more what I have and haven't said.'

'So that really changed your life – meeting Justin.'

'Yes, it did. But I was always clear that Danny and I would have been OK anyway. We didn't need somebody to take us on and look after us.'

'Was that what Justin wanted to do?'

'I think so, and I made it clear to him that we weren't interested in that. But he persisted, and in the end – I guess, I fell in love with him. It was odd, because he wasn't really my type.'

'He was a bit establishment for you?'

'Yes, I think that was part of it. He seemed like an older generation. Of course, he wasn't really, he was only a few years older than me, it was just because of his job and the people he mixed with.'

'Did you notice anything different about Justin over the past few weeks or months? Anything that suggested he was worried about something?'

Francine nodded. 'Yes, he had mood swings really for the past few months – short-tempered for a bit and then he would snap out of it, and then down again. It wasn't easy to live with.' Her face fell. 'But I'd still give anything to have him back. Maybe I only appreciate the good things about him now that he's gone.'

'That's often how it is,' said Murphy. 'Did you ever have any idea what was causing his mood swings? Was there something he was worried about?'

'There must have been, but he would never tell me anything.'

'Do you think he'd got himself involved in something he shouldn't have?'

'I don't want to think that about Justin.'

'I understand. But Justin's reputation won't matter to him now. And any information you have could help us find out why he died.'

'There was something going on' she said. 'He was getting phone calls that he would shut off if I came into the room. But I don't know who he was talking to.'

The was a ring at the front door. Francine started to rise.

'Don't worry,' said Murphy. 'Kevin will get it.'

They heard him open the front door to a burst of voices and barking.

Francine smiled. 'That's Ron and Wilfred' she said. 'They went to pick up Danny.'

Danny burst into the kitchen followed by a dachshund and Ron Warner, who looked surprised to see Murphy sitting there.

'Mr Warner.' Murphy smiled at him. 'As you can see, we're still on the case. What an excellent dog. I wish mine was that well-behaved.'

'Wilfred's full of beans' said Ron, 'and he does bark a lot, but that's how dachshunds are, especially puppies. He's very sociable.'

'Wilfred did a poo outside the school,' said Danny. 'We had to pick it up in a bag.'

'We did indeed,' said Ron. 'And Wilfred and I will now be off. See you tomorrow, Danny.'

Danny followed them out. 'That's great to have a chap doing the school run,' said Murphy.

'Yes,' said Francine. 'To be honest, I've never enjoyed the school run much. I'm not much of a networker.'

'I was the same,' said Murphy. 'Now that I have a dog, I think I would be better at it. They break the ice in all directions.'

Chapter Forty

ARTHUR WILKINSON, Adam Bryce's accountant, had an office above a shop in the Gray's Inn Road. The stairs were steep and creaked alarmingly and the upper floor was sloping in places.

'Built in 1905,' Wilkinson told them. 'So not particularly old. But I suppose the Edwardians had their fair share of jerry-builders, just like we do now. And don't let me get started on the wiring.'

'The building looks lovely from the outside,' said Murphy, 'but I guess the landlords don't spend any more than they have to.'

He nodded. 'You said it. Anyway, come and sit down on one of my rickety chairs and I'll show you Adam Bryce's accounts. I was very sorry to hear that he had passed. Not what you expect in the case of someone so young. I suppose there's no explanation?'

Murphy shook her head. 'No, we're still looking into it.' She thought how much she hated that euphemism 'passed'. At least 'passed away' sounded more realistic. 'Passed' made it sound like the person had aced their driving test, which was very much not the case.

Arthur Wilkinson sat behind his desk and rotated his mouse. 'Here we are. I was advised by Mr Lindsay – Adam's solicitor – that accounts would need to be drawn up, so that's what I have done. I'll print them off for you. There are separate accounts for Adam personally and for the band.'

A printer by the side of the desk sprang into life and four sheets of paper shot out. Wilkinson stapled them into two sets and passed them to Murphy, who had a quick glance and passed them to Wilcox.

Murphy stretched back in her seat. That was a bad idea. One of her chair legs seemed to stumble into a depression in the floor. She sat back upright. 'How long have you known Adam?' she asked.

He seemed to be thinking for a moment. 'It must be nearly four years now. It started when he got going with the band. I had done some work for Adam's father and he put us in touch. Of course, they were all still doing their normal jobs at that time and the band wasn't making much, but I think he decided that they needed a third party involved in the finances, so that they wouldn't think any one of them was ripping off the others. Quite a good idea.'

'Did the band ever make much money?'

He sighed. 'To be honest, not really. They covered their costs and they probably made about ten grand a year over and above that. So, it was never going to make them rich. I kept expecting to hear from Adam that they had folded, but they kept going. So maybe they would have made it in the end. Bit of persistence, one hit song, that might have been all it needed.'

'But then the money arrived.'

He nodded. 'Indeed. A huge amount of money. Six mil. And Adam deserves a lot of credit for not behaving like some brain-dead footballer. Expensive houses all over the place, fast cars, faster women. He banked it, invested it and left it alone while he thought about it. He took an income from it of course – it was generating plenty of income – but he left most of the capital alone.'

'That gave him money to invest in the band.'

'Exactly. They were now in a position where they could fund their own recording and their own publicity and appearances. Record companies were now approaching them, rather than them having to make their pitch all over the place. They were now in a good place. The band itself still wasn't making much money, but now it didn't matter too much. Of course, it did matter, because it mattered beyond money, but you can't buy musical talent or whatever the magic ingredient is.'

'How do you think the other members of the band felt about Adam's money?'

'I only met them once a year, because I would present the accounts to all three of them, although I can't say the other two had much interest in the financial side. And there wasn't much money showing up in the band's accounts. But once Adam had all this money everything changed. On the one hand, the band could now spend money, and it did, so they were pleased about that. But the fact was that the money they were spending had not been earned by the band and I think they were very aware of that. And now Adam was in a totally different income bracket to them, so that cut him off from the other two. The accounts for the band still showed very little income, although their assets were increasing through Adam's investment. Adam's personal accounts were where the money was, but of course the other two didn't have any right to see those. So, I think there were tensions.'

'Did you meet Mrs Bryce?'

'Adam's wife? Yes, I met her once, briefly.'

'What did you think of her?'

'Seemed like a very smart young woman. She proposed taking over the accounts, or the bookkeeping side, anyway. I would still have done the tax return.'

'But that hadn't actually happened.'

'No. Overtaken by events is probably what applies here.'

'Did you look after Adam Bryce's investments?' asked Wilcox.

Arthur Wilkinson nodded. 'Yes. It's not really my area of expertise, but I thought he should at least put the money initially into something where it was working – even if it was not working as profitably as it could. After all, he was going to have a hefty inheritance tax bill to pay. I channelled the funds into ISAs and unit trusts. Not the most cutting-edge financial instruments, but safe. Then, when he'd had a chance to decide what he wanted to do, he could find a reliable broker and maybe diversify into instruments which would bring him higher returns.'

'A person who gets a windfall like this,' said Wilcox, 'there must be a lot of people – or entities – who are looking to relieve him of some of it.'

'Of course. There are always grifters floating around. And I warned him about that. If anything sounds too good to be true, that's because it is. But, with such a large sum to invest, he didn't need to pursue some massive rate of return. And the fact that it was such a large sum, and that he could afford to tie most of it up long-term, meant that he got favourable rates anyway. He didn't need to look for get-rich-quick offers.'

'Do you think he would have been wise to anybody trying to get their hands on the money?'

'Totally. He knew he could trust me, because I knew his family, but he knew there were sharks around.'

'How did his family feel about the money?'

He shook his head. 'I don't know. I haven't been in touch with them for the past few years, just Adam. But this is awful for them.'

Murphy nodded. 'Certainly is.'

———

WILCOX SETTLED himself in the car, seat belt fastened and feet braced, and began to read Adam Bryce's financial statements, while Murphy barrelled back down the Gray's Inn Road.

'It looks kind of peculiar,' he said. 'The band's accounts show very little income but money going into the bank account and more in the way of fixed assets – equipment and…Christ!' His eyes snapped shut of their own accord and he waited for the impact. When it didn't happen, he opened them slowly. 'I think it was his right of way, the guy in the Audi.'

'Of course it wasn't,' said Murphy, seemingly oblivious to the horns sounding in her wake. 'He was just a road hog. So, you were saying?'

Wilcox breathed deeply. 'The band has assets but no income and Adam has massive assets and a lot of income – all unearned of course. Accountancy charges for the band are negligible, but Wilkinson's now charging quite a lot for

Adam. I suppose that's fair – assets under management or whatever.'

'Sounds like he was doing nicely out of this client,' said Murphy. 'So not much motive for topping him.'

Chapter Forty-One

'FIRST BUILT IN ROMAN TIMES' said Wilcox as they exited Liverpool Street Station and walked along Bishopsgate.

'Looks like it's had a few modifications since then,' said Murphy, indicating the high-rise block which appeared to be their destination. 'Seems like his solicitor is much more high-end than his accountant. Why would that be?'

Wilcox swerved round a bunch of tourists. 'Maybe he only engaged the solicitor after he inherited the money. The accountant was originally hired to do accounts for a not-very-successful band.'

The building had a double-height reception and a long list of occupants. 'Ninth floor' said Wilcox and they scrambled into the lift. The receptionist at Turner and Walbrook confirmed that Brian Lindsay was expecting them and he materialised a few moments later, a tall, spare man with thinning blond hair and an enthusiastic handshake. He led the way to an office with spectacular views of the City, marred only by another couple of high-rises.

'Thank you for seeing us, Mr Lindsay,' Murphy began.

'Can I start by asking when you were engaged by Adam Bryce?'

He nodded. 'We act – or we did act – for Mrs Daphne Billington. When Mrs Billington died, we were her executors, so we contacted Mr Bryce and he came to see me here. It was quite a large inheritance, so I asked him whether he had legal and financial advisors. He had an accountant, Mr Wilkinson, and he proposed to retain him, so that was fine. I offered him our services in respect of his legal affairs, so we became his legal advisors at that point. We drew up a provisional will at that time and about ten days ago he came in and made changes to his will. It is very shocking that he has died so young. I had no expectation that I would be executing the terms of his will so soon.'

'It's a bit unusual for somebody so young to be making wills, isn't it?'

'His financial advisors, the people managing his investments, will probably have required it. I assumed that it was just a formality for him, so I was a bit surprised when he wanted to change it. He took the whole thing more seriously than I would have expected.'

'Were you surprised that Mrs Billington had left so much money to him?'

He shrugged. 'Mrs Billington was a woman with no natural heirs. From comments that she made, I came to understand that she was not particularly close to the remaining members of her family and she talked about leaving the whole amount to charity. But then she told me that she had a nephew to whom she had decided to leave a large part of her fortune. She had not seen him since he was a child, but from what she had heard, she had come to the conclusion that he was what she called a 'free spirit'. I did attempt to impress upon her that this was not how these decisions are normally made, but she was adamant that this was what she wanted to do.'

'And his will?'

'His initial will left half to his wife, and the other half split equally between his parents and his brother.'

'I wonder if any of them knew that?' said Murphy.

'They would only have known if he told them,' Brian Lindsay said. 'I didn't enter into any communication with them.'

'And the amended will?'

He shuffled some papers and pulled one out. 'The new will leaves his fortune split six ways. The beneficiaries are his wife, his brother, his parents (a joint share), Bert Wilson, Lennie Bright and Daniel Beattie.'

'He left money to Danny?'

'Yes. I gather that Daniel Beattie is a minor, so I wrote to his guardian – a Mrs Francine Beattie. She will administer it on his behalf.'

'So all of these people have now been informed?'

'Yes, I wrote to them all four days ago. But I don't know how long the post took to arrive. I have applied for probate so it will be some time before they see any funds, but I felt it was my duty to let them all know as soon as possible. There were no provisions in respect of the funeral, which is usually the urgent information that is needed from the will. I was informed of Mr Bryce's death by his wife on the fourteenth of October.'

'Yes, I'm sure she wanted to get things moving,' said Murphy absently. 'And these six shares – how much will each of them be worth?'

'Allowing for expenses, legal fees, funeral costs, about nine hundred thousand. And they will all be subject to inheritance tax.'

She stood up slowly. 'Thank you very much for your help, Mr Lindsay. We may need to speak to you again, but I think that's all for now.'

'I'll tell you one thing,' she told Wilcox, as they went down in the lift. 'Everybody underestimated Adam Bryce. We'd better not do the same thing.'

Chapter Forty-Two

STANLEY FARROW WAS SITTING on the steps of his van, digging out the soles of a pair of walking boots, when they arrived. He waved a screwdriver in greeting.

'I'm glad you're out here, Mr Farrow,' said Murphy. 'Perhaps we can have a chat without disturbing Mrs Beattie.'

'Be my guest.' He led the way into the van. 'Very comfortable,' said Murphy, sitting on the window seat. 'And you even have a shower.'

'Yes. Everything a traveller needs.'

'Except you're not really travelling at the moment.'

'No. I can hardly go off and leave Francine at the moment. It's not as though she has a supportive family swooping down to look after her. We'll get through the funeral and then see how things look.'

'When we spoke some time ago,' said Murphy, 'you referred to the fact that Justin used to gamble. Do you think he carried on with that habit?'

'I don't know. I don't have any evidence. But that's what I was afraid of. I recognised some of the signs. He was getting nervy, bad-tempered. He was like that as a teenager when he was losing money.'

'If he was gambling' said Wilcox, 'where would he have been doing it? Slot machines or betting shops?'

'No, Justin would be into something more exclusive. He wouldn't want to be seen going into a betting shop. When he was a teenager he got into a poker club – until I found out about it.'

'In that case, a casino, a gambling club, something like that?'

He nodded. 'That would be my guess. You think this is relevant to his death? You think he killed himself because of gambling debts?'

'I don't really think that,' said Murphy, 'but we're still going over evidence and anything that was happening with Justin could be important. It did seem as if he had got himself into some sort of scrape and he needed money.'

'Needing money was his default position,' said Stanley. 'No matter how much he had, he always needed more. And I worried about what he might be prepared to do to get it.'

'Like kill somebody?' said Murphy.

'No, I'm sure he wouldn't and I shouldn't say anything,' said Stanley. 'I have no evidence.'

'Anything you say to us now won't matter to Justin,' said Murphy. 'And it might help us establish what happened to him.'

Stanley sighed. 'It was a few years ago, when Shirley was dying. But I've told you about this already, haven't I? Justin had been sitting with her, she was asleep. I came in to take over from Justin and the nurse came in a few moments later and said the morphine seemed to have gone down too far. Shirley died that night.'

'You think he could have done that?'

'I didn't want to think so, but I always wondered about it. I think he could have rationalised it to himself. She was dying anyway, it was just taking a long time, it was kinder to let her go. That sort of thing. I was very angry. I was determined that if he had done that, I was going to make sure that he didn't benefit from it. In the event, I did end up giving him money, but not as much as he wanted.'

'He must have been very angry when he didn't get the money from his mother.'

'He certainly was. He had just assumed she would have made a will in his favour. After that, the obvious person for Justin to murder was me.'

———

'WE MIGHT AS WELL CALL on the Warners now,' said Murphy. 'As we're here anyway. Then we'll have done the neighbourhood.'

It was Ron who answered the door, with his coat on and a dog lead in his hand, Wilfred bouncing up and down behind him.

'Oh, hello,' he said. 'We were just heading out.'

'We won't keep you long, Mr Warner,' said Murphy. 'Just a routine visit.'

'No, of course. Come in.' He stood back and held the door open. They followed him into the sitting room, where he shrugged off his coat and handed the lead to Wilfred, who took it off to his basket.

Murphy helped herself to a seat. 'As you know, Justin Beattie died on Monday night, so we're questioning everybody around here, to see if they can give us any information.'

He nodded. 'Of course. Happy to help if I can.'

'Can I start by asking what you were doing on Monday evening?'

He shrugged. 'I was just here. We both were. We don't often go out in the evenings. Not in the winter at any rate. Apart from Wilfred's final walk of the day, but that's just a quick fifteen minutes.'

'And did you see Justin Beattie at all that day?'

'No.' He shook his head. 'But then, he would have been at work, wouldn't he? In which case I wouldn't expect to see him.'

There was the sound of a key in the lock at that moment and Wendy came in, pulling a shopping trolley.

'Inspector, hello. It's getting really cold out there. Has Ron offered you a cup of tea? Of course he hasn't.'

'A cup of tea would be great,' said Murphy, and Wendy headed for the kitchen.

'Perhaps, if you don't need me anymore, Wilfred and I can head off,' said Ron.

'Fine by me,' said Murphy. Wendy looked like a better source of information. They followed her into the kitchen, where she filled the pot and produced a jar of biscuits.

'Can I start by asking you, Mrs Warner,' said Murphy, 'what you were doing on Monday evening?'

'Me?' Wendy shrugged. 'I was here at home, with Ron. Can't remember exactly what we were doing. Oh yes, I can. I was making a cake for the food bank and Ron was up in his den. Surfing the internet or whatever.'

'And did you see Justin Beattie at all that day?'

Wendy shook her head, 'He's somebody you only see around at weekends. I think he works long hours.'

'You've lived in this street a long time, haven't you?'

'Ages. We loved this house as soon as we saw it. Must be thirty years ago. And I've never wanted to move.'

'And it's quite a friendly neighbourhood.'

'Yes, it is.' Wendy poured the tea and handed it around. 'We've seen a few changes. People have come and gone, but we've all got along well with each other.'

'You would have known Justin and Francine Beattie from the moment they moved in.'

Wendy seemed to be thinking. 'Yes, I think I saw Francine around, pushing Danny in a buggy quite soon after they moved in and we said hello. It was good to see a young family arrive as some of us here were getting a bit ancient. Makes what's happened now seem so tragic.'

'You had plenty of time to get to know Justin,' said Murphy. 'What did you think of him?'

Wendy raised her eyebrows. 'The poor young man is dead, so I wouldn't…'

'Yes, we know all about that,' said Murphy. 'But his death is unexplained at the moment and it's my job to find out exactly what happened, so I would really appreciate an opinion not influenced by the fact that he's dead.'

'Yes, I do see that.' Wendy sighed. 'Justin was a great person to have around socially. He was quick-witted and he made you laugh. If you found yourself in a boring social situation, you would be pleased to see Justin there. Not that this has ever happened, but I think that's how it would be. But, people like that, they're often not so amusing in private. You do hear about famous comedians who actually suffered from depression, but their audience would never have guessed it. And I have occasionally seen Francine looking quite – drained. So, I think maybe Justin was not so easy to live with as you would assume if you just met him socially.

Also, as far as I understand such things, he worked in financial services, which can be a stressful environment. Very sad to leave a wife and two young children.'

'Yes, indeed.' Murphy helped herself to a biscuit. 'It's good that Francine has Stanley around to help.'

Wendy took a sip and put her cup down. 'Stanley seems such a decent man. At least Danny still has his grandad. Stanley did joke a few times about Justin wanting to throw him out, but I don't think he was serious.'

'Well, there's nobody to throw him out now,' said Murphy.

'No, I can't see Francine asking him to leave. Although he has always said that he plans to go travelling in that old bus of his, so I guess he will eventually. Wouldn't be my idea of fun, but we're all different. 'Specially not the fishing.'

'Apparently,' said Murphy, 'Stanley is a big name in the fishing world.'

'Really? Well, it's good for a man to have a hobby.'

'That's right,' said Murphy. 'I expect Ron has lots of activities he gets involved in.'

Wendy shrugged. 'Not so many. He spends a bit of time tracking his investments and reading the news and of course he's in and out with Wilfred. Seems to keep him busy.'

They heard the front door opening at that moment and Wilfred bounded in and made for his water bowl.

'Well, we'd best be off,' said Murphy, rising. 'Thank you for the tea.'

Wendy escorted them out and shut the door.

'I'm not sure that got us anywhere,' said Wilcox.

'Probably not, but it's as well to keep talking to people. It lets them know we're still around and sometimes they say something useful, whether they intend to or not. Wendy seems to think Justin was depressed and committed suicide.

Does she really think that, or was she expounding the theory for our benefit?'

'People don't like to think of murder, because that means it could have been somebody they know. Suicide is more acceptable.' Wilcox unlocked the doors and slid inside. 'And it makes no difference to the victim. They're still dead.'

Chapter Forty-Three

DCI ERNIE MILLBROOK was looking increasingly worried.

'Two deaths in two weeks in the same small area and the victims were known to each other,' he said. 'Are we assuming that these deaths are related?'

'They have to be,' said Murphy. 'But we haven't uncovered the way in which they are related, or any evidence against anybody. The main issue that links the victims is that they both had relationships with Francine Beattie, and it looks as if Adam Bryce wanted to get her back, away from Justin Beattie. That could conceivably have led one of them to kill the other. We thought Justin Beattie could have killed Adam Bryce, in fact that still seems the most likely explanation, but it doesn't explain why Justin Beattie's dead.'

'And the motive you are attributing to him is money?'

Murphy nodded. 'Justin wanted – probably needed – money. He was perpetrating a fraud of his own at work which was bound to be uncovered unless he found enough money to cover his tracks and, according to his stepfather, he had a gambling habit. But killing Adam would only bring in money if he had some arrangement with Rebecca Bryce. We haven't found any evidence of that. In fact, Rebecca Bryce was not going to get as much money as she thought, because under Adam's will the money is split six ways. One share actually goes to Danny – Justin's adopted son – so Justin could have got his hands on that amount if he managed to get himself named as trustee.'

'But he wouldn't have known that.'

'No. The letters to the beneficiaries went out a few days ago, so none of them knew at the time when we questioned them. Unless Adam told them, but I don't think that's likely. I think he was a lot smarter than anybody realised. He looked like some chap who played in a band, which was what he was, but he understood finance. He wasn't about to be ripped off by anybody.'

Ernie Millbrook sat back and folded his arms. 'If Adam Bryce left a large amount of money, which I understand it was, each of his beneficiaries had a motive. We think they probably didn't know about the bequests, but what if we're wrong?'

Murphy nodded. 'It's a possibility. The only person who could assume they would inherit was the wife. I think she may have been having an affair with one of the band members – Bert Wilson – so she might have wanted to get rid of the husband. If she'd just left Adam she wouldn't get a penny.'

'In that case, if she had made some arrangement with Justin Beattie, that perhaps he would do the deed in return for a share of the money, is it realistic that she would then kill him?'

'It would make sense,' Murphy admitted, 'if she then decided that she did not want to give him anything. Or, maybe more convincingly, she was afraid that he would be arrested and he would implicate her.'

'So, in order to avoid being implicated in one murder, she commits another one. That would be some ruthless woman.'

'Yes. We are probably in the realms of speculation here,' said Murphy, 'but if there is a link between these two people, we need to find it.'

Chapter Forty-Four

THE INQUEST on Justin Beattie took place on a grey morning in a room illuminated by stark LED lighting. There were very few windows, which Murphy decided didn't matter today, as there was no sunlight available anyway. And inquests were by their very nature miserable affairs, so why spoil the mood?

She saw Stanley and Francine enter and take seats near the front. Francine was looking surprisingly frail for a woman of her age, as if something had been stripped away from her. Stanley was looking combative. It was good that Francine had Stanley at this time, Murphy reflected. Unless it was Stanley who had killed Justin, in which case it wasn't good at all. At that point the coroner entered and business got underway.

The first responders gave evidence about finding Justin and then Linda Fleming took the stand and gave the post-mortem evidence. She stated that it was not possible from her examination to tell whether Justin fell, jumped or was pushed. The coroner seemed disappointed by this, but

Linda declined to modify her opinion. Stanley was then called upon to give evidence concerning Justin's state of mind. He said that Justin had appeared to be under stress of some kind over the past few weeks, but his family had seen no indication that he was suicidal. As far as they knew, he had no drug habit. Murphy then stated that police enquiries were still ongoing and the coroner sighed and brought in the only conclusion available to him - an open verdict. Something that satisfied nobody, as Murphy knew.

There had been only one junior reporter present and Murphy had noticed his head suddenly come up from his phone at the mention of GHB, but the verdict offered little for the press to get their teeth into. Hopefully, just something buried further down the newsfeed on the dangers of drugs, Murphy thought, as long as it wasn't a slow news day.

Outside, a light drizzle was falling, enough to wreck anybody's hair, but not enough to put up an umbrella. It was good that her hair was beyond any further damage, Murphy decided. She went over to stand with Francine while Stanley went scouting for taxis.

'I told him we could just call an Uber,' she told Murphy. 'Or get the tube, come to that. Stanley seems to feel that an event like this warrants a black cab.'

'At least it's over,' said Murphy. 'You should be able to have the funeral now. Although we still have to find out exactly what happened.'

'Do you know the worst thing?' said Francine. 'About a fortnight ago I was thinking that I'd like to get rid of Justin, that life would be better without him.' She shook her head. 'I had no idea.'

'Thinking these things doesn't make them happen,' said

Murphy. 'Remember that.' She looked up and saw Stanley waving from the open door of a black cab. 'Take care now.'

The taxi drove off and Murphy walked to the tube station. She would have liked to have a chat with Stanley, but in pursuit of what, she couldn't say. Was there something he knew that she didn't?

Chapter Forty-Five

WILCOX LIFTED his head from the screen and sat back. 'Got it,' he said. 'Justin Beattie was a member of Beadles in Upper Brook Street. They were about the twenty-fifth gambling club I contacted. None of them wanted to give out the information, but when I threatened to visit them with a uniform in tow, they all decided to co-operate. '

'Good job,' said Murphy. 'We'll now realise their worst fears by visiting them anyway.'

'We can get the Elizabeth Line' said Wilcox, shrugging into his jacket. 'If you don't mind a bit of a walk first. Then we'll go Farringdon to Bond Street – five minutes.'

Emerging at Bond Street Station, Murphy counted three fake candy shops without even moving.

'Why has nobody closed these places down?' she muttered. 'Everybody knows what they are, but they're still here, proliferating. Are the council really that useless?'

'Letting them get a foothold in the first place was the big mistake,' said Wilcox. 'We should be investigating how that happened.'

'Well, when people stop killing each other, perhaps we can move onto that.'

Beadles was housed in an eighteenth-century terraced property, its existence announced only by a discreet brass plate.

'Classy,' said Murphy. 'You wouldn't even know it was here.'

'They don't want rabble walking in off the street,' said Wilcox.

'Or not unless it's wealthy rabble.'

The door was opened by a diminutive woman in carpet slippers trailing an enormous vacuum cleaner, which looked like it was about to consume her whole. She squinted at Wilcox's badge.

'There's no-one here, love. Only me and Mr Parsons and he's nipped out for a sandwich.'

'So he should be nipping back in soon?' said Murphy.

'Yeah, won't be long. He'll only have gone round the corner. Shocking price those sandwiches are. I make me own.'

'Can we come in and wait for him Mrs…?'

'Wilberforce. Olive. I guess you can come in, love, being as you're the police.'

Wilcox closed the door behind them and they followed Olive down the hallway and into a huge room with marble-lined walls and velvet-covered sofas. A bar with a full set of optics nestled in the corner.

'This is the lounge, the bar, whatever,' she announced. 'Where they hang around when they're not busy losing their money.'

'That's right, isn't it?' said Wilcox. 'The house never loses.'

She smiled. 'You bet it doesn't. Otherwise, how could it afford me?'

'It's enormous,' said Murphy, looking around. 'You'd never guess from the front.'

Olive nodded. 'Go back a long way, these houses do. Very discreet at the front. That sounds like him now.'

Mr Parsons was less welcoming than Mrs Wilberforce. 'Really Olive,' he said. 'It's not your place to admit people.'

'She had to admit us,' said Murphy. 'We threatened to arrest her. Perhaps we can have a chat with you, Mr Parsons.'

He nodded and turned on his heel. They followed him into an office with three screens showing the front door, the bar and a large restaurant, from a number of different angles.

He sat behind his desk and they took seats in front of him.

'I spoke to you on the phone, Mr Parsons,' said Wilcox. 'As I explained, we want to talk to you about one of your members – Justin Beattie.'

Mr Parsons looked mutinous. 'We have a duty of confidentiality towards our members…' he began

'You don't have any duty of confidentiality towards Justin Beattie,' said Murphy. 'Because he's dead.'

He stiffened. 'Dead? Are you saying that this is something to do with the club?'

'No, not directly,' said Wilcox. 'But we are investigating a number of aspects of his life and the fact that he had a gambling habit is one of them. That being the case, we'd like to examine your records, to see how much he was staking, and how much he was losing.'

Murphy was looking round the room. 'Good that you

have CCTV, isn't it? We'll want to see the footage for the last month.'

He folded his arms. 'You'll need a warrant for that.'

'No problem,' said Murphy. 'We'll be back later this evening with a warrant and some uniformed officers.'

He glared at her, then turned around. 'Very well. Follow me.'

The room in the basement was much less luxuriously appointed than the office upstairs. Just a large desk with a bank of screens and three laptops. Murphy pulled one of the chairs out and sat down. 'The nerve centre,' she announced, looking at the screens. 'What's your maximum bid?'

'Depends what you're playing. Somewhere around £5,000.'

'In that case, it doesn't take a punter long to lose the farm.'

He narrowed his eyes. 'That very rarely happens. We encourage responsible gambling.'

'Excellent. Now let's have a look at Mr Beattie's account.'

He paged down a few screens and clicked. 'Can you print this off for me?' asked Murphy. He nodded and a few seconds later a printer in the corner spat out some pages. She scanned the list of dates and amounts. 'Doesn't seem to have stopped when he was winning.'

He shrugged. 'Not much we can do about that, is there? We certainly don't pressure people to carry on. We have an exclusive restaurant on the top floor, so a lot of our income comes from that. Gambling is provided as an additional entertainment for our members. We are not trying to screw the last tenner out of people.'

'And how much are your annual memberships fees?' asked Wilcox.

'£3,000' he replied. Wilcox raised his eyebrows.

'OK' said Murphy. 'Now for the CCTV. Do you want us to sit and watch it here or are you happy for us to take the disks away?'

His lips tightened. 'It's really not up to me. I would need to consult the management.'

'That's fine,' said Murphy. 'I guess the management will be around later this evening, won't they? In the meantime, we can just sit here and have a trawl. We won't get in the way.'

He opened his mouth, presumably to reply and then turned on his heel and walked out.

'Gone to 'phone a friend,' said Murphy. 'Let's see what we can see in the meantime.'

'I don't think we need to look through the whole thing,' said Wilcox. 'We can just pick the dates from Justin Beattie's account. No point looking at the nights he wasn't in.'

'Good thinking,' said Murphy, sitting back and waiting for him to page through. 'These seats are quite comfy, actually.'

'Ok. Here we go.' The high-speed movement on the screen in front of Murphy stopped and the figures resumed a more measured pace. 'Two cameras in the casino area and this is the front door.' Wilcox indicated the other two screens.

'If we start with the front, we should see him arriving,' said Murphy.

'Exactly. Then we can switch to the interior.'

After fifteen minutes speeding through arrivals, Justin appeared at 8.15pm, unaccompanied.

'Told the wife he was working late, I guess,' said Murphy.

'This was one of his winning nights,' said Wilcox. 'He had to come back the next night to lose it all.'

And the CCTV did indeed show Justin having a profitable evening at the roulette table and leaving with a spring in his step. The following evening was less jolly, but he took it well and didn't reappear until the following week.

'Looking like a man with a mission now' said Murphy and there was indeed a determined lift to Justin's chin as he rang the bell the following Wednesday.

'He's going to lose again,' said Wilcox. 'But not as badly as last week. Still, it's all cumulative…'

'Probably next visit they should let him win a bit,' said Murphy.

'Yes, they do,' said Wilcox. 'Just a small bit. Enough to keep him on the leash.'

Again, they watched Justin's evening unfold. 'He always arrives alone and leaves alone,' said Murphy. 'He doesn't seem to talk to anybody apart from the staff. And I'd have pegged Justin as quite a sociable sort of chap. It doesn't look like the sort of place you hang around in to make new friends.'

Eventually, after an intervening evening in which he lost £30,000, they arrived at Justin's final visit. 'Two weeks before he died,' said Murphy. 'Small win,' Wilcox informed her.

'Opening G&T to psych himself up,' said Murphy, watching him at the bar.

They followed him across to the roulette wheel where he seated himself and lined up his chips. For an hour or so, not much happened. Then Justin won a bit. A punter opposite him peeled himself away and was replaced by a younger man obviously the worse for drink, accompanied by two young women, staring over his shoulder.

'Well, look at that.' Murphy pointed at the unmistakeable figure of Rebecca Bryce. Justin seemed to note the appearance of three new people opposite him, but took no further notice of them. Half an hour later he cashed in his chips and made his way out.

'They didn't acknowledge each other at all,' said Wilcox, wonderingly. 'Do you think that was deliberate?'

Murphy was still staring at the screen. 'They didn't know each other,' she said. 'They hadn't met. Looking at the date, the Bryces were just about moving into the area. These two had not yet been introduced.'

'So when they were introduced…'

'They already knew something about each other,' she finished.

Mr Parsons reappeared at that point. 'Can you tell us who this is?' Murphy pointed to Rebecca's male companion. He started to shake his head. She raised her eyebrows. He sighed.

'Jeremy Wells' he said. 'He's one of our regular members.'

'What does he do?'

He shook his head. 'Don't know. His father runs a charitable foundation, so he probably works for that.'

'And the two young women with him?'

He shrugged. 'Never seen them before. He often signs in friends, most of them only appear once.'

'We may need his contact details,' said Murphy. 'I don't know yet. We'll let you know. I think that's all for now.'

Parsons had opened his mouth and now shut it again. He escorted them to the front door practically at a run.

'Think he might have been glad to see the back of us,'

said Murphy. 'But we've got what we wanted. Whether it will get us anywhere is another matter.'

Chapter Forty-Six

REBECCA BRYCE YAWNED WIDELY when Murphy mentioned Beadles. 'Not that I can remember,' she said.

'We have you on CCTV,' said Murphy.

Rebecca yawned again. 'Well, I must have been there then, mustn't I? There's quite a lot of after-work socialising in my job, entertaining clients and all that sort of thing.' She waved a hand as if to indicate the loftiness of her position. 'Really, I've probably been to loads of places I can remember nothing about.'

'The person sitting opposite you on the night you can't remember was Justin Beattie,' said Murphy.

'Really? Fancy that. Well, I don't remember meeting him anywhere. Am I on CCTV talking to him?'

Murphy had to admit that such was not the case. Rebecca smiled.

'There you are then. I didn't even see him.'

'You were with Jeremy Wells,' said Wilcox.

'Jeremy' she repeated. 'Yes, that would make sense. Jeremy's a chap who likes to gamble occasionally. I don't think he wins very often, but he probably doesn't need to.'

'He has lots of money, does he?'

'Oh, I think so. From my perspective, he's one of our donors, or at least his father is, so he's worth a bit of my time.'

'So how often have you accompanied him to Beadles?'

'Only that once, and I don't even have much recollection of that.'

'How about Bennie's Bar? How often have you been there?'

'Never heard of it.'

'Round the back of St Katherine's Dock,' said Murphy. 'Prime City location. Ring any bells?'

Rebecca shook her head. 'No, I'm sure I've never been there.'

Murphy looked around the room. Some of the shelves were now empty. 'Packing up to move, are you?'

Rebecca shrugged. 'I've started organising stuff a bit. I can hardly rattle round here on my own.'

'Has the will been read yet?'

'I've been informed of the provisions by the solicitor.'

'And the house is part of his estate,' said Murphy.

Rebecca nodded tightly. 'That's right.'

'I think that's all for now.' Murphy rose and Rebecca walked them to the front door

———

'SHE HAS to sell the house as part of splitting the proceeds,' said Murphy. 'Although I'm sure she'd be selling it anyway. This is not an exciting area for a young, newly-rich woman.

Bet she was spitting nails when she discovered he'd made a will.'

'She'll still have a decent amount of money,' Wilcox pointed out.

'Yes, but not what she thought she'd get. And at the time when Adam died, and some days later when Justin died, she was probably still assuming that she'd get the lot.'

'Justin would never have known that money had been left to Danny.'

Murphy shook her head. 'No. I wonder if that would have changed anything?'

'You still think he killed Adam?'

'We certainly can't rule him out. We don't have anybody else in the frame. What Justin was after was money. Would he have arranged to kill Adam in exchange for money? It seems really extreme.'

Wilcox started the engine. 'I know Lennie and Bert won't have known about the will until after Adam died, but maybe they did know in some way. Maybe he told them.'

'It would be a bit of a funny thing to tell somebody, wouldn't it? Unless you were expecting to die soon, which can't have applied in his case. The fact is that, at the time when he died, the only person that we know had a motive was Rebecca. But motive doesn't get us far. What we need is some evidence. Let's go and have another word with Bert.'

———

BERT WILSON OPENED the door with a beer in his hand and the sound of football blasting away behind him. He didn't look pleased to see them, but sighed and let them in.

'Sorry to interrupt the match,' said Wilcox, 'but it wasn't a great result.'

Bert fixed him with a look and clicked the remote to turn it off.

Murphy sat down in the best-looking armchair and stretched her legs. 'So happy days are here for you, Mr Wilson,' she said.

'Dunno what you mean.'

'Haven't you had a letter from Adam Bryce's solicitor?'

'Oh that. Yeah.'

'I'd have expected you to be out celebrating, not sitting in here watching Chelsea get thrashed.'

Bert gave up and sat down. 'That's right,' said Murphy. 'Take the weight off your feet. Did you have any idea Adam was going to leave you money?'

He shook his head. 'None at all. I would have expected it all to go to his wife. Well, we didn't expect him to die, so we never thought about it.'

'Did you feel he should have given you money while he was alive?'

He shrugged. 'Why should he? It was his money. He spent it on keeping the band going, so in that sense he was sharing it with us. If we'd made it big, we wouldn't have needed money from him.'

'So now you and Lennie have money to keep the band going,' said Wilcox.

'Yeah, we'll have to find someone else first.'

'I guess,' said Wilcox, 'Adam won't be hard to replace as a musician, will he?'

'Not particularly, no.' Bert was looking a bit wary now.

'So, it's turned out well for Dead Cells, hasn't it?'

Bert shook his head. 'I don't like where you're going with this. As far as Lennie and I are concerned, we'd rather have him back.'

'Talking about the wife,' said Murphy, 'have you seen much of her?'

Bert shook his head again. 'No.'

'Only I got the impression you and she were rather close. Wouldn't she be turning to you for support at this time?'

'She doesn't need me. She has a sister, friends, whoever.'

'Good-looking woman, isn't she?'

Bert rolled his eyes. 'I'm in the music business. It's full of good-looking women. She's nothing special.'

'She's selling the house,' said Murphy. 'Where do you think she'll go?'

'How would I know?'

'She might have discussed her prospects with you. In her case, she's getting a bit less than she expected, isn't she?'

'That's none of my business.'

'OK' Murphy stood up. 'We'll leave you to get back to the match. Try not to watch that penalty shootout.'

'There was no penalty shootout,' Wilcox pointed out as they walked back to the car.

'I know. I think that's what they call fake news. Thought I'd give it a go. Seeing as he wasn't very forthcoming. I'm pretty certain he's had a fling with Rebecca, but there's no law against it. And he's right, he can probably get any number of groupies, he's an attractive guy. Rebecca might have found him more attractive than Adam Bryce.'

'You think they could have offed Adam for the money?'

She sighed. 'It's possible. None of them have cast-iron alibis. But she already had the money, she'd married into it, and he doesn't look to me like the sort of chap who would rouse himself to commit murder. They could have had an affair and she could have stayed married to the money.'

Wilcox unlocked the car door and slid inside. 'But maybe she didn't want to stay married to the money, living in a boring residential area. Maybe she wanted to go travelling, get rid of Adam, find somebody more exciting, but she wanted the money. She wouldn't have got much in a divorce.'

Murphy climbed in and sniffed. 'You been shampooing the car seats again?'

'I try to keep the interior of my car clean' he said, pointedly.

Murphy nodded. 'Don't ever get a dog. For my money, if Rebecca wanted a partner in crime, poor old Justin would have been a better bet. A man desperate enough to do something stupid.'

'The MO fits him,' said Wilcox. 'A punch to the jaw. But that's usually something done in anger, rather than an attempt at murder.'

'It could be,' said Murphy, 'that somebody knocked Adam over and was then going to stab him, but they didn't need to because he just died. It was very sudden and very quick.'

She fastened her seatbelt. 'And then they just had to make their escape. Wouldn't have been so difficult. It's not an area where everybody watches the neighbours and most people would have been at work. If we're saying it was Justin, then it's easier to understand what happened to him.'

'You think Rebecca killed him?'

'Somebody was in that bar with him. Somebody drugged his glass of wine. Somebody was there when he went over the balcony. We have no trace evidence, but she's got to be the prime suspect. She won't be easy to nail, that's for sure.'

'If Justin was hoping to get money from Rebecca, he

would have had to wait a while,' said Wilcox. 'There would have been probate to go through. It would have been months before she got her hands on it. He needed money more urgently than that.'

'He could have been pressuring her to take out a loan. She could have got some sort of bridging loan on the basis of the inheritance. Then she could pay him off. But he might have lost it all, and then come back for more. She knows he's a gambler. And if the police catch up with him, he'll probably drop her in it. Justin then becomes a serious liability.'

'What about Francine?' said Wilcox, as they negotiated a hold-up on the Holloway Road. 'She's got rid of both men in her life and her son is now well-provided for. She'll probably be able to use that money for school fees and all that. He might have told her he was going to leave money to Danny.'

'The thing is,' said Murphy, 'men of his age don't go round talking about their wills. Not unless they've got a life-limiting illness, or something like that. It would be a weird thing to say. Whereas Rebecca didn't need to know anything about wills, she could just assume she would inherit.'

'OK, let's go in and show our faces,' said Murphy, as they pulled into the car park. 'If we're really unlucky, Bellweather might be back.'

But it was DCI Millbrook who approached as they sat down in the CID room.

'Call came in for you on the switchboard' he told Wilcox. 'A Mrs Bailey. Said you'd been wanting to speak to her. She's left a number.' He handed them a slip of paper.

'Bailey?' said Murphy, as Ernie wandered back to his office.

Wilcox logged in and typed the name into the search

bar. 'The Baileys' he said. 'They were on holiday when it happened. In which case they probably won't know much.' He tapped the number into his phone.

Chapter Forty-Seven

SANDRA BAILEY SHOWED them into a room festooned with clothes, piles of them on every surface. 'I hate the unpacking and laundry business' she said. 'It's the downside of going on holiday.'

'Thank you for getting in touch, Mrs Bailey,' said Wilcox. 'You'll have heard about what has been happening.'

She nodded. 'I heard about it from Ted when I popped in to see how Molly was. It's really hard to believe. We hadn't kept in touch with anybody. We were doing a digital detox – Eddie's idea. He thinks it's good to keep the kids off their phones. It just made them both really bad-tempered.'

'I gather you were at this house-warming party,' said Murphy. 'Can you tell us what you remember about it?'

'Not a lot, to be honest. We didn't stay long because we were off on holiday the next day and we'd done no packing or anything, let alone organised the kids. It was very classy, good food and drink. They seemed like nice young people. We chatted to a few of the neighbours, it was all very friendly. Those poor young men, who could have guessed…?'

'Did you see either Adam or Justin talking to anybody in particular?'

Mrs Bailey grabbed a couple of T-shirts and threw them into the washing basket. 'I saw them talking to each other at one point, don't know what about. Then I saw Justin talking to the man's wife – Rebecca she's called. They were laughing about something. That's just like Justin, he always had a joke ready.' Her expression became sombre.

'So that was the last time you saw either of them,' said Wilcox.

'What? No, we saw Justin the next day. But not to speak to.'

'What time was that?'

She thought for a minute. 'Early evening. Must have been nearly seven. We were getting the seven-thirty Eurostar from St Pancras. And when we went past the Booking Office – clever name for a restaurant, I suppose – there he was, sitting at the bar.'

'On his own?'

'Yes. I wanted to go in and say hello, but Eddie hurried me past. He was worried we'd miss the train. If Justin had looked up, I would have waved, but he didn't.'

'And you're certain it was him?'

'Of course. I've known him for years.'

Murphy had to sit down. She wasn't sure where to go from here.

'You were around most of that day, the day after the party,' said Wilcox.

Mrs Bailey waved him into a seat. 'That's right. We were coming and going all day, in and out to the shops, the kids have forgotten this and then that, you know how it is, and we finally got away about five. Then we did a bit of food shopping, just stuff to eat on the train, and got on the bus down to Kings Cross.'

'It would have been just after you left that Adam Bryce died,' Wilcox said. 'Did you see anybody around that afternoon?'

She shook her head. 'No. Well only Ted. I saw him knock on the Bryce's door about three o'clock as I was going past to the pharmacy. But there was no answer. He came back down the path and we waved. That's all. Actually, I knew there was nobody in at the Bryces' because I'd seen the chap – Adam – ringing the bell at Francine's about half an hour earlier.'

Wilcox shook his head as if to clear it. He pulled out his notebook. 'Let me make sure I've got this straight,' he said. 'At two-thirty you saw Adam visiting the Beattie's house. Did you see him go in?'

'No, I was just driving past, I think that was when I was picking Felicity up from her swimming lesson. That's right. She was already changed, so we got back quite quickly. Then she said she hadn't got any contact lens fluid – talk about leaving it till the last minute – so I was just nipping out for that when I saw Ted.'

'And then a few hours later you saw Justin at Kings Cross.'

'Yes. Poor Justin. I still can't take it in.'

Murphy also felt she couldn't take it in. She rose and they made their way out.

'That woman has just destroyed my life,' she told Wilcox, as Mrs Bailey waved them off with a smile.

'Well, she's destroyed your working hypothesis, that's for sure.'

Chapter Forty-Eight

TED YARDLEY WAS COOKING dinner when they presented themselves at the front door. A smell of frying onions reminded Murphy that lunch had somehow been missed out.

'I'll just go and switch the cooker off' he said as he left them in the front room. He returned a moment later, having removed his apron.

'There's something you omitted to tell us, isn't there?' said Murphy.

He nodded. 'Yes. I realised Sandra would probably tell you.'

'OK, let's hear it from you.'

He took a deep breath. 'It was about three, I think. Mollie had had a really bad night but she'd just gone off to sleep. Then there was the most awful racket from next door. He must have had his speakers turned up as high as they would go. I went round and knocked on the front door but there was no answer.'

'But you knew he was in there.'

'Well, yes, because of the noise.'

'What did you do then?'

He hesitated. 'I went round the back and knocked on the back door.'

'What, you climbed over the fence?'

'Well, yes, it doesn't take much climbing over. We've got a stile there. He opened the door and I followed him in and asked him to turn the noise down. He – I don't really understand this, because I had up to that point thought him a very decent young man – he told me to f... off and slammed the door after me. I just came back home.'

'And you didn't tell us this before because...?'

'Because I knew we'd be having the conversation we're having now. I knew I hadn't done anything wrong and I didn't want to risk being hauled off and having to leave Mollie.'

'You must have been the last person to see him alive,' said Wilcox.

'Yes. I mean, no. He was perfectly fine when I left.'

'Why do you think he was so abusive to you?'

He scratched his head. 'I've thought about that and my impression is that he was already angry about something, he didn't just get angry with me for knocking on the door. He was already furious and I just happened to intrude at that moment.'

'Were you wearing gloves when you went round there?'

'Gloves? No, of course not.'

'And nobody else was there with him?'

'No, nobody that I saw.'

'OK' said Murphy. 'You'll need to come down the station and make a statement about this.'

He nodded. 'Let me just phone Wilma and tell Mollie what's happening.'

———

TWO HOURS in the police station did not produce anything Murphy could have classified as a result. Ted Yardley did not deviate from the story he had originally told them and he was not tempted to add in any details or justifications. He declared that he did not need legal assistance, as he had done nothing wrong. Murphy tried to tell him that these were not necessarily related issues, but he brushed that aside. He was unimpressed by suggestions that confessing to an accidental killing would mean a short sentence. His only concern appeared to be how quickly he could get home to his wife. Eventually, Murphy threw in the towel and let him go.

'I feel just like him' she told Wilcox. 'I'm going home.'

The roads were so deserted and the drive so uneventful that she pulled up outside the house without any recollection of how she had arrived there. Had she been asleep? Where was everybody else? Why was nobody on the road? What was going on? Surely not football?

It was indeed football. A bunch of people she had never seen before were gathered around the TV waving bottles of beer and shouting. Clive had forsaken cooking for watching, and Murphy's arrival was followed in short order by that of a motorbike rider bearing a stack of pizza boxes. This was fine, Murphy decided. She helped herself to a bottle and a slice of pizza and joined in the general denunciation of the referee. At the end of two hours, she realised she hadn't thought about the case once. Maybe the break would do her brain good.

Chapter Forty-Nine

FRANCINE BEATTIE SEEMED surprised when Murphy told her that Adam Bryce had been seen knocking on her door on that Monday.

'I must have been out,' she said. 'You mean the day…?'

'Yes, that day.'

'In that case, I can remember. Stanley had gone to Syon Park with Ted, Danny was at school and it was a lovely day, so I settled Tommy down in the pram and we went to the park. We stayed there till it was time to collect Danny. Adam must have come while we were out. 'Can't think what he would have wanted. We'd said everything we needed to.'

'He didn't leave a note, he didn't contact you again after that?'

She shook her head.

'You knew him well at one time,' said Murphy. 'Can you think of any reason somebody might have wanted to get rid of him? Did he get into fights?'

'Fights? Adam? No, he was not that sort of person at all. If anything, I'd say he didn't like confrontation.'

'Did anybody see you leave the house that afternoon – anyone who knew you, I mean?'

Francine sighed. 'Not that I saw. 'Street was pretty deserted as far as I remember, and I didn't see anybody I knew in the park. Not much of an alibi, is it?'

Chapter Fifty

JUSTIN BEATTIE HAD NOT BEEN a churchgoer and his funeral service took place at the local crematorium on one of those bright, unseasonably sunny days that sometimes happened without warning. Just to show the deceased what they were missing, Murphy thought.

She sat on a bench a short distance away and watched people assemble outside – waiting for the previous service to empty out before they were allowed in. Business was brisk and all of her suspects would probably be here – apart from Rebecca Bryce.

Tom and Louise Fraser were the first to arrive. Louise was wearing a bias-cut black wool coat, which Murphy thought was probably very expensive. Joining them next in the queue was a delegation from the office – David Cargill, Melanie Fisher and Jim Saxon. Melanie Fisher's coat looked like something she had kept in her wardrobe for decades and brought out for funerals. And of course, Murphy admitted, there was nothing wrong with that. Funerals tended to increase as one went through life, it was as well to have your outfit ready. It was smart of Watson Fullerton to turn out for Justin, to demonstrate that they were mourning him as a valued colleague. Made it easier to keep whatever he had been doing under wraps while they busied themselves with the damage limitation. For them, having him die was a better solution than having to fire him.

Ted Yardley was next to appear. He and Ron Warner climbed out of a car being driven by Wendy, who locked the doors and hurried them along. Wendy's black coat had an unforgiving belt, which made her look like a trussed-up barrel. Ted and Ron both looked awkward and ill-at-ease. Probably wishing they could escape to the pub, Murphy decided.

Eddie and Sandra Bailey arrived just as people began filing into the chapel and Murphy followed them in. Francine and Stanley then appeared and took their places at the front. Danny was not with them. He'd be at school and maybe six was too young for a funeral. Yes, thought Murphy. She wouldn't have brought him either. Francine was looking better than she had at the inquest. Maybe she was now getting more food and sleep. She was wearing a small amount of makeup and black definitely suited her.

The service was brisk, the woman conducting it obviously mindful of the time constraints and the eulogy was given, surprisingly, by Stanley. Although, when Murphy thought about it, who else was there? Justin had spent his working life in an industry not much conducive to forming personal relationships. He hadn't been into golf or cricket or rugby or football, as a participant or even as a supporter. He hadn't been a pub regular, on the darts team or a quiz team. He hadn't engaged in any of those pursuits through which men accumulate friends, or, if he had, none of them had lasted long. It looked like he was no longer in touch with any of his friends from university. He had no brothers or sisters. He had made plenty of money, but here he was now, having his funeral eulogy given by the stepfather he had never much liked. There was a lesson in there somewhere.

Stanley had obviously put a lot of work into his short speech, emphasising the positive aspects of Justin's character – his love for his wife and son, his brains and success in his career, his enjoyment of being a father, his sense of humour and good company. It was a good performance and Murphy thought his last point was undoubtedly true. Justin had a lot of faults, but he probably wasn't boring. If you found yourself sitting next to him at a dinner, he would keep you entertained. There was a lot to be said for people like that.

In what seemed like no time at all, the service was over and they were filing out, the crowd for the next funeral already assembling outside. Francine and Stanley were thanking people for coming and inviting them back to the house. Murphy found herself included in the general invitation, whether by accident or design, so she parked outside Francine's house half an hour later. Not a suitable environment in which to be questioning people, but right now she'd take any options on offer.

Inside was a blur of activity. Stanley and Tom were dispensing drinks, Louise was handing round crisps and olives and then the front door opened to admit Wendy bearing an enormous plate of smoked salmon sandwiches. This was what you called people pulling together, Murphy thought, as she accepted a drink and went over to talk to Ted.

'Hello,' he said. 'Am I still your number one suspect?'

'I have about a dozen number one suspects, Ted. I'm having a hard job keeping track of them all.'

Ted nodded and took a sip of his beer. 'I really thought the next funeral I would be attending would be Mollie's,' he said. 'I could never have expected this. Two much younger men dead in this street, and she's still alive.'

'Life surprises us all the time,' said Murphy. A meaningless platitude, but all she could come up with at short notice. 'Did you see much of Justin?' she asked him.

He shrugged. 'Not really. Only the odd neighbourly get-together, of which we've had a couple recently. And I hardly knew Adam Bryce at all. But it makes you think about your interactions with other people, doesn't it? You never know when it may be the last time you'll see them.'

Murphy knew the interaction he was referring to, but they'd already done that to death, no point bringing it up again. Wilma suddenly appeared at Ted's side.

'No hurry,' she said. 'She's asleep.'

But Ted was obviously going to grab this opportunity to leave. 'I'll get back anyway, now,' he said. He deposited his empty glass, exchanged a few words with Francine, and then he was gone.

'Poor Ted,' said Wilma. 'He loves her very much.'

Murphy was saved from having to reply by the appearance of Wendy, determinedly handing round food. She accepted a sandwich. It was easier than arguing. Wendy and Wilma embarked on a discussion of changes in the parking regulations, leaving Murphy free to accost Stanley.

'It was probably good that you didn't bring Danny,' she said.

'We thought about it, but in the end, we decided not to. Although kids are far more robust than we think.' He took a sip of his drink. 'At the moment Danny's going through the scatological phase, which I think is quite common. They love jokes about poo.'

Murphy smiled. 'Yes, I remember that,' she said. 'Especially little boys.'

'We were laughing about it just a week ago. Justin went to collect Danny from Ron's and Danny was showing him where Wilfred had done a poo in the tree next to the fence. Justin said that he had been shown the evidence and that Wilfred must be the only tree-climbing dachshund in the world. I looked it up and we found lots of pictures of dachshunds climbing trees. It was so funny. You never know these things. But Danny thought the tree-climbing was less interesting than the pooing.' His face fell. 'How suddenly things can change. I wish we could have him back.'

Murphy nodded. 'Of course. Every death is a loss and life will always be different afterwards.' Where was she getting all these banal statements from?

'It's going to be different for me,' said Stanley. 'I expected to be across the Channel by now. But now, with Justin gone, I can't very well leave Francine on her own. Not that I would want to.'

'I'm sure she's very glad to have you here,' said Murphy. 'Now I must be getting back.'

There seemed little point saying goodbye to Francine as Murphy wasn't sure she had even been invited in the first place, so she slipped out quietly and then spoilt it all by making a lot of noise trying to start the car.

Chapter Fifty-One

BACK IN THE OFFICE, Wilcox was scrolling through a set of alarming photographs on his laptop. Murphy went to look over his shoulder.

'What's this? Some sort of advert for teeth?'

'It's a bunch of selfies. We took details of all the people in that bar and we asked them for any selfies they took that night, remember? Well, they've all been coming in and I'm putting them up.'

Murphy pulled up a chair. 'Seen anything yet?'

'Not so far. It's a pretty long shot, I guess. You'd think people would want to show something of their surroundings, rather than just their faces, but no.'

'I guess it's not an iconic location, could be a bar anywhere. Hey, what about that one?'

Wilcox laughed. 'That one looks like an accident. Somebody fired one off without turning it to selfie. That could have been our best bet, but I don't see anybody who looks like Justin.'

Murphy rubbed at her eyes. 'I'm not sure what I'm

looking for anymore. If Justin didn't kill Adam, which seems to be the case, why would anybody want to kill him? Maybe there's no connection between their deaths. Could there have been some other reason to kill Justin?'

Wilcox sighed. 'Maybe Stanley killed him – he might have been his stepfather but I don't think he liked him much and Justin was trying to throw him out of the house. Maybe Ted killed him because he knew Ted had killed Adam, although we think he probably hadn't. Maybe Francine killed him because she knew about Louise, or just because she was tired of him. Maybe Tom killed him because he found out about Louise. Maybe Louise killed him – maybe he chucked her, not the other way round, and she got angry. Maybe his boss at the bank killed him so that the fraud wouldn't be uncovered and ruin the bank's reputation. How many is that?'

'Enough to be going on with. It could be any of them. The only person we can definitely rule out is Adam.'

Wilcox moved along to the next photo. 'Just a minute…'

Murphy narrowed her eyes. 'That's him. Right behind the woman with the green hair. Just raising a glass. And that person opposite – navy-blue coat and a beanie hat. Do you recognise that back view?'

'Bit hard to tell. It's definitely a woman. Could be Rebecca, Francine or Louise. They're all about the same size. Or it could be some woman we know nothing about.'

'Ok, let's park that last suggestion for the time being. Keeping your hat on in the bar implies a certain level of not wanting to be seen. If we could track down that hat and coat, we'd be getting somewhere. Let's start with my preferred suspect.'

'You want to search Rebecca Bryce's wardrobe?'

'Yes. We'll tell her it's to do with Adam's killing. That we want another look at the crime scene. Phone her at work, ask for the keys.'

―――――

'SHE WASN'T HAPPY ABOUT IT,' said Wilcox, as he twisted the yale in the front door. 'But she couldn't really refuse without it looking suspicious.'

'It's looking a bit bare,' said Murphy as they entered the sitting room. 'All the books have gone.'

'She's clearing it out, isn't she?'

'Let's hope she hasn't cleared out her wardrobe.' Murphy made her way upstairs.

The bedroom had two large built-in wardrobes. One of them, presumably Adam's, was completely empty. The other had a good selection of clothes, but no navy-blue coat. She wandered back downstairs.

The back door was open and Wilcox was in the back garden. She followed him out.

'What are you doing out here?'

'Can't you hear it?'

After a few seconds Murphy heard it, a hollow clunking sound. 'A woodpecker.'

'That's right. It's in that tree somewhere.' He pointed to a tall tree next door, in Ron and Wendy Warner's garden. 'They're much smaller birds than you think. You can really only spot them from the pecking movement.'

'OK. Good to get some fresh air and a look at the natural world. I think we need to get on now.' Murphy headed back into the kitchen. 'I didn't find anything interesting in her wardrobe. And the contents of his wardrobe are all gone.'

'So, what do you think she did with all that stuff?'

Murphy stopped to think. 'She would have taken it to a charity shop. That's really all you can do with clothes. And if she wanted to get rid of something of hers, she'd just bundle that in too.'

'There's a charity shop just round the corner, in the high street.'

'Lock up again and let's get round there.'

Chapter Fifty-Two

MURPHY LIKED CHARITY SHOPS. Lots of it was just rubbish, of course, but there was always the chance of happening upon something really good, for just a few pounds. That chance had diminished with time. People running these shops now had a good eye for what they were dealing with, and anything with a designer label would be priced accordingly. The backlash to that had been people cutting the labels out of their decent clothes before they brought them in. It was an interesting social phenomenon and she hesitated for a few minutes over a linen jacket that looked very much like one she'd seen in a glossy magazine.

'I thought we were looking for a navy-blue coat,' Wilcox hissed behind her. Wilcox didn't like charity shops; they were way outside his comfort zone. Murphy nodded and moved onto the coats. Black coats, red coats, camel coats, fake fur coats, denim coats, dark brown, white, but no navy. She approached the woman at the counter and showed her badge.

'We're trying to trace some articles of clothing that may have been brought in here.'

The woman looked alarmed. 'What, you mean like stolen goods?'

'No, not necessarily that. But somebody may have brought in a large number of men's clothes and a woman's navy-blue wool coat, sometime in the last few days. Do you have any stuff that's not appeared on the hangers yet?'

She nodded. 'We have a couple of bags that Letty will be dealing with tomorrow. She comes in three afternoons a week and she does the steaming. We steam-clean everything that goes out, and I don't have time to do that.'

'Can we have a look at those bags?' asked Murphy.

'I guess so. They're through here.' She led the way to the back of the shop and into a poky room full of clothes and hangers. 'Here, these two.' She pointed to two bulging black bags. 'We haven't even looked in them yet.'

'Right. Let's see what we've got.' Murphy pulled on gloves, wrestled with the knot at the top of the first bag and pulled out a pile of men's clothes – jeans, shirts, T-shirts, sweaters.

'Good quality stuff,' she said. 'Looks like the sort of stuff Adam Bryce would have worn.'

At the bottom was a logo T-shirt – Dead Cells. 'OK, I think that seals it' she said. 'Let's try the other bag.'

Halfway down the other bag, there they were. A navy coat and a grey woollen beanie.

'OK, let's ask her to come back in here,' said Murphy.

The woman, who gave her name as Brenda Mitchell, acknowledged that the items in question must have been in the bag and could not have been introduced by the officers and agreed that she would make a statement to that effect if called upon to do so.

'There are Gift Aid stickers on both of these bags' said Wilcox. 'Which allows you to claim back the tax. That means you have to have the details of the taxpayer.'

Brenda looked a bit uncomfortable. 'This was a bit of a funny one,' she said eventually 'but I didn't see why we shouldn't get the tax back.'

'What happened?' asked Murphy.

'This young woman brought those two bags in and I asked her if she was registered for Gift Aid and she said 'No' and hurried off. But I remembered her because she brought some things in a few weeks ago and it was really good stuff. We made quite a lot of money on it. One of her pieces was still unsold, so I got it down and it had a Gift Aid sticker on it, so that gave me the donor details. So, I went ahead and marked these two bags as Gift Aid with the same reference. I guess I shouldn't have done.'

'Have you still got that unsold item?' asked Murphy.

She nodded. 'Yes.' She walked over to the rack. 'It's this sweatshirt. Brand new. Probably for some band, but good quality.'

'Good old Dead Cells,' said Murphy.

'So where do you keep the taxpayer details?' asked Wilcox

'We keep them in a log.' She led the way back to the desk and pulled out a notebook. There it was, the tenth name down – Rebecca Bryce of 17 Windworth Road.

'And you have the actual gift aid declarations?' asked Wilcox?'

'Yes.' She reached under the counter, produced a box file and showed them Rebecca's declaration.

'And you're certain that it was the same woman?' asked Murphy.

'Yes, I am. I've always been good on faces. She hasn't done anything wrong, has she?'

'We don't know yet, maybe not. So, you can tie these taxpayer details to those items?'

'Yes. It's the reference number on the sticker. We would transfer that number to the individual garments and when we sell any of them, we can then reclaim tax.'

'Alright, I think we're there.' Murphy pointed towards the back room. 'We'll need to take both of those bags and the box file and the log.'

Brenda looked pained. 'We would have made a lot of money on those items.'

'I know and we will return most of them to you at some point. In the meantime, we'll give you a receipt. And thank you very much for your help.'

They staggered out, carrying the two sacks of clothes. 'I've got a horrible feeling this one's going to split,' Murphy gasped.

'Not far now.' Wilcox strode ahead and got the boot unlocked.

Murphy dumped her burden thankfully and raised a fist in the air. 'At last! Something!'

'I wonder why she left her name and address?' Wilcox said. 'She didn't have to do that.'

'She works for a charity,' said Murphy. 'They all get a lot of income from Gift Aid, so she probably felt she should. And in respect of the first consignment, that was before any of this happened, so she wasn't bothered about being anonymous.'

'I wonder why she didn't take the second lot somewhere else.'

Murphy shrugged. 'Maybe she's not as smart as we're

thinking she is. Maybe she forgot she'd already taken stuff there. And if she did think about it, she must have thought there was no chance we would ever track down her old clothes.'

'It's not conclusive,' Wilcox pointed out, fishing in his pocket for the car keys. 'It's pretty good evidence that she met him for a drink, but it doesn't prove she killed him. And she might not have killed him. What motive did she have?'

'Maybe she killed Adam, and Justin knew about it and was blackmailing her.' Murphy climbed in and slammed the door shut.

Wilcox shook his head. 'Now you're just scrabbling around. We weren't really able to check much about her alibi for Adam's death, were we? She's in the sort of job where nobody will really clock what time she leaves, and the time taken to get home on the tube is infinitely variable. Nobody spotted her around late afternoon – not even Mrs Bailey, who seems to have seen everything else that went on.'

'The thing is' said Murphy, 'she had a reasonable motive for killing Adam, but we can't place her at the scene. She had no motive that we know about for killing Justin, but in that case, it looks like we can place her at the scene. It's very unsatisfactory.'

'I guess we need to forget about motive and concentrate on evidence,' Wilcox pulled into the police station car park. 'If forensics can match that coat to any fibres found on Justin's clothes, we'll be getting somewhere. Oh my God, look at that.'

They both stared in horror at the maroon Lexus. 'He's back,' Murphy breathed. 'How can he have recovered so fast?'

'He was desperate to get back and see what you were up to,' said Wilcox. 'Good job we're bringing in some spoils.'

Bellweather's eyes widened as they hauled the bags into the office. 'Been to a jumble sale, have we DI Murphy?'

'Charity shop, actually,' she replied. 'Looks like we've found the outer garments worn by the last person to see Justin Beattie alive.'

'Excellent. I've been reading the case files. Who's the person in question?'

'Rebecca Bryce.'

'The merry widow, eh? I'd have thought she'd be more likely to have killed the other one. Or are you thinking she killed both of them?'

'We're trying not to speculate at this stage,' Wilcox replied. 'Just getting the evidence together.'

'Of course. Quite right. Let's push on and get a result.' He turned to Murphy. 'These cases have been outstanding for far too long. Two people dead in one street – it can't be that hard to fathom out.'

'Yes, well we'll get all this over to forensics,' said Murphy.

He nodded and headed back into his office.

'I should just leave you to deal with him,' she said. 'Being ill doesn't seem to have changed him at all. But I wonder if he could be right. Could she have killed both of them?'

Chapter Fifty-Three

MURPHY WAS HALFWAY home when she remembered. This was the evening she was supposed to be having dinner with Jack. At the time when she had agreed to it, it had seemed far enough away, but now it had caught up with her. She could put him off of course. He knew all about the demands of the job, it would be no surprise to him. But she couldn't put it off forever. Time to front up.

Two hours later she sat opposite him in a very decent Italian restaurant. At least he was easy to be with. No need to impress each other. They spent a bit of time discussing the children, who were both doing well without any interference from either of them, and then relaxed into a peaceful silence, during which Murphy had a good look at her ex-husband and noted that he was wearing what looked like an expensive shirt. Definitely looking a lot better than last time she saw him.

She took a sip of wine and waited for him to make his pitch.

'I do have something to tell you,' he began.

She nodded. 'I thought maybe you did.'

'I've met somebody.' Something thudded in Murphy's heart. She was pretty sure it was relief, but he was certainly looking good in his nice shirt. Then she thought about taking him back and what that would mean and was immediately reassured. Definitely, it was relief.

'That's fantastic' she said, and noticed that he looked a bit insulted. 'That's really good, Jack' she amended. 'Tell me all. Not another millennial, is she?'

'No, actually Shelley's a bit older than me.'

'Really? How much older?'

'Not so much. Five or six years. Maybe seven. Or eight.' He waved a hand.

'And what does she do?'

'Well… not so much really. She's retired.'

'Oh. Retired from what?'

'Property management. She and her husband had quite an extensive property portfolio.'

'What happened to the husband?'

He folded his arms, just as a plate appeared in front of him. 'What is this – the third degree? He died.'

'I'm just showing an interest. Watch your sleeve in that. Died of what?'

He was silent for a moment. 'He fell.'

'What do you mean, he fell? Fell out of a window? Toppled off a cliff? Fell into a pool and drowned?'

He narrowed his eyes. 'I don't think I want to discuss this with you anymore.'

'Sorry. Professional curiosity. I need to curb it.'

'Yes, you do. If you must know, they were hiking a trail in Greece and he lost his footing and fell.'

Murphy tried to look suitably chastened. 'That must have been a horrible shock.'

'Yes, it was, but it was over a year ago, so Shelley's over it now. She's trying to rebuild her life.'

'That's good. It's good that she has…funds. To rebuild with.'

'Yes. He left her well provided for.'

'So, are you going to be a kept man?'

'No, I'm not going to be a bloody kept man! Why do you always have to reduce everything to the lowest common denominator?'

'Sorry, didn't mean that. Have you told the kids yet?'

'No, I thought I'd tell you first. Why I bothered, I don't know.'

'I appreciate that you told me first. And I'm glad you've met somebody. I'm just processing it, that's all.'

'One thing I thought you'd be happy to know. I'm not bothered about you selling the house.'

'Because your accommodation needs are now taken care of.'

He nodded. 'That's right. Shelley has a house in Surrey and a villa in Greece.'

'Greece? That's good.'

'But we'll mostly be living in Surrey.'

'Very nice. Bit different to Queen's Park.'

'Very different. But it's on a good commuter line. Anyway, that's my news.'

'That's great Jack. Maybe I'll get to meet Shelley at some point.'

He shrugged. 'I don't know about that. Well, maybe.'

Murphy nodded. 'Plenty of time. But I'm sure she's dying to meet the kids. Does she have kids of her own?'

'No, they weren't able to have children.'

'Well, that's something you can bring into her life. Shame she's missed the teenage years.'

He narrowed his eyes again. 'I'm sure they'll get on fine. Not something I'm going to rush into anyway. They're leading their own lives now.'

Murphy swallowed a mouthful of pasta and waved the fork at him.

'Wait till they hear about the Greek villa. They'll be all over you.'

Chapter Fifty-Four

REBECCA BRYCE STRETCHED her legs and scrutinised her fingernails. Her lawyer, a middle-aged woman who Murphy knew to be the most expensive in the business, rolled her eyes as if this was just one more farrago of nonsense she had to listen to.

'Let me get this straight, Inspector. You have forensic evidence that my client's coat brushed up against the clothing of the victim. That is surely not so remarkable considering that my client has admitted that they had a drink together in this bar. After which, as you've just been told, my client left by the front door and the victim carried on drinking alone.'

'Your client was the last person to see the victim alive, so it is expected that we will want to question her. And she has not freely admitted to this meeting, which must make us suspicious. That being the case, I would like to know everything about this meeting, how and why it was arranged, and what was discussed.'

Mrs Winthrop nodded at her client.

'He phoned me up at work and asked me out for a drink,' said Rebecca. 'He knew I would be feeling depressed about Adam. And we met at Bennie's.'

'He phoned you up on a work landline?'

She shrugged. 'I guess he was at work too.'

'And it didn't leave any record on his mobile,' said Wilcox.

'Didn't you wonder why a married man was asking you out for a drink?' asked Murphy.

'I assumed he fancied me.'

'Did you fancy him?'

Mrs Winthrop made to intervene, but Rebecca answered. 'A bit. Not awfully, but he was amusing.'

'What did you talk about?'

Rebecca shrugged. 'Nothing much. He talked about his business and I talked a bit about mine. We're both in the finance field in different ways. That's it.'

'Doesn't sound like a very exciting date. Did you discuss your late husband?'

Mrs Winthrop held her hand palm up.

'That's all you're getting Inspector. My client has nothing further to say.'

Murphy waited till they had left and turned to Wilcox.

'OK, we need to investigate her a bit further. We need a warrant to access her bank accounts. We need to trawl her social media. Let's get onto it.'

———

CLIVE WAS COOKING when Murphy arrived home.

'Wow! You knocked off at a normal person's time! You'll be glad you did. Vegetable gyozas and stir fry with lime and ginger. What's not to love?'

'Absolutely nothing. I love it already.' Murphy sank into a seat.

'And how did the date night go?'

'It wasn't a date night. Date nights are not part of an ex-relationship. Except for Hollywood people, I think. And the food was very good. Vita's in Bayswater. Jack paid the bill, which was decent of him, so it was all good.'

James came in at that moment with a garlic bulb and handed it to Clive.

'But you don't look like it was all good,' he said. 'So, what was wrong?'

Murphy leaned her elbows on the table and rubbed her face. 'Nothing really. He's met somebody else, which is a good thing.'

'That's what you wanted, isn't it? Or has he picked another twenty-something?'

'Not at all. This one's an older woman. A wealthy older woman.'

'Good for him,' said Clive. 'Wealthy makes up for a lot of the older bit.'

'I wouldn't want to think he's with her for the money.'

'No, of course he isn't, but a bit of money makes life more enjoyable, doesn't it?'

'I guess so.'

'So, what is it you're not happy about?'

'She's a widow.'

'Well, OK. Lots of older woman are. We men die younger.'

'Her husband didn't die of natural causes. He fell off a mountain trail in Greece. Hiking. With her.'

Clive brought the pan to the table. 'And you're thinking … no, you can't be serious.'

Murphy shrugged. 'I'm not really seriously thinking that. But it just made me wonder.'

James passed her a plate. 'Was her husband rich?'

'Yes.'

'That's alright then, isn't it?'

'Is it?'

'I would say so. She might have had a motive to knock off the rich older husband and get her hands on the money. But she'd have no reason to off Jack. He's got no money. In his case, she's just after his body.'

'Thank you for making the point so sensitively.'

'But the whole idea's ludicrous, don't you think? Wouldn't the Greek police have looked into what happened?'

Murphy nodded. 'Yes, they would. I am just letting my imagination run away with me.' She swallowed a mouthful. 'This is really good.'

'If I wanted to murder my husband,' said Clive, 'which of course I don't.' He directed a glance at James. 'I wouldn't do it myself, and certainly not in a situation where I was the only person on the scene. I'd get somebody else to do it and make sure I was a long way away.'

'That's all fine,' said Murphy. 'But how would you deal with the somebody else?'

Chapter Fifty-Five

REBECCA BRYCE'S social media postings seemed to fall into three distinct phases. The period before Adam came into her life was full of clothes, nights out, airports, hanging out by pools, bikini shots, visits to the hairdresser, girly groups in bars, posing with various unnamed men. Then in phase two came shots of the band, the band performing at various venues, lots of shots of Bert, Rebecca posing with Bert, then posing with Adam. This was followed by the engagement, the ring, the hen night and the wedding, at which Adam's family made their first appearance, looking not too over-joyed. Phase three was married life, and the number of posts was definitely dwindling. Shots of the apartment in Notting Hill, posing in Portobello market, then a number of shots of the pair in hiking gear, in what looked like Wales, one of Adam standing at the top of a crag looking through binoculars, another taken from below, showing Adam at the top of a cliff path.

'Tells a story, doesn't it?' said Murphy.

Wilcox nodded. 'Sure does. Starts with the usual girly

stuff, then the band comes on the scene. She fancies Bert, but suddenly Adam is rich, so she transfers her affections, then they're engaged. Fast work. And the hen party. I was in a pub one night when one of those hen parties arrived. Bloody terrifying. Wedding straight away, no messing. And then she finds being married isn't so much fun. He's an outdoor chap at heart, likes climbing hills in remote places. Probably not her scene at all. No grinning selfies here.'

Murphy nodded. 'That's a pretty good summing up.'

'But none of it's illegal. You're entitled to marry some-body for money.'

'Of course. It's a respectable option with a very long history. But sometimes buyer remorse sets in, and if that's combined with a desire not to give up the money – that's when stuff takes place which we have to take an interest in.'

'We have no evidence tying her to Adam's death. We have no evidence tying anybody to it.'

'We just have to keep poking away at it. Something will surface. Hopefully before Bellweather demotes us both to traffic, or crowd control. What about her bank accounts?'

'The permission for that came in about an hour ago. Let's have a look.' He paged down and clicked a few times. 'Very healthy balances. She's on a good salary. That's her personal account. And there's a joint account which trans-fers £2,000 a month into her personal account. Looks like most of the money stays in Adam's personal account though. The joint account is topped up from his personal account and looks like it pays the utility bills and insurance and stuff. But she will have had no access to his personal account. Most of the money will be invested elsewhere, of course.'

Murphy frowned. 'That's interesting. Adam wasn't that

dumb. He gave her a large monthly allowance, but she had no access to the big bucks.'

He nodded. 'Not while he was alive. Once he was dead, she could expect to get her hands on all of it. Only, it hasn't worked out like that, because of the will.'

'Yes, she probably didn't count on him making a will.'

'Here's something interesting.' Wilcox pointed at the screen. 'Ordered a new debit card, existing card reported as lost. On the twenty fourth of October. Just last week.'

Murphy squinted at the screen. 'That's the day after Justin Beattie died. I wonder if she lost it in the bar? If she left it lying around, somebody might have picked it up. Let's get onto the bank, see if it was used in the hours before they stopped it.'

———

'BAKED BEANS' said Wilcox. 'Washing-up liquid, tea bags, eggs, margarine, instant coffee, marmalade, sliced bread, value-pack sausages. Amazing, the information you can get these days. And another haul of similar stuff a few hours later at Tesco.'

'Certainly not somebody with expensive tastes' said Murphy. 'And not what you'd expect from a thief. I would assume they'd buy a couple of bottles of vodka and maybe cigarettes, not their weekly boring groceries. Where were these stores?'

'Wapping. Wapping High Street.'

'So that suggests that the person who picked up the card lives near where we found Justin. And they're not some young tearaway, they're an older person, somebody who washes the dishes by hand and drinks instant coffee.' She stopped and thought for a minute. 'What about that old guy with the saucepan on his head? Where does he live?'

'The dangerous cyclist? Granger, wasn't it? Just a minute.' Wilcox pulled up another screen and paged down. 'Fenham Street, E1.'

'E1. That's Wapping, isn't it?'

He nodded.

'OK. Let's get round there.'

Murphy was out of the door waving her car keys before Wilcox had time to protest.

'My car's just round the corner' he shouted.

'No time. Just get in.'

Wilcox climbed in, fastened his seat belt and braced his feet.

'You're looking apprehensive Kevin,' said Murphy, as they shot off. 'Don't worry. I know the way. There are lots of back routes round here if you know where they are.'

Murphy's back routes were soon leading her in ever-diminishing circles. 'What the hell is going on?' she yelled, confronted with yet another 'No entry' sign. 'That wasn't here last time I came down.'

'It's called pedestrianisation,' said Wilcox. 'They're trying to force cars off the road and improve access for … people, I suppose.'

'I don't see how tying more cars up in knots in ever smaller areas makes anything better for anybody' Murphy muttered. 'More likely to lead to incidents of road rage. And I'm starting to feel that now. OK, here's where we get out and back onto the main road. Knew I'd find it eventually.'

Wilcox seemed about to say something, but just covered his eyes instead. 'That was a one-way street,' he pointed out, when they were safely away from it.

'No, it wasn't. I know that street. It's never been one-way.'

'It's one way now. They're making lots more streets one-way. We went past a 'No-entry' sign.'

Murphy felt genuinely puzzled. 'Did we? I didn't see it. Anyway, there was nobody coming in the other direction. That was lucky.'

Wilcox didn't look like a man who felt lucky. He fixed his attention on his phone. 'It's a social housing block,' he said, 'where Mr Granger lives. Just off Cable Street. Turn left here.'

Chapter Fifty-Six

'BAKED BEANS' Murphy intoned, reading from the list in her hand. 'Washing-up liquid - Sainsbury's own brand. Tea bags - box of 100. Eggs - medium, free range. Don't believe that for a minute. Margarine − sunflower. Instant coffee. You won't catch George Clooney drinking this stuff. Marmalade -thick cut. Sliced bread − white. Sausages - value-pack.'

Edward Granger was looking more and more alarmed. 'What is this?' he whispered.

'This,' said Murphy, 'is a list of items fraudulently obtained from a supermarket, using a card in the name of Rebecca Bryce. You don't look like a Rebecca Bryce.'

He felt behind him for a chair and lowered himself into it. 'I can explain.'

'That's what I was hoping,' said Murphy. 'Go ahead.'

'It was just lying there.'

'What was it?'

'A wallet. I saw him on the ground and I went over and I could see he was probably dead, but I called the ambulance. Then, while I was waiting for the ambulance, I saw it on the ground. I looked inside and the card belonged to a woman, so I knew it wasn't his.'

'You also knew it wasn't yours.'

'Yes, that's true. I wondered if maybe he had stolen it from a woman. Or it could have been nothing to do with him at all.'

'Then what did you do?'

He looked at the carpet. 'I put it in my pocket.'

'Where is it now?'

'I have it here.' He opened a drawer in the sideboard and handed it to Murphy.

She opened it. A driving licence, the debit card and a few business cards, including one from Justin Beattie. 'What else was in it?'

'Nothing.'

'No cash?'

He sighed. 'Ten pounds. That's all.'

'This is very serious,' said Murphy. 'This wallet is important police evidence. That means that you are guilty of both theft and perverting the course of justice. I think that carries a substantial penalty, probably a term of imprisonment.'

Edward Granger was starting to shake.

'Your best chance of avoiding a long sentence,' said Murphy, 'is to give us all possible assistance. We will be taking you to the station now to make a statement. Get your coat on.'

———

'THAT WAS A BIT MEAN,' said Wilcox after they had deposited him in an interview room. 'Telling him he could go to prison.'

'Well look at the time he's cost us. If he hadn't picked that wallet up, we would have found it at the time. You said yourself, he's a public menace. Anyway, as long as he co-operates, I'm not going to press charges. Has it been checked for prints?'

He nodded. 'Yes, that didn't take long. Nothing useable on the wallet or the cards. Looks like Granger gave it all a good wipe over. Probably wanted to remove his own prints. Why he bothered when it was sitting in a drawer in his house, God knows.'

'That's unfortunate. Justin's prints on it would have been useful.'

'It still wouldn't have been enough,' said Wilcox. 'Rebecca Bryce is not stupid and she can afford the best legal brains. They would, probably still will, say that Justin must have stolen her wallet and she did not discover it until she got home. After all, we know he was desperate for money.'

'I don't think the contents of Rebecca's wallet would have been enough to ease Justin's financial problems. But you're right, we need something else. Have we had the lab report on that substance we found in her kitchen cupboard?'

He shook his head. 'I chased them up yesterday. Usual story. Staff holidays, people off sick, staff training, backlog of cases, maybe next week if we're lucky.'

Murphy sighed. 'OK. Call them up again and tell them that DCI Bellweather has threatened to visit them in person if the results are not back by the end of today.'

MRS WINTHROP REGARDED Murphy with the jaded expression for which she was paid a large amount of money per hour.

'I assume you have a good reason for hauling my client back in here, Detective Inspector. If this is just a fishing expedition, we won't be staying long.'

'I just have a few additional points to put to your client,' said Murphy. 'Shouldn't take too long. I'd like you to take a look at this, Mrs Bryce.' She slid the wallet across the table and described what she was doing for the tape.

Rebecca's bored expression gave way to one of apprehension.

'Have a look inside,' said Murphy.

Rebecca looked inside and brought out the debit card and driving licence. There was silence.

'It's mine,' she said, after a few moments. 'I lost it. Where did you find it?'

'It was found next to Justin Beattie's body,' said Murphy.

Mrs Winthrop swooped. 'OK. That's enough. I'd like to speak to my client alone.'

'No problem.' Murphy and Wilcox gathered up their papers and left the room.

Chapter Fifty-Seven

'GHB,' said Wilcox, reading the email from the lab. 'It's amazing the effect that can be produced with a significant threat. Gamma hydroxybutyrate. How about that?'

'That's good,' said Murphy. 'Very good in fact. But I wonder if it's enough. She will say the stuff belonged to Adam and she knew nothing about it. See if that jar was fingerprinted at the time – hopefully her prints are on it.'

'She wouldn't have been able to mix powder into his glass of wine – much too messy and obvious. It would have had to be already in liquid form. It would need to be in a container of some kind.'

'Some container which would dispense it quickly,' said Murphy. 'Maybe something squeezable, small and squeezable.'

Wilcox rummaged in his rucksack. 'Something like this,' he said.

'Eye drops, yes,' said Murphy. 'That would do it. And it wouldn't look suspicious. Wait for him to go to the bathroom. Bring it out, pretend to drop a bit into your eye, quick squirt as you bring it down. And what would you do with it then?'

'Drop it in the nearest bin.'

'Maybe. But what if you don't pass a bin? Or you're more concerned with just getting away from the area. You might just leave it in your handbag and put it in the rubbish when you get home. I wonder when her rubbish was last collected? Most places it's only every two weeks now.'

Wilcox shook his head. 'That is such a long shot. Are you really suggesting we go through her rubbish?'

'I think we start with her rubbish and then we start scavenging in bins round the scene of the crime. You go to her house now, while she's still here, and bring her black bags back. Hopefully they haven't been collected.'

'I don't want rubbish bags in my car.'

'No, I don't suppose you do. Take a pool car. Give the neighbours something to see.'

———

TEN MINUTES later Murphy was informed that Mrs Winthrop and her client were available to continue the interview. In the absence of Wilcox, she pulled PC Avril Duffy in with her. Avril would be able to work the equipment.

Mrs Winthrop was looking a bit less confrontational.

'My client can explain the loss of her wallet' she said.

Murphy nodded and transferred her attention to Rebecca.

'Actually,' said Rebecca, 'I don't know exactly what happened to it. I lost it in the bar at some point, or that's what I think happened. It's possible that Justin took it while

I was in the bathroom, or I just left it behind and somebody else picked it up.'

'And went out and tossed it over the balcony?' Murphy enquired.

Rebecca seemed to be stopping to think. 'Maybe they took the cash and just dumped it.'

'How much cash was in there?'

She shrugged. 'I dunno. About forty pounds.'

'Strange not to take your debit card,' said Murphy. 'Everybody knows you can go to the supermarket with it, if nothing else. And you think Justin Beattie might have taken it? Was he that hard up?'

Rebecca looked momentarily uncomfortable. 'He did seem to have a need for money.'

'Asked you for money, did he?'

She shook her head. 'No, but he talked a lot about money.'

'I imagine he wasn't talking about amounts like forty pounds.'

'Well, no.'

'But as it was found near his body, would you say the likeliest explanation is that he took it?'

Rebecca nodded. 'Yes, he must have done.'

'Strange, then, that we didn't find his prints on it.'

Rebecca flashed a look at her solicitor who shook her head.

'No comment.'

'In that case,' said Murphy, 'we will hold you here while we make further enquiries. I am not presently charging you with an offence, but I'm sure you appreciate that we are talking about a possible murder here, so it is a serious matter.'

'I don't think that's necessary Detective Inspector,' said

Mrs Winthrop. 'My client is co-operating and is not a flight risk.'

'Oh, I think your client is well able to afford a plane ticket,' said Murphy 'and I am not satisfied with her explanations so far, so I am minded to keep her here for a short while pending further investigation.'

Mrs Winthrop made the usual standard protests, but Rebecca was eventually deposited in a cell and Murphy went in search of Wilcox. She found him on the ground floor in the evidence room, wearing a plastic suit and sporting a mask. At his feet was a black bag and a number of bulging pedal bin liners.

'It doesn't smell so bad' she said.

He shook his head. 'I think she doesn't cook at home and she's not into cheap takeaways. The odd pizza box, but no chicken bones or half-eaten burgers. Nothing disgusting. In fact, a lot of this stuff should have been recycled.' He looked up. 'She doesn't even separate her rubbish.'

'Well, if we don't find anything else, we'll do her for that,' said Murphy. 'It's surely been brought into law by now. Let's get through this lot quickly and send people round to check bins in the vicinity. Then I want to have another look round her house. We'll need a warrant. We can hold her for 24 hours, let's make the most of it.'

Chapter Fifty-Eight

THE HOUSE WAS LOOKING EVEN LESS lived -in than on their last visit. The bookshelves had been cleared and most of the furniture was now gone. Pale shapes on the wall showed where pictures had been taken down.

'Probably took the books and pictures to the charity shop,' said Murphy. 'Don't worry,' she added. 'I won't make you go back there.'

The kitchen and bathroom had not been emptied. 'People leave the functional rooms till last,' said Wilcox. 'You still have to shower and make coffee up to the last minute.'

'And to think this place was newly fitted out, at no doubt vast expense, only about a month ago,' said Murphy. 'Nobody ever knows what's round the corner. If I was Rebecca Bryce, I'd be wanting to get rid of this place as fast as possible and move somewhere else.'

'Well, we are trying to get her fixed up somewhere else, aren't we?'

'If it turns out that she killed Justin Beattie, yes, for sure we are.'

The kitchen was tidy but a thin layer of dust lay over the surfaces. Murphy drew a finger along it.

'No cleaning being done. Not surprising really. And some of these really dusty patches are where we were dusting for prints. The scene of the crime.'

Wilcox opened the back door and stepped outside. 'Can you hear it?'

'What?'

'The woodpecker. Listen. That hollow, tapping sound.'

Murphy joined him and strained her ears. 'Yes. It's coming from next door. Can't see it though.'

Wilcox walked back into the kitchen and came out with a pair of binoculars. 'I remember seeing these, last time we were here.'

He held them up to his eyes. 'They're really powerful. I can see every leaf on that tree quite clearly, but the bird is still hidden. Can't see it from this angle. You'd need to be up that tree to get a good view.'

'Well, we won't go climbing their trees' said Murphy.

Wilcox stood there for a moment. 'That's what Adam would have done,' he said.

'What?'

'He would have climbed that tree. It's quite an easy tree to climb. Didn't Bert or Lennie say he'd been climbing it? Adam was into birdwatching and climbing, wasn't he?'

'Yes, so we were told, but...'

But Wilcox was no longer listening. He was already halfway up the tree with the binoculars hanging round his neck. He stopped near the top.

'Come down now,' Murphy yelled. She could already envisage the health and safety investigation. But he was ignoring her and fiddling with the binoculars. That didn't say much for her authority as his senior officer. Then she saw him pull his phone out of his pocket and he seemed to be doing something with it, taking a photo, presumably, but it was taking a long time. Really, she'd lost interest in this bloody bird.

A few minutes later she saw him descending, then dropping lightly to the ground.

'I hope you enjoyed that,' she said, 'but now I think we'd better get on.'

'I think you'd better look at this,' he said, holding out his phone.

The video was fuzzy and jerky but after a few seconds Murphy could definitely see what she was looking at. She turned to look at him. 'You took this through the window?'

'Yes. The laptop screen faces the window. You could only see it with really good binoculars.'

'And nobody sitting in front of it?'

'There was at first, but then he wandered off and I could see the screen properly, so I took the shot.'

'You think Adam saw this?'

He shrugged. 'It's possible, isn't it?'

Murphy pulled out a chair and sat down. 'And what would he have done then?'

Wilcox sat down facing her. 'He'd have gone round to see Francine. That would be his priority.'

Murphy scratched her head. 'And that's what he did. Sandra Bailey told us that. But she wasn't home. So...' She thought for a minute. 'He came back here. He was angry. He wanted to see her. He could have gone ahead and contacted us, but first he wanted to talk to her. He wanted to point out her mistake, show her that she needed him after all. But she wasn't there. He was pissed off. He put on some loud music. Ted came in to complain. He told Ted to fuck off, or whatever he said. Ted went back home – and what happened then?'

'I think,' said Wilcox, 'that we need to ask that question next door.'

She nodded and they locked the back door and went out of the front.

It was Ron Warner who answered the door, looking crumpled and rubbing his eyes.

'Ah Detective Inspector' he said. 'Excuse the state of me. I was just having forty winks. I'm afraid my wife isn't here.'

'That's OK, Mr Warner,' said Murphy. 'It's you we've come to see.'

'Oh.' He looked momentarily taken aback. 'In that case you'd better come in.'

He held the door for them and pointed the way to the sitting room.

'We'd like to talk to you up in your office,' said Murphy, leading the way upstairs.

Wilcox went up after her and Ron scampered behind.

'You're wearing gloves, Mr Warner,' said Murphy.

'What, these? Yes, I wear them when I have a sleep, just to stop scratching.' He pulled one of them off and Murphy could see the sore patch underneath.

'Eczema?'

He nodded. 'Had it all my life. Bloody nuisance. Sometimes it's not so bad.'

Wilcox was standing at the laptop. 'Mr Warner, can you come and put your password in please.'

Alarm flashed across Ron's face. 'What? Why?'

'Because we need to see what sites have been accessed. Or we can take the laptop away with us.'

'Don't you need a warrant for that?'

'We are allowed to remove your device for inspection under Section 22 of the Police and Criminal Evidence Act,' said Wilcox.

Ron went over and typed in a password. Then he sank onto the sofa and covered his eyes. Murphy went over, had a look and shook her head.

'How people can do all of that without putting their back out is beyond me,' she said. 'It'll catch up with them in later life. But it's the part with the children that we're really interested in. That's what Adam Bryce saw, isn't it? Now do you want to tell us what happened when you went round to see Mr Bryce?'

His shoulders shook. 'Wendy will kill me,' he said.

'I think you might find that Wendy is the least of your problems,' said Murphy.

Ron went over to the table, grabbed a tissue from a box and blew his nose. Then he straightened his back.

'I'd just drifted off to sleep,' he said. 'I don't sleep well at night, so I usually have an afternoon nap. Then there was this awful noise. I guess it was music, but so loud it just sounded like noise. I went down and knocked on the front door but there was no answer. They don't have a bell and he probably couldn't hear me knocking over the noise. So, I went round the back. I just climbed over the fence. It's very easy. I used to do it a lot when Ted and Dorothy were there. I knocked on the back door but there was no answer. I opened it and took a few steps in and called out. He came out and he just went for me, called me a pervert, said I shouldn't be allowed near Danny. He punched me hard in the stomach and when I straightened up, I could see he was ready to punch me again, so I got in first. It wasn't a hard punch, I didn't intend to do any damage, although I did a bit of boxing at college but it knocked him back and he slipped. Those polished stone floors are lethal if you're just wearing socks. He hit his head on the way down and I knew it would be bad. Massive head injury. He was dead immediately. I felt for a pulse but there was nothing there.'

'You didn't call the emergency services.'

'There was no point. I knew he was dead. I was the first aid rep at the office and I've done a lot of training courses, how to resuscitate people and all that. I would have done CPR, but it was too late. I still should have called the emergency services, I know that.'

Murphy nodded to Wilcox who turned off the record button on his phone and read Ron Warner his rights.

Chapter Fifty-Nine

'SO NOW WE KNOW FOR SURE,' said Wilcox, 'that Justin
didn't kill Adam. So why would Rebecca, or anybody else
need to kill Justin?'

Murphy sighed. 'We know that Justin didn't do it. Justin
knew that Justin didn't do it. But it may have looked to
somebody else as if he did. Anyway, motive isn't what we're
after. We need evidence. We've found nothing in her
rubbish at the house, but there should be some stuff coming
in from the bin searches.'

The phone started ringing at that moment. Wilcox
picked it up. 'Mrs Warner has arrived,' he said. 'With the
family solicitor in tow. Sounds like she's making a bit of fuss
in the reception.'

'I did get the impression he was scared of her,' said
Murphy. 'Good job she won't be there when we interview
him. Hopefully this solicitor won't persuade him to retract
his confession. How long have we got left to hold Rebecca
Bryce?'

Wilcox looked at his phone. 'Just over three hours.'

'OK. You go and rummage through whatever's been brought in. There may be something there. We'll definitely need prints to tie anything found in a public bin to Rebecca, but we might be lucky. I'll go and brief Bellweather. Unless you'd rather do that and I'll do the rubbish?'

Wilcox shook his head vigorously and Murphy made her way into Bellweather's office.

'So, what's going on?'

'We have a suspect in custody for the death of Adam Bryce.'

'Have you indeed? Well, I suppose I should thank God for that. At long last. Are you going to charge him with the other death?'

Murphy shook her head. 'No. There's no evidence he had anything to do with that.'

'What evidence do you have for the Bryce killing?'

'None really. But,' she added hastily as his eyebrows shot up, 'he's already confessed and I don't think he'll retract. Although it looks more like manslaughter than murder.'

'We'll let the CPS decide that,' he barked. 'And he'd better not retract. So, you're thinking a different suspect for the second killing?'

Murphy nodded. 'Yes. I still think Adam Bryce's wife was responsible for that one.'

'Wouldn't it make more sense for her to be responsible for Bryce's killing? Are you sure you haven't got them the wrong way round?'

'I think she killed Justin Beattie because she thought he'd killed her husband.'

'What, some sort of retribution killing?'

'No, I don't think that was the motive. I think she was afraid of being implicated.'

'In a killing that he hadn't done? That you've now

arrested somebody else for? That makes no bloody sense. Are you quite sure Justin Beattie wasn't guilty?'

'It would have been very neat if he was,' said Murphy, 'but no, I'm satisfied we've got the right person for the Bryce killing.'

'In that case you'd better get them both wrapped up and quickly. Next twenty-four hours would be good.'

Murphy nodded again and made her escape.

Wilcox was waiting by her desk. 'Fifty-one soft drinks cans, thirty-seven water bottles, fifty nitrous oxide canisters, twenty-seven disposable vapes. The rest was newspapers, cigarette packets, sandwich wrappers, fried chicken boxes and generally extraneous stuff. I don't think any of it meets what we're looking for in a container.'

He pulled his gloves off. 'The water bottles are probably the best bet. I sniffed all of them and they all just smelled like water, but I've sent them to the lab anyway. We won't be getting results inside the next few hours, so I guess we'll have to let her go.'

Murphy sighed. 'I'm afraid you're right. Go and tell the duty sergeant. I'll go and see her.'

———

MURPHY WAS HEADING for the cells when Wilcox caught up with her.

'Just a minute,' he said. He was holding a large, expensive-looking handbag.

'Look at that,' said Murphy. 'Looks like a Birkin bag or some such. Probably cost about three thousand pounds. Is that Rebecca Bryce's? Guess she can afford it.'

'The thing is,' he said, 'it hasn't been searched. They were too busy downstairs and we didn't think of it.'

'How long do we have left?'

He checked his phone again. 'Half an hour.'

'OK, bring it into the office quickly.'

Wilcox dumped it on the desk, put on gloves and began to pull out items.

'Make-up bag.' He opened it. 'Tube of foundation.' He squirted a bit out. 'Yes, that's what it is. Black pencil. Lipstick. Some sort of spot concealer stick. Cotton wool buds. A tin of small round wipes.' He looked puzzled.

'They're for removing eye make-up,' said Murphy. 'Keep going.'

'That's it for the make-up bag. Phone – she'll have been missing that. If we charge her, she'll have to unlock it. Plastic water bottle. Sunglasses – two pairs. Two biros. One pencil. A packet of – what are they? It says panty liners. A packet of tissues. A pre-wrapped sandwich – cheese and tomato. Half a Kit Kat. Two condoms. One of those things for tying up hair.'

'A scrunchie,' said Murphy.

'Yes. One of those. Another biro. This one seems to be leaking.' He grabbed a tissue from the desk and wiped his fingers. 'A hairbrush. Half a bag of crisps. A comb, with lots of hairs attached. And the bottom half of the bag seems to be composed of biscuit crumbs, used tissues, hairs. This is disgusting,' he pronounced.

'What else do you expect from a woman who doesn't separate her recycling?' said Murphy. 'Just tip the bottom half out and we'll pick through it.'

'What? On my desk?'

Murphy rolled her eyes. 'OK, do it on my desk.'

She cleared a space and he upended the bag and shook it. A cloud of dust and biscuit crumbs showered over the desk, followed by four shop receipts, five crumpled tissues, two boiled sweets, a pencil sharpener, two fake nails and a small plastic squeezy bottle.

'Ear drops' said Wilcox. 'We weren't so far out.' He sniffed it. 'Difficult to tell. Smells like nothing much. That stuff probably smells weird anyway. If this is it, all the time we were scavenging in bins, it was sitting here in the police station.'

'It's a good argument for clearing out your handbag,' said Murphy, 'but she might really be an earwax sufferer. We won't get too excited yet. However, this is grounds to hold her for another twelve hours at least. Send it to the lab and I'll get Bellweather to call them. That seems to work well.'

Chapter Sixty

MRS WINTHROP WAS WEARING a pinstripe suit and an outraged expression. Power-dressed and ready to perform. Rebecca Bryce was looking dishevelled and apprehensive. As well she might, Murphy thought. The lab report had been timely and positive.

'Justin Beattie,' she said. 'He was probably smart in some ways, but very stupid in others. Justin got himself into a trap. Gambling habit on one side, serious financial irregularities on the other. And he could see no way out other than a large injection of cash. Then he meets you and Adam at a party. Adam isn't interested in Justin's investment scheme, but Justin has a good chat and a laugh with you. Tells you he'll knock off the rich husband for you and you can split the proceeds. It's a joke. Justin was big on jokes. But then, suddenly, Adam is dead. And Justin decides to play a dangerous game.'

'But none of this involves my client,' said Mrs Winthrop. 'Justin Beattie's problems were nothing to do with her. She hardly knew the man.'

'Bear with me,' said Murphy. 'Your client will soon be entering the picture. So, Adam is dead. And we know that Justin Beattie had nothing to do with it.'

'But he said…' Rebecca began. Mrs Winthrop held up a hand to silence her.

'We can imagine what he said,' said Murphy. 'He decided to pretend to you that he'd done it. He knew he hadn't, so he was sure there could be no evidence connecting him to a crime he hadn't committed. But you didn't know that. You'd seen him taken away by the police, so you believed him. He probably told you that he had been carrying out what you had both agreed upon. What he wanted now was his share of the money. He was pretty sure the police wouldn't have enough evidence against him, but if he did get caught, he would keep you out of it as long as you paid up. I guess he wanted you to take out a loan on the strength of the inheritance from Adam. You had no intention of doing that and you could see that Justin was going to be an ongoing nuisance. If he was arrested and claimed it was joint enterprise, how could you prove it wasn't? And Adam's wealth could then be classified as proceeds of crime, stopping you from inheriting anything.'

'This is all just surmise,' said Mrs Winthrop. 'You have no evidence.'

'Well, we do have a few bits and pieces,' said Murphy. 'Justin had GHB in his stomach when he died. You probably know something about GHB, Mrs Bryce. It's a depressive. The effect is increased if it is combined with alcohol. Induces relaxation, euphoria, loss of inhibition, desire for sex. Was that what you led him out onto the balcony for? A quick fumble? Anyway, to get onto the evidence, we found a peanut butter jar in your kitchen containing GHB. It might have been Adam's originally, him being music business and all, but your fingerprints were on it. And we found this in your handbag.'

She slid the ear drop container across.

'This contains GHB mixed with water. So clever, already in liquid form. Pretty much tasteless, certainly wouldn't taste it in red wine. Wait till he goes to the bathroom, quick squirt and you're done. So, he got woozy, maybe a bit amorous and you tempted him outside, down one floor where nobody could see you. Now it's not that easy to sling a fully-grown man off a balcony, you need to unbalance him a bit, or get him to lean over it. I guess at this stage there's a bit of hugging and giggling going on and he's probably got his arms wrapped round you, which is not quite where you want him. You want him leaning over. Then you have an idea. You let your wallet fall to the ground and maybe you get your phone out and switch the torch on and challenge him to see who can spot it first. He's up for that. Then you grab him round the ankles, and the rest is history. His phone torch was still on when we found him. All that remained then was to nip down, retrieve the wallet and be on your way.'

Rebecca Bryce shrugged. 'This is all just rubbish. The GHB was for my own use.' She turned to Mrs Winthrop, who was uncharacteristically silent.

Murphy ignored her and carried on. 'It's at this point that things start to go a bit wrong. An elderly cyclist, going past the other side of this bit of waste ground, spots the body. He wheels his bike in, has a look at Justin, calls the emergency services and then spots your wallet. Well, this is a disaster. You can hardly rush over and grab it off him. Then you see him look inside it and stuff it in his pocket. He's not going to hand it in. That's a relief. Good to be able to rely on the baser instincts of other people.'

'But none of that happened,' said Rebecca. 'I had already left by the front door.'

'Are you saying you just drugged him and left him sitting there?' asked Murphy.

'Yes. I knew we had that stuff in the cupboard, so I decided to give him some, but that's all I did.'

'You thought the GHB would kill him?'

'No further comment,' snapped Mrs Winthrop.

———

'WE NEED MORE EVIDENCE,' said Wilcox. 'We've got her up to the drugging bit, but we can't yet prove she chucked him off the balcony. What we've got might not even be enough for attempted murder. The defence can say there's no proof he didn't just jump. The CPS will want more than that to take it any further. Surely somebody must have seen her taking him out there.'

'A lot of people had already left the bar before we arrived,' said Murphy. 'One of them might have seen something. I wonder if there's any way in which we can trace any of them?'

Wilcox sighed. 'We'd have to go back there in the evening. Maybe there are some regulars we can identify who might have seen something. It's a bit of a long shot.'

'You go back tonight,' said Murphy. 'Take Riley, he'll appreciate being paid overtime to sit in a bar. See what the bar staff can tell you. Put it on expenses.'

Chapter Sixty-One

VALERIE WAS GETTING something out of the oven and Susannah was opening the wine when Murphy let herself in.

'God, it smells wonderful in here,' she said. 'I am so hungry.'

'You're always hungry, Miranda,' said her mother. 'You never eat properly. Clive is just wasted on you.'

'I know, I just can't fit my schedule to his most of the time.'

'As a DI, aren't you supposed to be more office-based?' asked Susannah. 'Surely, it's the DCs and DSs that do the running around and you could just be doing co-ordination or something. Then you could leave at a decent time and get some meals in.'

Murphy shook her head. 'What, sit around the station all day, looking at Bellweather and organising duty rotas? I'd rather be on door-to-door. Actually, I think he prefers having me out of his sight, so it suits both of us. I get

Wilcox to deal with the paperwork; he's much better at it than me.'

She took a glass from Susannah and took a seat at the table. 'Now that I think about it, I have sent Wilcox and a PC off investigating tonight, while I sit here on my arse, so I guess that's the correct use of resources. Anyway, enough about me.' She turned to Valerie. 'So, what's Mark doing tonight?'

Valerie put the dish on the table and took off her oven gloves. 'I don't know.'

Murphy frowned. 'Oh. Have you had an argument?'

'No, of course not. But we've kind of called time on it. We're still friends, but that's all.'

'Have you?' said Susannah. 'Whose idea was that?'

Valerie pushed a plate towards her. 'Mine, actually.'

There was silence for a moment.

'OK, don't tell me,' Valerie said. 'You think a woman of my age, right at the end of the runway, has been lucky to find a man to spend my declining years with. You think I should be hanging onto him.'

'No, of course not,' said Susannah. 'We're just surprised, that's all. He seemed like a very nice man.'

Valerie sighed. 'He is a very nice man. And, God knows, there aren't that many of them around. But he was a bit too much *there*, if you know what I mean. I think they call it presenteeism.'

Murphy wondered if Susannah felt as confused as she did. Valerie looked at them both and then waved a fork. 'He wanted to come shopping with me.'

Murphy shook her head and then nodded. 'OK, now I get it. That's a deal-breaker. Jack, for all his faults, which were many and various, would never have wanted to do that. He had a healthy disregard for whatever I was doing.'

'Exactly,' said Valerie. 'Same with your father. I did my thing and he did his and we met up at mealtimes. But I see these older couples going round the supermarket together and I know that's not for me.'

'I think maybe I wouldn't mind it so much in dress shops,' said Susannah. 'If it was a really expensive dress shop and he was paying.'

'I can see that being a good argument from a purely mercenary point of view,' said Murphy. 'But it still means you've saddled yourself with a man who likes hanging round women's dress shops. Wouldn't you prefer to have somebody who has better things, or at least other things, to do? Even if it's only fishing or watching football or gambling. Well, maybe not gambling.'

'Maybe you should look for a younger man, Mum,' said Susannah. 'One that still has a job. That will keep them out of the way.'

Murphy nodded. 'That's a good point. Jack has just taken up with an older woman. A wealthy older woman.'

'Good for him,' said Valerie. 'I always liked Jack and I don't think you gave him too many chances, Miranda.'

Murphy decided to let that pass. 'Well, he's happy now, anyway,' she said. 'Or I hope he is. This woman's husband fell off a mountain while they were hiking, but I've decided not to worry about that.'

'What?' said Susannah. 'You thought she might have killed him?'

'That's an awful suggestion,' said Valerie. 'The poor woman. I think it takes a particular type of person to do that. Most people wouldn't be capable.'

Murphy sighed. 'I'm constantly surprised to discover what people are capable of,' she said. 'But I think you're right. It does take some degree of cold efficiency. I'd be no good. I'd definitely mess it up.'

Chapter Sixty-Two

WILCOX WASN'T sure how well it would work, unleashing Riley Prendergast on an investigation. Riley took his duties very seriously and his interpretations of orders were sometimes a bit too literal. But anyway, this was only one step up from going through the motions. The chances of them discovering the evidence with which to nail Rebecca Bryce from this excursion were somewhere below zero. In which case, no need to worry about Riley messing it up.

Riley had dressed for the occasion in jeans, a white T-shirt and a leather jacket and his hair was slicked back with some sort of gel. Obviously trying to look as if he'd left the motorbike outside, when Wilcox knew for a fact that he'd come on the bus. 'Keep your notebook handy and leave the talking to me,' he hissed, as they went up the stairs.

Business was quieter than last time they had been here. A few groups dotted around, the odd couple in a corner and background music just loud enough to ensure they weren't overheard. The blonde barmaid (barperson, Wilcox corrected himself) saw him and smiled. She remembered him. That was good. Maybe this jaunt wouldn't be a dead loss in all aspects.

The barman saw them and came over and joined her, addressing himself to Wilcox. 'We weren't expecting to see you back,' he said. 'Still about this business last week?'

Wilcox nodded. 'Just a few ends we're tying up and we're hoping you can help us.'

He shrugged. 'Sure. Janine can probably tell you whatever you need to know and I'm around if you need me.'

'Thanks.' Wilcox turned to Janine. 'What we're interested in is any customers who were in that night, but had left before anything happened. Do you know who any of those people were? It could be that one of them saw something.'

Janine sighed. 'Now you're asking.'

Riley climbed onto a barstool and took out his notebook.

'Do you want a drink while I'm thinking about it?' she asked.

'Yes please,' said Riley. 'I'll have a beer.'

Wilcox was about to say something about drinking while on duty, but could immediately see how this would look to Janine, so he nodded and ordered the same. She winked at Riley and reached down into the fridge for the bottles.

'One of my friends was in that night' she said, putting them on the counter. 'I didn't get time to talk to her. She was here with her boyfriend. Do you want me to give her a ring?'

'That would be really helpful,' said Wilcox. She pulled her phone out of her pocket and walked to the other end of the bar.

'OK, that's sorted,' she said, coming back. 'She lives just round the corner, so she's coming over. You'll have to buy her a drink. I told her there were two cute police officers here.' She smiled at Riley.

Wilcox nodded and took a swig of his beer. Really, this was getting a bit out of hand.

Mandy walked in five minutes later and took a seat next to Riley at the bar. She had long, red hair tied up in a very high ponytail and multiple piercings. Like him, she was wearing jeans and a leather jacket. Wilcox experienced the unsettling feeling of being the adult in the room, in charge of a pair of teenagers.

'I'll have an espresso martini,' Mandy announced, getting the important business out of the way first. Janine went off to make it.

'Thank you for coming to talk to us, Mandy,' Wilcox began. 'We'd just like to see if there's anything you can tell us about that evening, any people you remember being here.'

'OK.' Mandy took a first sip and sat back. 'Well, I remember that evening very well and Janine knows why, don't you?' Janine nodded and moved off to serve another customer. 'And I'll tell you why,' Mandy continued. 'I remember it because it was the night I broke up with Olli. Not likely to forget that, am I? I hadn't come here intending to break up with him, before you ask. I mean, we'd been together six months, and that's quite a long time, isn't it? People get married after dating for less time than that. And I had thought we were doing pretty well together, but it just goes to show, doesn't it? You don't always know what's going on. Now, don't get me wrong, I'm not the sort of girl who would look at a guy's phone. I know some women do that, but as far as I'm concerned, it's just wrong, on so many levels. If you can't trust somebody, you shouldn't be with them, should you? And if you're looking at their phone, that means you don't trust them, doesn't it?'

Ryan seemed to be concentrating hard, shaking his head and nodding in what he thought were the right places. Wilcox was just wondering how to get this back on track.

'So, I was really not expecting it,' Mandy declared, 'when my friend, Riva, told me what he was posting on Facebook. Can you believe, I wasn't even following him on Facebook – trusting or stupid or what? Of course, it's also that the people I hang out with don't bother much with Facebook – we have other platforms. Which means he probably knew I wouldn't check in there, see who he was sending private messages to.'

Mandy drained her glass and pushed it across the bar. Riley signalled to Janine to make her another, Wilcox tried not to think about the bar bill.

'Thanks.' Mandy took a sip. 'So, there we were,' she said. 'And I had decided that I would give him a chance to explain. Everybody deserves one chance, don't they? And if he had had a decent explanation, or if he had even made a proper apology and promised not to do it again, I would probably have taken him back. But do you think he did? Not a bit of it. What I got was a whole raft of lies and excuses. It was like he thought he hadn't done anything wrong.'

'Do you remember seeing this woman in here? Or this man?' Wilcox put the photos of Rebecca and Justin in front of her, on the bar. 'She was wearing a woollen hat.'

Mandy shook her head. 'It was still quite crowded when I left, and I wasn't really looking at other people. Apart from one guy. He was with a crowd of people in the corner and we looked at each other and our eyes kind of locked. You know how it is? Across a crowded room, and all that. And I thought to myself, Mandy, I said, there's lots more fish in the sea, maybe even lots like that guy over there, so man up, girl, and stop allowing your time to be wasted. And do you know what I did then? I got up and walked out and left Olli sitting there. Just like that. It was a moment. It was empowering.'

Her glass was empty again and Wilcox could see a third round coming up if he didn't move fast. 'This guy Olli,' he said, 'can you give us his details?'

'With pleasure. Give him a good working-over, won't you?' She scrolled on her phone and Wilcox tapped the data into his.

'Brilliant' he said, signalling to Janine with his debit card. 'Thank you so much for your help. We'll be off now.' He paid the bill, grabbed Riley by the arm and hurried him out.

———

OLLI MASON LOOKED SERIOUSLY worried when he opened the door and scrutinised their warrant cards.

'Are you sure you guys are police? I can smell beer, and you hear so many stories these days…'

'The people you're thinking of are usually targeting pensioners, not fit young men, but I understand your reservations,' said Wilcox, thinking that he wouldn't have had this problem if he'd been with Murphy. Riley's biker look was obviously not inspiring confidence. He pulled out his phone. 'I'll just call some uniformed chaps to come and vouch for us.'

'OK. It's fine.' He held the door open and they followed him inside.

'We won't keep you long,' said Wilcox. 'It's just something that you might be able to help us with. Do you remember being in Bennie's bar in Wapping last week with a girl called Mandy?'

Olli sat down and momentarily covered his face. 'God, yes,' he said. 'Although I'd prefer to forget it. Don't tell me she's complained to the police about me?'

'No, nothing like that. But an incident took place in that bar, probably after you had left. So, we're talking to everybody we can trace who was in there and might have seen something.'

'I dunno, I didn't see anything happen. I was too busy being verbally abused by Mandy. That woman doesn't draw breath. There could have been a saloon fight going on in there and it wouldn't have shut her up.'

'I gather she left before you did?'

'That's right. Knocked back her drink and walked out. I was afraid she was going to make a scene, so it was a relief when she just left.'

'And how long did you stay after that?'

'About fifteen minutes, I think. It was nice to sit and finish my beer in peace. Also, I wanted to give her time to get far enough away. Didn't want to run into her at the tube station.'

'Can you remember any other people that were there that evening?'

'Not really. I do remember that there was a large, noisy group in the corner – somebody's leaving party, I think. I only noticed them because, there was a guy in that group that Mandy was making eyes at. I think she thought that would make me jealous but, to be honest, all I thought was 'come and take her off my hands, mate. I won't stand in your way.''

'Do you know where this group came from?'

'No.' He shook his head. 'Except I heard one of them refer to 'ward something-or-other' and they all laughed, so maybe they were from one of the hospitals.'

'Were they all men?'

'No. Pretty mixed bunch, I think. And not all young.'

'OK. And do you recognise either of these people?'

Olli looked at Justin and Rebecca and shook his head.

'The girl could have been wearing a grey beanie hat,' said Wilcox.

'Oh.' He studied the picture again. 'In that case, there was a girl in a grey beanie who left just before me. She walked past my table.' He took another look. 'It could well have been this girl.'

'What else was she wearing?'

'I dunno. Long dark coat, I think. Nothing very memorable.'

'And which door did she leave by?'

Olli looked confused. 'There is only one door isn't there? She went out the same door as me.'

'She didn't go out the other door, onto the fire escape?'

'No. Not if it's the person I saw.'

'She was with a man,' said Riley. 'Did you see him still sitting there when she left?'

Olli shook his head. 'I never saw who she was with. So that was what happened, was it? She walked out and left him sitting there just like Mandy did to me. Poor chap. Or maybe he was glad, like I was. We should have had a drink together, celebrated our lucky escapes.'

Chapter Sixty-Three

MURPHY STARED at them both and slowly shook her head. 'I send you off to get evidence that she pushed him off the balcony, and you bring back evidence that she didn't. This is not what I ordered.'

Wilcox shrugged. 'No. It wasn't what we were expecting to find, but people say what they say.'

'Well thank you for that insightful observation. Maybe it was another woman that this guy saw. Maybe he has bad eyesight. Maybe she went out the front door and ran round the back to the fire escape, ran up it and pushed him off.'

'Maybe you're clutching at straws' said Wilcox.

She nodded. 'I'm certainly doing that.' She looked at her watch. 'Our twenty-four hours are almost up. We'll have to let Rebecca go. Riley, you go and do that. Tell her the investigation is ongoing and she's not to leave town.'

'I suppose,' said Wilcox, 'that the GHB in his system was not enough to kill him, if he hadn't gone off the balcony?'

'It wasn't the cause of death, so we didn't ask that question. But it's a good one. We'll ask Linda. And if he fell off the balcony accidentally because of the GHB in his system, we would be able to charge Rebecca with manslaughter at least. But I don't see how it's possible to accidentally fall over a quite high set of railings like that. Defence counsel would tear that to shreds and I'd have to agree with them.'

'Suicide is the other option.'

'But it doesn't make sense on so many levels. Justin Beattie was in a bit of trouble, but he was the sort of chancer who would always think he could get out of it one way or another. If Rebecca wouldn't give him any money, he'd go back and have another go at Stanley. I can't see him deciding to just end it all. And if you do want to kill yourself, why choose such a terrifying way to do it? Why not take some pills, they can't be that difficult to get hold of. No, I don't buy the suicide theory.'

'In that case' said Wilcox, 'we are either saying that Rebecca left by the front entrance and ran round to the back, which seems a bit bonkers, but maybe she did that to avoid being observed. Or we are looking at somebody else killing him.'

'That's what I don't want to confront,' said Murphy. 'Back to square one.'

JANINE WAS STANDING by the dishwasher when they walked in and failed to hide her surprise at seeing them.

'I know, love,' said Murphy. 'Here we are again. Looks like you guys here are the only ones who can help us.'

Janine lifted the tray from the dishwasher and began unloading it. 'The problem is, I don't think there's anything more we can tell you. Was Mandy not able to help you?'

'Mandy did have a few … observations,' said Wilcox 'but she hadn't seen anything significant.'

'What we really need' said Murphy, 'is to trace some of the other people who were in that night. Anybody at all. They may have seen something that looked normal to them but would be important evidence for us.'

'There was nobody else that I knew,' said Janine. 'But Russell or Wanda might know who some of them were.'

Wanda simply shook her head. Russell maintained that he hadn't moved from the bar all night and didn't know who anybody was.

'There was a large group that could have been from a hospital,' said Wilcox.

Russell frowned. 'Was that the night they were in? Yes, it was. I think it was somebody's leaving drinks. But that was earlier. They weren't here when the alarm was raised.'

'But they might have left just a few minutes before.'

He nodded. 'They might have. But we don't actually know them. They probably came in early to bag a table and maybe they then went off to dinner somewhere. We wouldn't know how to get hold of them.'

'No' said Murphy. 'But we might.'

Chapter Sixty-Four

'OK,' said Murphy. 'We'll start with the hospitals in east London. Go straight to HR, don't waste the time of the clinical staff. We want a list of anybody who left their job in the week up to that date and the week afterwards. Most people have the party on the day they leave, but best be sure. We want names and contact details. Get them to email it over. Tell them it's urgent.'

Wilcox nodded. 'Let's hope it was a leaving do, otherwise we're stumped.'

Murphy shrugged. 'Stumped is how I'm feeling right now. According to the lab, the GHB in his system was something short of a fatal dose, so there's nothing we can pin on Rebecca. It would be good to have another witness who saw her leave, and then we can take our attention off her. Where we can direct it after that, I really don't know. Anyway, I'll leave you to it. I'm going back to see Mrs Beattie, see if she has any further information to give me.'

FRANCINE WAS WEEDING the front garden when Murphy pulled up with a screech.

'Need new brake pads on that.' Stanley emerged from round the back of the van.

Murphy shook her head. 'No, they're fine. 'Been like that for ages.'

Stanley frowned. 'They're not fine. They'll take longer to stop and that wears out your tyres. Just saying.'

Francine stood up and peeled off her gloves. 'I'm sure that's not what DI Murphy is here to see us about.'

'I'm just here for a chat,' said Murphy, following them into the house. 'We're still investigating what happened.'

'To be honest,' Francine turned around to look at her, 'it doesn't much matter to me anymore what happened and who was responsible, if anybody was. Justin's dead and nothing you uncover is going to change that.'

'You said 'if anybody was'. Does that mean that you think it could have been suicide?'

'I don't know. I would have said that Justin is not the suicidal type, but now I've come to the conclusion that I didn't really know him all that well. Maybe he was capable of killing himself.'

'I don't think he was the suicidal type,' said Stanley. 'He was a risk-taker. All his life he got away with things. He could charm his way out of trouble. He would have assumed that he could go on doing that.'

'There were a couple of things going on with Justin that we've been made aware of,' said Murphy. 'I don't know whether they would have made him more or less likely to have committed suicide, but I'd be interested to hear what you think.'

'In some ways, I don't want to know,' said Francine. 'But go ahead.'

'Justin was frequenting a gambling club,' said Murphy. 'One of the posh ones in the West End. They play for big stakes in these places and once you win a bit, they suck you in. Then you start losing and you keep going, trying to win it back. Justin was following that predictable pattern and he ended up with substantial losses.'

Stanley nodded. 'That's what I was afraid of,' he said. 'If there's such a thing as a gambling personality, Justin probably had it.'

'That will be why he got so moody,' said Francine. 'I used to ask him what was wrong, but he would never tell me.'

'And there's something else,' said Murphy. 'It looks as if he was carrying out some kind of fraud at work, involving misappropriation of other peoples' money.'

'I wondered about that.' Francine sank into a seat and put her hands over her face. 'All the phone calls he didn't want me to hear.'

'It looks like he began that as a way to handle his gambling debts,' said Murphy. 'And then it all ran out of control, as these things do. His firm are looking into it now and they will need access to his records and his bank accounts. I don't think they will come after you for money, they will probably take the hit themselves to avoid any adverse publicity. And quite right too. Their procedures and controls should have made a fraud like this impossible. But I thought you should know.'

Francine looked up and nodded. 'So it doesn't all end with him being dead.'

'Not many problems are solved by someone being dead,' said Murphy. 'There are always unforeseen consequences.'

Chapter Sixty-Five

'RIGHT.' she walked back in and slung her bag on the desk. 'Francine Beattie. I didn't pay enough attention to Francine Beattie. Who's the obvious first suspect? It's always the spouse, isn't it? We certainly went after Rebecca Bryce over Adam's death, but we didn't really look into Francine when Justin died. She looked like the more sensitive type and she had young children, as if that gave her some sort of immunity from guilt. I'm thinking maybe we've been fooled. Because I went and told her about Justin's misdemeanours and she put on a good show, but I just had the feeling that she already knew.'

'She didn't have a very convincing alibi,' said Wilcox.

'No, she didn't, did she? Something about wandering around looking in shop windows. And if you look at it from her viewpoint, she's discovered that her husband is gambling and committing fraud, and maybe she also discovered that he's screwing the next-door neighbour. That means he's now a serious liability, because everything is soon going to come crashing down. She's got a new baby to look after, she doesn't have a job, so she's not well-placed to just walk out on him. Then her old boyfriend turns up and wants to take her away from all this. At first, as she said, she probably told him to get lost. But then she started to think maybe this would be a good solution. Next thing you know, the old boyfriend has been murdered and we're making it clear we think Justin did it.'

'It's a theory,' said Wilcox. 'But we have nothing to back it up.'

'If she did know what Justin was doing, how would she have found out? She was in no position to go following him.'

'She could have hired somebody else to follow him.'

'Alright.' Murphy shrugged her jacket off and sat down. 'So where would she have found somebody? What's the first port of call for somebody who's never done this before?'

'Google. Private detectives in London. That's what I'd do.' He clicked and typed. 'Let's see who comes up. Here we are. First up is Ronnie Banks – he's obviously done his SEO optimisation.'

'We'll work our way down the list, starting with Ronnie. We want to know if they've done any work for Francine Beattie.'

———

TWO HOURS later they sat opposite Wesley Fitch in a coffee bar in Camberwell.

Murphy sipped her flat white and had a good look at him. 'You're looking prosperous, Wesley.'

'That usually means fat, doesn't it?'

'Well not necessarily, although you're not the skinny young thing I remember. So business is good?'

He nodded. 'It's been really good the last few years. Everybody wants to know what's going on. They all want to get an edge.'

'OK, tell us about Mrs Beattie.'

'There's such a thing as client confidentiality.'

'When it's a murder investigation, client confidentiality goes out of the window. You should know that.'

'You mean the husband…?'

'Yes, he's dead.'

'Oh my God.' He shook his head. 'And you think she did it?'

'Let's say she's a person of interest.'

'She didn't seem like that sort of person. Not at all.'

'Let's have the full story from the beginning. She called you up to begin with?'

'That's right. She said she wanted some information about her husband. Well, that's the usual thing in my business. Evidence for divorce.'

'Did she say she wanted evidence for divorce?'

'No. She just said she wanted to know what was going on.'

'And when was this?'

He pulled out his phone. 'Nineteenth of October. We had a face-to-face meeting that day and I worked for her for the next two days.'

'And what did you discover?'

He shrugged. 'The usual. Gambling and womanising.'

'What did the woman look like?'

'Blonde. Good-looking, late thirties.'

Murphy nodded. That would fit Louise Fraser. 'So did you catch them in flagrante?'

'No. I saw them meet up for a drink, and it was just one drink. Bit of intense discussion and then she walked away and left him. But you could tell they were familiar with each other.'

'And the gambling?'

'Followed him to one of these members clubs in Mayfair. Slipped a few quid to the doorman, who told me he's a regular. Well, there's no other reason to be going in there, is there?'

'Anything else?'

He shook his head. 'I knew where he worked, of course, but I couldn't get any information out of there. These places keep everything wrapped up tight as a duck's arse.'

'And when did you report back to Mrs Beattie?'

'Twenty-first of October.'

'What time and place?'

He consulted his phone again. 'Lunchtime. 1.30. Regents Park.'

'Met on a park bench, did you? Like the Cambridge spy ring? Doing a dead drop?'

He shrugged. 'It was her idea. Said she could do with the fresh air. She had a baby in one of those slings. Luckily, it wasn't raining.'

'What did she say when you told her?'

'Not much. She said it was pretty much what she had expected and she paid me off.'

'In cash?'

'Of course.'

Murphy drained the last of her coffee and stood up. 'Thank you, Wesley. If we think of anything else we need to know, we'll be in touch.'

They came out onto Camberwell Green and walked back to the car.

'Francine had that information on the twenty-first of October. How does that date fit into our schedule?'

'I just had a look. It's the date of the inquest on Adam Bryce.'

'And two days later Justin was dead.' Murphy snapped her seat belt on. 'I think we'll get her in.'

Chapter Sixty-Six

FRANCINE BEATTIE WAS LOOKING APPREHENSIVE. As well she might, Murphy thought. The duty solicitor was looking solicitous. Francine was obviously one of those women who men feel should be looked after, the current incumbent in the role being Stanley Farrow. But maybe Justin Beattie had become tired of all that. Maybe he'd been looking for something sparkier.

Wilcox set up the equipment and recited the who's who in the room. Francine looked around, licked her lips and began scratching varnish off her thumbnail. Murphy sat forward and rested her elbows on the table.

'We'd like to revisit your movements on the twenty-third of October, Mrs Beattie. That was the day your husband died. Can you tell us again what you were doing that afternoon and evening.'

Francine looked at the solicitor who gave her a nod. 'It's just as I told you. I met a friend for the afternoon and then I walked around Mayfair for a while and then I came home.'

'When you first told us this, we checked with your

friend, as you would have expected us to. Her recollection was that she had left you at six, because her train was at six-thirty. You told us you were with her until six-thirty. OK, we weren't going to make a big fuss about half an hour, so we left it at that. But we've since discovered that your phone was not wandering around Mayfair from six-thirty. For some part of that evening, it was actually located in the same vicinity as your husband. So, now can we have the truth?'

Francine sat back in her chair and sighed. 'I didn't want to tell you this, because I would then be suspected of having something to do with Justin's death.'

'As it happens, you're under far more suspicion now for the fact that you didn't tell us, so let's see if we can rectify that.'

She nodded. 'Marianne went off and I realised that I had the whole evening free, so I thought I'd go and see what Justin was up to. He had said he'd be late, some evening meeting with clients, but now I didn't believe him.'

'You thought he was seeing somebody else.'

'Yes. I assumed it was Louise. I had thought I wouldn't be bothered if he was seeing someone else. But then I found I was.'

'OK. Go on.'

'I got to that huge building where he works and I hung around over the road until I saw him come out. He was on his own and he looked like he was heading somewhere, so I decided to follow him. It was a stupid thing to be doing. I followed him to the DLR station and got on the same train and he never saw me. We changed at Poplar and then on to Tower Hill. I'd never been on the DLR before, but it's easier when you're following somebody else, you don't have to worry about where to go.'

'Where did you go from Tower Hill?'

'Round the back of the Tower, onto East Smithfield and then round a few twisty little streets. And then we came to this building where the top floor was all lit up. There was a neon striplight with the name – called Beanie's, I think.'

'Bennies.'

'Yes. That was it. It looked like a bar, so I thought he must be meeting somebody. I saw him go up the stairs. I gave him five minutes and then I followed him up. It was quite crowded in there, but then I saw him sitting with a woman. She had a woolly hat on, like she'd just arrived. I thought it must be Louise, but then she turned her head and I saw her profile, and it was Rebecca Bryce. It was such a shock. He stood up at that moment and he was obviously heading for the bar, so I just ran. I hadn't had any sort of plan, I didn't know whether I wanted to confront him, and when it came to it I didn't. Maybe I should have.'

'What did you do then?'

'I made my way back to Tower Hill station and came home on the tube and bus.' Her voice fell to a whisper. 'And I never saw him again.'

'Did Rebecca Bryce see you?'

Francine shook her head. 'No, I'm sure she didn't.'

'Did anybody you know see you, on the way home, perhaps.'

'No.'

'It was a noisy, busy bar. You could have sat quietly in a corner for a bit. Nobody would have paid you much attention. Rebecca Bryce left at some point and then Justin was on his own. That was your chance to approach him, wasn't it? And then he left by the fire escape. And you followed him out. Good place for a quiet chat.'

The solicitor stirred himself. 'Do you have any evidence for that, Inspector?'

Francine shook her head again. 'None of that happened. I never saw Rebecca leave. I'd already gone.'

'Justin was in a fair amount of trouble, wasn't he?' said Wilcox. 'You knew about the gambling. Did you know he was in trouble at work? That there were financial irregularities going on?'

'What? No. Well I guessed something was wrong, but I didn't know what it was.'

'He was becoming a liability, wasn't he? You were starting to think you'd be better off without him. And he was cheating on you.'

'Yes, I was upset about that. But we hadn't been getting on that well...'

'I think 'no comment' is advisable here,' said the duty solicitor. 'If you have no actual evidence, then my client has nothing further to say.'

Wilcox terminated the interview and they went back to the CID room.

'It's true,' said Murphy, dropping into a chair. 'We have no evidence. We need a witness. Somebody who saw her. Do we have a photo of her?'

'I can copy something off Facebook.'

'OK. Do that. Then we'll have to go back yet again to this bar. They'll be sick of the sight of us.' She sighed. 'It's sounding like a bad play. Justin was at Bennie's, Rebecca was at Bennie's, now we discover Francine was at Bennie's. I wonder who else was there? Maybe Tom and Louise were in the other corner and Stanley was sitting outside in his van.'

Wilcox frowned. 'Before we go back there, it might be worth trying somebody else.'

Chapter Sixty-Seven

OLLI MASON ARRIVED at his front door just as they pulled up outside.

'Whoa,' he said, as they arrived behind him. 'Am I supposed to have done something wrong?'

'Not that we know about,' said Wilcox, following him inside. 'We just have another photo we want to show you.'

He dumped his rucksack and shrugged. 'OK. Go ahead.'

Wilcox handed him the photo and he sat down on the sofa with it. 'Good-looking woman.'

'That's right,' said Murphy. 'It's a face you'd notice.'

He sighed. 'There is something familiar about it. Except I feel like I've seen an older version. She looks younger here.'

'This picture is off her Facebook page,' said Wilcox. 'She's a few years older now.'

'OK, let me get this right. We're still talking about this evening at Bennies, right?'

'That's right.'

He closed his eyes for a second. 'OK, I've got it. There was a moment when Mandy was still there, laying into me. She suddenly started making eyes at some poor innocent chap sitting in the corner and I looked behind me to see who she was staring at. And there, standing by the door, was this woman. She was scanning the room, obviously looking for somebody.'

'OK,' said Murphy. 'What did she do then?'

'I dunno.' He handed the photo back. 'I didn't see her after that.'

'You didn't see her walk further in, approach anybody?'

He shook his head. 'No. I turned back to Mandy at that point. Mandy finished saying her piece and walked out a few minutes later and I sat back then and looked around the room, but I didn't see the woman again. She maybe didn't see her friend and left.'

'And how long after that did the woman in the grey hat walk past you?'

'Very soon. Maybe five minutes.'

'OK.' Murphy stood up. 'Thank you, Olli, that's very helpful.'

'What we can be sure about,' said Wilcox, as they walked back to the car, 'is that she didn't approach Justin while Rebecca was still there. Rebecca would have told us that straight away. That means Rebecca didn't see her.'

'If you see your husband with another woman,' said Murphy, 'it goes one of two ways. Either you go in and tackle them, or you don't. You don't hide in the corner and watch them and wait for a chance to get him on his own. Francine could not have predicted that Rebecca was going to leave, so she could have been sitting there all evening. I don't think Francine is the sort of woman who enjoys confrontation, I think she'd have done what she said and just left.'

'Also,' said Wilcox. 'If she was getting tired of him, passing him onto Rebecca might have been a good move. He would still have provided for her and the kids. Much less problematic than killing him.'

'This Olli Mason is a bloody nuisance,' said Murphy. 'I don't think he's a reliable witness.'

'The fact that he keeps blowing our suspects out of the water doesn't make him an unreliable witness. Maybe neither of them did it.'

Murphy fastened her seatbelt. 'It must have been one of them. Or maybe it was both of them together? Maybe it was a joint enterprise killing?'

Wilcox shook his head. 'Maybe we're back at square one.'

Chapter Sixty-Eight

'HE'S HERE AGAIN,' said Murphy, scanning the vehicles as they drove into the car park. 'I'm sure he should have taken longer to recuperate. He'll have a relapse if he's not careful.'

'He'll have a relapse if we don't bring this one in soon, that's for sure.'

Bellweather looked up as they came in and narrowed his eyes. 'So where are we at?'

'We're still collecting evidence on the Justin Beattie killing,' said Murphy. 'Both Justin's wife and Rebecca Bryce were in the vicinity, but we haven't yet found the evidence to charge either of them.'

'Surely this killing must be related to the other one.'

'Tangentially, yes, but that one was more like manslaughter – or I think that's what the charge will be. This looks like murder.'

'Well, keep at it. The evidence must be there somewhere.' He walked back into his office and shut the door.

'OK. These lists are coming in from the hospitals now,' said Wilcox as he logged in. 'There are loads of them. No wonder the health service is in such a mess. Everybody's leaving.'

Murphy sighed. 'Maybe there's an outside chance one of these people may have seen something,' she said, 'but I'm not hopeful.'

After an hour of phone calls, Wilcox raised a fist in the air.

'Bingo,' he said as he put the phone down. 'Retired staff nurse Moira Freeman. Leaving party at Bennies. We can go and see her now and she's preparing a list of her attendees. One of them might have something to tell us. She's off the Seven Sisters Road. We can take my car.'

Moira Freeman lived in a terraced Victorian house with a frail-looking husband and three energetic corgis.

'Don't mind them' said the husband, as he opened the door. 'Just walk straight through them.'

'You don't often see corgis' said Wilcox, bending down to stroke one of them. 'Apart from with Royalty.'

'I think that's why my mum got them in the first place, to be honest,' said Moira. 'And as they died, she replaced them. We've inherited them now, but I think these will be the last ones. Might outlive us anyway. Come through and have a seat.'

They followed her into the kitchen where she brandished the kettle. Murphy nodded.

'The reason we wanted to talk to you is because you were in a bar near Tower Hill called Bennies last Thursday. It was your leaving do, so I'm sure you remember it well.'

Moira nodded. 'It wasn't a place I'd have chosen, but Trisha, she seems to be our social organiser so to speak, she seems to like the place, so it's become the place we go whenever somebody leaves. Bit crowded and noisy for my taste. But still, it was nice to see everybody.'

'There was an incident at this bar, probably after you had all left,' said Murphy. 'I wanted to see if you recognised any of the people that we're interested in.' She took out photos of Justin, Rebecca and Francine and placed them on the table.

Moira spent a few minutes looking at them and her husband came and peered over her shoulder. 'Not much point you looking, Derek,' she said. 'You weren't there.'

'A man and two women,' he said. 'Is that husband, wife and mistress?'

'Not exactly,' said Murphy.

He pointed at Justin. 'He looks like a man who's had too many options available to him. Not enough hard times, no weathering, nothing to rub the edges off. He's never been tested.'

'Not like you, you mean,' said Moira. 'This man and this woman,' she pointed at Justin and Rebecca, 'they look a bit familiar.'

'She was probably wearing a grey woollen hat,' said Wilcox.

'In that case I did see her. She walked past us and out of the door and I remember wondering why she was wearing a hat indoors.'

'Yes,' said Murphy. 'That agrees with other sightings we've had. How about the man?'

Moira shook her head. 'As I said, he looks a bit familiar, but I can't actually picture him there.'

'And the other woman?'

'No, I didn't see her at all.'

'OK' said Murphy. 'And can you let us know who else was there? One of them might have seen something.'

Moira stood and walked over to the worktop. 'I've written them all down here. Most of them are from my ward – ten years I was on that last ward. I'm missing a lot of them already. A couple of other old friends and three people who were long-term patients of mine and have now recovered. That's when you feel a medical career is really worthwhile.'

Murphy scanned the list and suddenly realised what she had been missing.

Chapter Sixty-Nine

WILCOX CAME BACK LATER that evening with the additional samples.

'It was no trouble' he said. 'I think eventually people don't care anymore when you turn up.'

'I should have thought to do this in the first place,' said Murphy. 'I didn't pay enough attention to what Stanley was saying. He's one of those people that makes me mentally switch off when he's talking. I think it's something to do with the fishing.'

Wilcox nodded. 'Let's hope we can still get a match off those samples. Ron was easy enough to crack. This might be more difficult.'

'I think in his case,' said Murphy, 'it's because he has his sordid secret. Something like that makes you vulnerable, it chips away at the self-confidence. You're not in a good place from which to brazen things out.'

'Not sure what we're going to tell Bellweather,' said Wilcox. 'If we're now writing off the two suspects that we told him about. He's expecting us to charge one of them.'

'We'll tell him as little as possible. At least until we've got those samples analysed. And I think we'll threaten the lab with a visit from Bellweather again. Seems to work well.'

———

DESPITE ALL THREATS, it was two days before the lab came back with the results.

'To be fair, that's still faster than normal,' said Murphy. 'Let's go and bring her in.'

Chapter Seventy

WENDY WARNER SAT in the interview room wearing a smart suit and a truculent expression. The duty solicitor was a timid-looking man who was keeping his attention on his paperwork.

'Mrs Warner,' Murphy began after the preliminaries had been completed, 'you have been charged with the murder of Justin Beattie.'

'Absolute rubbish. You can't possibly have any evidence. Why would I want to kill Justin Beattie?'

'Because he was blackmailing you. Or rather, he was blackmailing Ron. Justin came to suspect that Ron had something to do with Adam Bryce's death. In fact, he had no evidence, but Danny showed him where Wilfred had done a poo in the tree and I think he wondered to himself why Wilfred would have been in the tree. He would only have climbed up there if he was following Ron, who would only have climbed up there to get into the Bryces' garden.

'This made him wonder whether Ron had gone into the

house through the back door on the day that Adam had been found dead. For Justin, who was looking for the means to raise some cash, this presented an opportunity. Ron had retired with probably a substantial pension pot and Justin saw his chance to get some of that. He didn't have any evidence, but he figured he knew enough to point us in Ron's direction. And Ron, as you will know, is not a robust character. Instead of telling Justin to get lost, which is what a lot of people would do, definitely what you would have done, Ron crumpled, which showed Justin that his suspicion was correct.

'You had probably been wondering what to do about Justin, when there you were sitting in Bennies bar with your old friend Moira Freeman and he suddenly walked in and was joined by Rebecca Bryce. I think you watched them very carefully. You may even have seen Rebecca put something into Justin's drink. Then Rebecca walked out and left him and a bit later you saw him stagger towards the fire exit. Now, you know the layout of this place, because you'd been at a previous event there in the summer, when the fire doors would have been open and the balcony in use. It's the usual place for leaving drinks. Moira told us that. Getting hold of Justin when he was a bit wobbly on his feet seemed like a good idea, so you said your goodbyes, left by the normal door and ran round to the fire escape.

'We think Justin had been looking in Rebecca's wallet, when he suddenly dropped it and he got his phone out and turned on the torch to try and spot where it was. He probably wasn't afraid when he saw you coming up the steps, he would have been feeling pretty spaced out by then. He probably said something like 'Hello Wendy, fancy seeing you here. I've dropped my wallet.' Was it something like that?'

Wendy folded her arms. 'Of course not. This is just a fantasy.' The solicitor nodded his agreement.

'Well, let me imagine a bit further,' said Murphy. 'You came up next to him. You could see he was about to collapse anyway. You probably pointed to some spot a bit further away where you thought you could see it and he stretched out with his phone to have a look. Then you just picked up one or both of his ankles and pitched him over. Just like that. No hesitating. Just as if you were turning a patient over. Then you made your way out and went home. Job done.'

The solicitor now leapt into action. 'This is a good story Inspector,' he said, 'but do you have any evidence? If not, I don't see that my client has any charge to answer.'

'As it happens,' said Wilcox. 'We do have evidence. We have your DNA, Mrs Warner, matched to traces around the bottoms of Mr Beattie's trousers, where you will have grabbed his ankles.'

Wendy shrugged. 'DNA evidence. Can be planted.'

'We also have the testimony of your husband, who knew what you had done and tried to persuade us that it was not premeditated.'

Wendy closed her eyes and then opened them again. She shook her head. 'The stupid bastard.'

Murphy nodded. 'I'm afraid he's not much of a partner in crime. I wouldn't choose him for a joint enterprise job.'

When Wendy had been taken away, they walked slowly back up to the CID room.

'All wrapped up?' Bellweather barked.

Murphy nodded. 'Yes. The CPS will go with this one.'

'Good. About time too.' He swept back into his office.

'I think that's what they call damning with faint praise,' said Murphy.

'It's a successful result, whatever he says.' Wilcox yawned and stretched.

'Yes, but he is right to some extent. I should have looked more closely at the Warners. Even after we discovered that Ron had been involved in Adam's death, I never looked at them in regard to Justin.'

'You were too fixated on Rebecca Bryce.'

Murphy nodded. 'I was fixated on Rebecca and then I moved on to suspecting Francine. But really, neither of them had what it took to pull this off. Rebecca is a fairly tough nut, tough enough to marry for money, but despatching Justin like that had to be done with cold efficiency. Rebecca's a woman who's so disorganised that she makes a half-assed attempt to poison Justin and then leaves the evidence festering in the bottom of her handbag with the biscuit crumbs. And Francine, well she looked in and saw him with Rebecca and didn't even have what it took to create a decent public scene. So really, neither of them was a proper contender. Whereas Wendy, yes, Wendy's a woman I'd put my money on. She had what it took to do that – no messing, no hesitating.'

'I wonder what will happen to Wilfred?'

'I think,' said Murphy, 'that Francine and Danny may give him a home. He'll certainly miss Ron.'

'It would have been better for Ron if he had called the emergency services. Adam's death would probably have been ruled as accidental.'

'Yes. But we'll never know what might have happened in that case. There's possibly a slim chance Adam might have survived, and that wouldn't have been good for Ron. Adam would have denounced him to Francine and to us. He felt safer with Adam being dead and maybe he waited just long enough to be sure he was dead. Now he'll probably face a manslaughter charge. One thing's for sure. If Ron had called the emergency services, there would have been no need for Justin to die.'

Wilcox closed up his laptop. 'Justin was a stupid man. Highly intelligent, but he made some stupid choices.'

'Justin was a very smart guy caught in a trap of his own making,' said Murphy. 'His mother had always given him money to get himself out of scrapes and now Stanley had control of the money and wasn't co-operating. So Justin played this charade with Rebecca, pretending to have killed her husband for her. But Rebecca wasn't coming forward with the money. It takes time to raise a loan, especially when you don't really want to, and Justin's problem was getting urgent. He just needed one of his clients to ask to withdraw their cash and the whole thing would have come crashing down. He could have gone to prison. But he really over-played his hand by taking on the Warners.'

'Ron and Wendy wouldn't have looked dangerous to him. He'd have thought they were no match.'

'That's probably true of Ron, but she's the one in charge. When we arrested him and he said 'Wendy will kill me' he didn't mean that Wendy would be angry when she found out about what he'd done. She already knew all about that. What he really meant was that Wendy would be angry with him for getting caught, for confessing like that. She's a tough woman. It takes a lot of nerve to seize an opportunity like that and just act, no dithering.' She sighed. 'I'm hoping the woman my ex-husband's taken up with isn't somebody who can dispose of a man just like that.'

Wilcox shook his head. 'It's not the sort of thing you can interfere in.'

'I'm not going to interfere personally,' said Murphy. 'I'm going to weaponise the kids and send them in there. They've both been good at staying in touch with him, so I'll just get them to increase the level of engagement. She's going to find that she's become a de facto stepmother. Let's hope she likes it.'